KT-477-963

-9
05

-6

2

20
??

A Full
Churchyard

A Full Churchyard

NICHOLAS RHEA

ROBERT HALE · LONDON

Robert Hale Limited
Clerkenwell House
Clerkenwell Green
London EC1R 0HT

www.halebooks.com

2 4 6 8 10 9 7 5 3 1

Typeset in Palatino
Printed in Great Britain by Berforts Information Press Ltd

Chapter 1

IT WAS MONDAY and Detective Inspector Montague Pluke was at breakfast with a boiled egg before him. It was accompanied by buttered soldiers of brown bread neatly arranged on his side plate, standing to attention as he waited patiently for Millicent. In the Pluke household it was bad manners to begin a meal before everyone was seated. Millicent, who insisted on preparing Montague's meals, was finalizing her own breakfast in the kitchen, but within minutes she joined him. Her tray bore a bowl of milky porridge, a peeled orange and a handful of fresh grapes. The teapot and milk were on the table as she smiled her usual greeting, unloaded her tray and settled down. It was time for Montague to begin his feast.

With his knife, he decapitated the egg with practised precision, scooped out the juicy bit from the detached cap and swallowed it. Leaving the empty cap to one side, he tackled the rest of the egg, which Millicent had boiled to perfection. A Millicent Pluke home-boiled egg was a treat above all others.

'Is the egg to your liking?' she asked.

'Perfect as always, my dear,' he acknowledged. 'It is a tribute to your culinary skill and now I must tell you this. When I'm away from home and hard at work detecting major crimes, I never fail to tell my colleagues that my wife is the world's finest boiler of eggs. There are few to equal you.'

'You shouldn't reveal such intimate matters to strangers and colleagues!' she blushed.

'Credit given where credit is due,' and he stabbed a soldier deep into the receptive yolk. As an authority on folklore and superstitions, and as Britain's most superstitious police officer, he knew the egg had been brought into the house during daylight hours. It was unlucky to bring eggs into the house after sunset and it was also worrying to dream about eggs. If you did dream about eggs, it foretold a death in the family and to date, Montague had never dreamt about Millicent's boiled eggs.

As Montague savoured his breakfast, Millicent broke the silence by announcing, 'You might like to know that dear old Mrs Langneb has passed away, Montague. Mrs Barnett told me only half an hour ago when I was collecting our paper from the shop. It's quite a shock. She was such a lovely person, a true lady.'

'She was a good age, I would imagine.'

'Eighty-nine,' she responded. 'A good innings but she will be missed. Amelia Langneb was very good at cleaning the kneelers in church; even at nearly ninety, she never gave up. She wouldn't have anyone else touch them, they were her special responsibility. It won't be easy finding such a devoted kneeler-cleaner to replace her.'

'Another death for Crickledale! There's been such a lot lately. Natural causes, was it? Like the others?' Pluke asked almost as if he was conducting a preliminary enquiry into the death.

'It was nothing more than old age, Montague. She's never been ill although she was confined to bed for the past few weeks. Crickledale Carers have been wonderful, bathing her, changing her clothes, doing her hair, preparing her meals.'

'She was very fortunate to have them on hand. Many in similar circumstances have to cope alone.'

'I saw her only a few days ago. She was quite alert and eager to chat over a cup of tea and a scone. She looked as fit as ever. It seems she passed away peacefully in her sleep last Thursday. She has sons who live down south but no relations in Yorkshire. Her husband, Harold, went to his eternal rest a few years ago. Anyway, Montague, that's my bit of news. Her funeral is tomorrow and I shall attend.'

'So how many deaths have there been in Crickledale this winter?' Pluke asked. 'Funeral corteges seem to be coming thick and fast these days. They're like buses that arrive in threes! I'm sure the local undertakers and gravediggers are having a busy and profitable time and the economy of Crickledale must surely benefit. It's an ill wind. . . .'

'She's the ninth in the last three months,' responded Millicent. 'But that's not particularly unusual, Montague. All were in their eighties or nineties. It's winter when we always get a crop of deaths among the elderly so don't go looking for sinister reasons.'

'I'm merely expressing an interest . . .' he began.

'Montague, listen to me. These deaths are of no interest to the police, so stop being a detective when you're at home, especially at breakfast. All those people, men and women, were well cared for and died in their homes from nothing more complicated than old age. That's what their doctors decided and there's no reason to question their decisions. I know that through my work for the Carers.'

'I was not being critical, Millicent. . . .'

'Yes you were – and suspicious too! There's no need to behave like an inquisitive policeman at home. Now listen to me.'

'You misunderstand me . . .'

'No I don't! I know you too well, Montague Pluke. The Crickledale Volunteer Carers looked after them all and Mr Furnival, our boss, made sure that everything that could be done was done. Nothing was overlooked and nothing was too much trouble. Mr Furnival is very good, Montague, all the carers are pleased he came to take charge. He has moulded us into a truly effective unit. . . .'

'You say all the deceased were cared for by Crickledale Carers?'

'There you are! Finding villainy where none exists! There's nothing suspicious in what we do, we care for almost all the elderly in Crickledale so it's quite normal for some to die in our care.'

'Millicent, you can't deny it's rather curious, nine deaths in this small community in such a short time and all cared for by the same organization! But if the doctors were happy to certify the causes of the deaths without any suspicion being attached to them, then we must accept their opinions. It's all probably due to the exceptionally mild winter. You know what they say: "a green winter makes a full churchyard."'

'It's often surprisingly true, Montague.'

'I wouldn't use the term *surprising*, Millicent. Such sayings are invariably based on ancient wisdom and acute observation. It's the same when people say deaths come in threes, except on this occasion it's been three-times-three so far. It makes me wonder about such things especially as we haven't even reached Candlemas Day!'

'Don't poke your nose in, Montague. It's nothing to do with you and your detectives even if you've nothing to do with your time. Sometimes I wonder what you do all day at work!'

'I am a leading detector of serious local crime, Millicent. That awesome responsibility remains with me all through my working hours and at home. Even in the peace and tranquillity of Crickledale, time and crime waits for no one.'

Millicent did not reply. Having scooped all the tasty bits from the eggshell, he prized it from the cup, turned it over and replaced it upside down. Then he whacked it several times with the back of his spoon to smash it to smithereens. He believed that this would ensure good fortune during the forthcoming days – it was one of his regular habits based on age-old superstition. If pressed to be more specific, he would deny that it had anything to do with preventing witches from using eggshells as tiny boats or any other means of transport as they went about their evil spells and trouble-making. Belief in witches had long gone and the eggshell smashing ritual, once such a feature of witch-lore, was now used to attract nothing more complicated than good fortune and general happiness. On the coast, however, an eggshell left intact would cause ships to turn around at sea or even produce a shipwreck. Montague did not wish to be responsible for such disasters and was always exceedingly careful to prevent them by smashing his eggshells into fragments.

When Millicent had finished her breakfast, he left the table with his right foot first and kissed her farewell with a light peck on the cheek. So far, all his preparatory omens had been successfully completed which meant his day had had a very good start. It had begun by him getting out of the right side of the bed before his ablutions and then putting on his right shoe first before settling down to breakfast. To add to his happiness he had found a knot in his right shoelace, a very positive indication of forthcoming good fortune. En route to work, he would take immense care not to walk under any ladders and would ensure he caught sight of that black cat that always sat on the mat outside the Town Hall.

He hoped he would not see any crows perching in the churchyard, either on the boundary walls or upon any of the tombstones – a crow in such a position was a sure sign of a funeral in the very near future. Then he realized he had seen a lot of crows in and around Crickledale during the last few months, so had one been sighted in the churchyard ahead of Mrs Langneb's death?

'Montague, have you got your mobile?' came Millicent's voice from the kitchen.

'Yes my dear, I have.'

'And is it switched on?'

'I'll check.' It wasn't, so he switched it on. 'It's on now.'

'Then make sure it stays on all day.'

'Yes, dear.'

Detective Inspector Pluke's morning walk through the streets and marketplace was as regular as the striking of the church clock, the queue at the newsagents and the buses that carried people into York. People checked their watches and clocks upon the appearance of Mr Pluke as he strode towards his office on the hill. Inevitably, his timing was immaculate. At 8.30 a.m. precisely he left home, a pleasant house not far from the town centre and arrived at the police station near the church at 8.50 a.m. precisely. He took the same route every day and passed the same pillar boxes, shops, bus stops, pubs, lamp posts, people, prams and dogs.

He offered his sincere 'good mornings' to those he passed and raised his blue-ribboned panama to every lady he encountered. The sight of Mr Pluke's hat rising and falling among the throng of early shoppers and hurrying workers was one of the familiar sights of a Crickledale morning. He was even reputed to have patted some dogs and admired babies in prams, inevitably without losing a precious second.

A Crickledale workaday morning without Mr Pluke was rather like the London rush-hour without Big Ben, red buses and crowds of moving people.

Much of the mystique and interest that surrounded Detective Inspector Pluke was due to his curious style of clothing. His wide-brimmed straw panama hat with its pale blue band was most distinctive when perched on his head of thick grey-black hair. Montague had always worn his hair far longer than some thought suitable or advisable for a senior police officer. Indeed, when he was a young constable in uniform, his hair was always so long and untidy despite admonitions from his senior officers that he was eventually considered unfit to wear police uniform and so he was transferred to the CID. It was customary that detectives did not look at all like police officers and there was no doubt that the then Detective Constable Pluke looked nothing like a police officer. With his heavy-rimmed spectacles, long hair and curious dress style, he exuded the demeanour and air of a bespectacled and absent-minded professor who wrote learned articles and tomes about horse troughs, which was exactly what Pluke did in his spare time. He had become a noted authority on horse troughs and their history, being the author of *The Horse Troughs of Crickledale and district since the 16th century – fully illustrated by the author.*

There is no doubt that many ageing male Crickledonians were overtly envious of Mr Pluke's thick hair and wondered if he used a secret horse-based recipe to maintain it. Did horses provide a secret potion that made Pluke's hair look like an untidy mane or long horsetail? Or did he wash his hair in horse troughs? But if there was a secret to his wonderful head of dark untidy hair, he had never revealed it.

In addition to his hair, his heavily patterned beige-coloured overcoat was equally striking. Some believed it was the very first overcoat manufactured by Burberry but Montague Pluke had always denied that, claiming it was a very old coaching coat that had belonged to an ancestor who was a coachman on the famous *Highflyer*. Made by a Pluke matriarch, it had been passed down the male line whilst retaining its fitted cape on the shoulders, numerous huge pockets inside and out, splendid epaulettes and wide belt. There were those who felt the coat ought to be placed in Crickledale Folk Museum but Montague would not do such a thing with a treasured family heirloom. He wore it every day, summer and winter alike, and it was said to have survived at least two major horse-drawn coach crashes, one stable fire and a motorcycle-and-sidecar accident. His heavily chequered beige trousers matched the coat but were rather shorter than was fashionable. Some thought he resembled a circus clown because when he walked, his trousers revealed pink socks, grey spats and brown brogue shoes. His overcoat's amazing colour scheme was said to be rather like a Macmillan tartan with faulty shades.

His jacket, worn under that greatcoat, was of similar style and design, rather like one designed for gamekeepers to carry guns and pheasants, except that his pockets bulged with fountain pens, propelling pencils, a pocket watch, digital camera, mobile phone, several notebooks and other assorted things that might come in useful sometime. Some notebooks were to record new discoveries relating to horse-troughs whilst his official police notebook was for police duty records. To enhance the appearance of his jacket he always wore brightly coloured shirts with white collars, meticulously maintained and ironed by Millicent. There was little doubt that his skill in discovering long-hidden horse troughs on the North York Moors and his remarkably sharp powers of observation, were strong aids in his ability to detect crimes.

And so it was on that morning in late January that Detective Inspector Montague Pluke wove through the crowds of

Crickledale as he progressed towards the police station. He was heading towards his office on the first floor of Crickledale Sub-Divisional Police Headquarters. The police station boasted splendid views across the little town and in some ways was ideal for keeping observations on streets and their possible trouble spots and to check whether people were behaving responsibly. As he neared his destination, he passed the Town Hall where his highly trained eye had, some years earlier, discovered a huge stone horse trough that had been almost invisible among the stonework. It had been laid on its side and filled with rubble, then used as a gigantic building block and, thanks to his powers of observation and his resultant lobbying, a replica had been constructed. It was now a handsome feature of the town centre, complete with flowing water and a tethering ring that had once featured in a bull's nose. As he passed that edifice every morning, he always felt a glow of pride – he believed he was upholding and indeed furthering the Pluke family's impressive contribution to the illustrious history of Crickledale.

For example, sir Wylyngton Pluke had occupied the Manor House in 1422 whilst Wortham Pluke (1349-93) had been a wandering minstrel. However, it was Justus Pluke (1553-1609) who had established the Pluke dynasty's long association with horse troughs through his futuristic design of horses' heads that he had carved upon the water inlets to stone horse troughs throughout England. He had received national commendation for that innovative work.

During his walk, Pluke was pleased there were no crows in the churchyard, no church-bells ringing without human aid and no reports of death watch beetles tapping in old houses. That suggested no ominous deaths were imminent, and, after all, it did suggest that Mrs Langneb and the other eight had died naturally.

Nonetheless, as he approached the end of his walk to work he did experience nagging feelings that there could have been a cover-up of some kind. He found those thoughts distinctly disturbing.

When Montague Pluke arrived at the police station – a handsome Victorian pile – he stepped through the impressive main door by using his right foot first. But instead of climbing the stairs to his office, he diverted, as always, to the tiny Control Room. The officer in charge was Sergeant Cockfield-pronounced-Cofield and, as ever, his Control Room door was standing open.

'Good morning, sir,' beamed the sergeant, as Pluke entered on time. It was precisely 8.50 a.m. Sergeant Cockfield-pronounced-Cofield left his computer and approached the counter.

'Good morning, Sergeant,' responded Pluke. 'Not a bad morning for the time of year. Now, before I head up to my office, have we, over the weekend, received any reports of sudden or suspicious deaths, major incidents, aircraft crashes, train derailments, arson and other malicious fires, motorway blockages, major crimes, robberies, criminal damage, riots, floods, drug-fuelled outrages, mass shoplifting expeditions and looting, thefts of bicycles from garden sheds or people drinking alcohol in the streets?'

'No, sir, I've just carried out an up-to-date review from all sources and it's been an exceptionally peaceful and quiet weekend, both here and throughout the entire Force area. There is absolutely nothing to report. We've not even had any cats marooned up trees, lost dogs or stray homing pigeons.'

'Thank you, Sergeant. It proves we are keeping crime and social disturbances under control so, in this welcome lull, I propose we undertake a cold-case review. We need something interesting and demanding to occupy us during quiet times.'

'Anything particular in mind, sir?'

'I'm sure there must be an old unsolved crime that will keep our CID officers fully occupied. Could you search your records, Sergeant, and we shall do likewise with CID files? We need something serious, like an unsolved murder or rape.'

'I feel sure there must be something outstanding, sir. I will conduct a comprehensive search, beginning immediately.'

And so, having alerted the station's complement of officers

to his plans, Detective Inspector Pluke led once more with his right foot and climbed the stairs where the magnificently upholstered Mrs Plumpton, his secretary, would be waiting with undivided attention. As he ascended he recalled that the arrival of a pigeon could herald death and wondered if any of the Crickledale deceased had been visited by pigeons? But the sergeant had said no stray pigeons had arrived at the police station. So had they gone elsewhere?

It was not the sort of occurrence a doctor or police officer would have recorded but it was something which he, with his specialist knowledge, could consider with due solemnity.

Chapter 2

RIGHT FOOT FIRST, Montague entered his office and removed his panama, then with a practised swing threw it towards the hat-stand just inside the door. With all the precision of a thrown discus, it settled on its regular hook. Years of practice had polished that modest display of useless skill and then he hung his voluminous old overcoat on another hook before approaching his desk.

But he did not immediately sit down. As always, the office cleaner had moved his desktop treasures to unwelcome locations and so he returned them all to their proper places. He inched his blotter and its load of correspondence to the right, put the coaster for his coffee mug even further to the right so that spilt coffee would not stain official papers, and then moved his model horse-trough full of paper clips towards the rear. He aligned his in-tray, out-tray and pending-tray, and took out of his drawer a rounded stone paperweight known as a witch-stone. It served as a useful paperweight which he placed on top of the correspondence heaped upon his blotter. It would prevent papers blowing all over the office should anyone open the window.

Witch-stones, known also as hag-stones, were circular pieces of rock about the size of one's hand, and they had a hole through the centre. They were formerly thought to deter witches or protect livestock when displayed in houses or stables but Montague preferred to use his as a paperweight. He had found it during one of his trough-hunting expeditions on the North York Moors and had recently discovered it made an ideal resting place for his mobile phone.

Having restored his desk to its state of normality he sat down. Mrs Plumpton in her adjoining office with the door open heard the movements of his chair and recognized it was time to visit him.

She floated into his office amidst a dress of flowing gossamer-like fabric in soft purple shades. It did little to keep her warm or conceal her well-rounded figure but she liked the dress and often wore it because she sensed it intrigued Mr Pluke. However, he wasn't unduly distracted by the vision that regularly confronted him and with an immense display of willpower, was able to dismiss all erotic thoughts and so avoid accusations of sexism. After all, he *was* the Detective Inspector in charge of Crickledale Sub-Divisional CID and must distance himself from any such carnal distractions especially when on duty. After all, he enjoyed a very comfortable home life where he had Millicent and her boiled eggs to admire.

'Good morning, Mr Pluke,' Mrs Plumpton beamed as she bore down upon him with a mug of steaming coffee in her hand. As she bent low to place it on his desk, she remarked, 'A nice morning for the time of year.'

'There is an old Greek saying, Mrs Plumpton, that if January had its own way, it would be a summer month. It is quite often the case that we can enjoy fine and sunny weather in January.'

'I pretend it's summer all the time, Mr Pluke. I do believe in being cheerful and sunny.'

'An admirable trait. So did you know there is an old saying in France that if the sun shines on the feast day of St Vincent, we shall have more wine than water?'

'You know such a lot of interesting things, Mr Pluke.'

'It comes from years of experience and research, Mrs Plumpton. And you should know that St Vincent's Day occurred on January 22nd. You may recall that the sun did shine that day. Now, am I right in thinking there is not the usual amount of incoming correspondence? My pile of mail seems smaller than usual.'

'Certainly that's true, Mr Pluke. Computers and emails are combining to reduce your morning mail. However, there are one or two items that require your signature and a few emails for attention but there's nothing of an urgent or contentious nature. There are a few circulars and routine matters I can deal with.'

She left him in a cloud of something that smelled like hyacinths, whereupon he promptly started to sneeze. Hyacinths had that effect on occasions but once she was inside her own office, his sneezing stopped. Was he allergic or sensitive to Mrs Plumpton, her perfume or hyacinths? Or all three?

'Bless you, Mr Pluke,' her voice wafted through the door. 'I hope it wasn't my perfume.'

'Perhaps I should unearth my wartime gas mask,' he retorted.

With his morning's entertainment over, he found most of his correspondence was boringly routine. There were Home Office Circulars announcing new regulations about motor scooters, crash helmets for invalid carriage drivers and a new range of controlled drugs. In addition, there were leaflets providing details of forthcoming changes and improvements to the Force's official computers along with a new system for checking motor vehicles via the Police National Computer (PNC) and the Driver and Vehicle Licensing Agency (DVLA). He initialled all the documents to indicate he had seen them, then placed them in his out-tray for Mrs Plumpton to deal with. He didn't know what she did with all the paper that flooded in and then disappeared.

With no new crimes reported over the weekend, therefore, it was time for his daily conference with Detective Sergeant Wayne Wain, his deputy. Rather than use the intercom or his mobile, he called to Mrs Plumpton.

'Mrs Plumpton, would you contact Detective Sergeant Wain and tell him I am available to receive him when convenient.'

'Of course, Mr Pluke.'

Detective Inspector Pluke never used an informal manner

of addressing his work colleagues and always addressed his secretary as Mrs Plumpton, never using her forename. In fact, he didn't know her first name. Likewise, he always referred to Detective Sergeant Wain by his surname but because his forename sounded exactly the same as his surname, everyone thought DI Pluke was mellowing. He wasn't, of course and would never contemplate a change of routine or a decline in standards. Soon afterwards, there was a knock on his door and he called, 'Come in.'

Detective Sergeant Wayne Wain entered. In his early thirties and not yet married, he was very tall, dark and handsome with winning ways among all the female persons he encountered. His cheerful disposition endeared him even to some of the suspects he interviewed, especially females and they would readily confess to all manner of exciting things. Some wondered whether he would search them for drugs or stolen goods they had shoplifted but, of course, there was a very strict and formal procedure for searching everyone. Immaculately dressed as always in his dark suit, white shirt and blue tie, Wayne smiled at his boss, pulled out a chair and settled down.

'Good morning, sir, I trust you had a pleasant weekend.'

'Most pleasant, thank you, Wayne but I have not discovered any more new horse troughs. Even on fine days, the winter weather is not conducive to searching those moors but I believe I have discovered an ancient route across the heather, now obliterated but which in times past would have linked several villages. It is highly likely there would have been horse troughs along its route.'

'If there are troughs to be found, sir, I'm sure you will trace them.'

'Indeed I shall. We all know that horses and their owners would require refreshments during their journeys but because this track is ancient and disused with troughs probably buried under earth and vegetation, or even stolen or destroyed, it will not be easy to locate them. But I shall ensure they all become a visible part of our moorland heritage and will take the necessary steps to preserve and protect them.'

'And now it's back to work. What have we on the cards for today? I can't find anything that demands our attention.'

'It's abnormally quiet even by Crickledale standards, Wayne, but I have been thinking it is a splendid opportunity to re-examine old unsolved crimes. I think we should use this opportunity to initiate a cold-case review. I was hoping that with your astonishing memory you might recall some older case – serious or slight – that has never been detected.'

'Leave it with me for an hour or so, sir. I'll go through our records. Shall I check back, say, over the last ten years? And refer only to major crimes?'

'That's a good start and if it doesn't produce anything, we can go back a further ten years. And if that doesn't produce a task for us, we can examine minor unsolved crimes especially those that appear to be the work of serial offenders.'

'I'm sure I'll find something. I'll report back soon.'

'Good, and while you are searching, I'll take a short walk into town. Walks in the fresh morning air do provoke my brain into creative action and I might recall a few cases. I'll return for coffee by which time you might have found something.'

His walk took him past the churchyard and instinctively he checked to see whether any crows were lurking on tombstones or sitting on the boundary walls. In fact he noticed one – it was perched on a tombstone and he realized it was heralding Mrs Langneb's funeral tomorrow in this very churchyard.

As he walked, one regular and oft-recurring memory was that Millicent had referred to the high number of deaths this winter – nine, she'd said. All were due to natural causes and none was considered suspicious. But were they all buried in this Anglican graveyard or were some in other cemeteries? Had some been cremated? Millicent had said that all had been under the care of Crickledale Voluntary Carers. As he pondered the likelihood of something nasty in the filing cabinets, did their number and frequency give rise to suspicion? Indeed, should he and Wayne investigate those deaths as their cold case review?

With that possibility in mind, he required a few moments of

total peace and solitude to develop his idea. There was a lot to think about – would his review lead to scandal in Crickledale? Would there be rumours of a mass killer at large and suspicions against ordinary innocent people? By strolling through the churchyard, he might meet the vicar or one of the churchwardens or possibly the man who tended the graves and graveyard. Informal chats with people involved in local funerals would surely produce some useful gossip laced with valuable information. It was amazing how many times shreds of evidence arose from very diverse and unlikely sources.

If he was *officially* investigating the deaths he would interview all the church officials, families, doctors and so forth, but this was not an official enquiry. Or so he told himself. As he turned into the churchyard and passed through the ancient oak timbered lych-gate to wander among the tombstones, the visiting crow flew away.

During this very early research, he would seek fresh graves or newly installed cremation memorials. This simple task would advise him of those who had been buried recently. If the graves were too new to have attracted inscriptions or headstones, he could check funeral reports in the local paper and if that did not produce results, there was always the Registrar of Births, Deaths and Marriages.

As he began to realize the fear that would be generated by news of a serial killer at large in Crickledale, he accepted that, at the moment, his actions were unofficial. Nonetheless, his enquiries were bound to set tongues a-wagging and rumours abounding. That was precisely what he did *not* want. To maintain secrecy, he and Wayne must therefore resort to subterfuge. It was vital they avoided mass panic with lurid headlines in red-top newspapers. There would be letters in the press and questions in Parliament asking what the local police were doing about it.

Meandering among the monuments, he became aware of a man working with a small digging machine and excavating mounds of earth. This would be Linton Farewell, the man who cared for the graveyard and dug the graves. His odd and rather apt name suggested links with the Potteries because that name was fairly common in that area, if little known in Yorkshire. There was no one else in the graveyard, not even Linton's assistant, 'Sooty' Black. Sooty would be sweeping chimneys in town, which was his full-time profession, and only helping with funerals if he needed extra income.

As Pluke wandered up and down the well-tended rows of tombstones, old and new, the noise of the digging machine came to a halt as the driver noticed Pluke.

'Mr Pluke,' he dismounted and headed in Pluke's direction. 'Good morning to you. It's not often we see you in here.'

'And a good morning to you, Mr Farewell,' responded Pluke in his formal tones. 'Indeed a nice morning.'

'Just off for my break, Mr Pluke, so is there anything I can help with before I go?'

Linton Farewell, the official gravedigger for Crickledale Anglican parish church and church caretaker (which included tending the graveyard, graves and grass-cutting) was a cadaverous fellow in his early fifties who always dressed in black. He wore smart black on funeral days and casual black when at leisure. At work he wore old black clothes, because tending the graves and graveyard necessarily involved a lot of wet earth, mud and clay. His black woolly hat, black jacket and trousers, and heavy black boots, all showed many signs of staining from the strong brown earth of this place. When away from work, he dressed in clean and well-tended clothes, but always black. A lifetime Crickledale resident, his father and his grandfather had been gravediggers here before him but Linton was unmarried and lived in a church-owned cottage in a corner of the churchyard. 'Very handy for work, and dead quiet,' he would often boast.

'I'm not here on official police business,' acknowledged Pluke. 'I'm taking some fresh air as I ponder the pressures of work away from the constant demands of office. As a senior detective with heavy responsibilities, I do need to get away from telephones and callers if I am to think deeply and be creative. I find that the peace of a churchyard is ideal.'

'I know what you mean, Mr Pluke, and this is normally a very quiet place but I'm busy this morning, making enough noise to waken the dead,' and he laughed at his own joke. 'So how can I help you? Is there something you want?'

'Perhaps you can tell me who is going to occupy this patch of ground,' Pluke indicated the newly dug patch.

'Mrs Langneb, you'll have heard she's gone to meet her maker? Well, her husband Harold is already buried here, so I have to dig hers beside him without interfering with his patch of ground. East-to-west orientation, head to the west. Her funeral is tomorrow.'

'It can't be the easiest of jobs, Mr Farewell, accommodating two bodies in one grave without causing undue disturbance.'

'True, but I am very experienced, Mr Pluke, a highly diligent craftsman, and I won't disturb him. Even so, it's not easy with a powerful and fast-moving digging machine, believe me. The old pick-and-shovel system had its merits, even if it was hard work. But Mrs Langneb was a lovely lady, Mr Pluke, I shall do my best for her.'

'Most considerate of you, Mr Farewell.'

'Well, she passed away very nicely and in peace, so I'm told, and the funeral's at 2pm. We're not expecting a big crowd, she lived alone, you know, since Harold died. Her sons are both living down south. There's no family hereabouts so the CVC will rustle up a few mourners from regular churchgoers, then there's always those who come only for the funeral tea. You're welcome to join us.'

'I didn't know the lady, Mr Farewell, and will have to check my diary, on top of which there is much to keep me busy fighting crime,' but Pluke could not let this opportunity pass without a comment to the official gravedigger about the recent high rate of deaths. He said, 'I hear you've been very busy in recent weeks.'

'I have indeed, Mr Pluke, me and my mate Sooty. Lots of funerals close together but good for business. I'm sure the undertakers aren't complaining and certainly their customers aren't!'

'Are all those recently deceased people buried here?'

'Most are here but not all. Here we've got good Anglicans who think they're Catholics and won't tolerate the idea of cremation. They do like to be buried beside their friends or relations with a dash of papist pomp and ceremony.'

'I can appreciate that thought, Mr Farewell.'

'It's very fitting they're all here, Mr Pluke. You'll find a graveyard plan in the porch with their names on it. All were members of this congregation, you know; all old folks living alone due to various circumstances but all remaining loyal to this church and to those who cared for them. They all used to come to our old folks' teas and bingo games. We are very lucky in this small town, Mr Pluke, having people who care so well for others, and with such devotion, and who work in their spare time to provide entertainment and care for the elderly. Here in Crickledale, the CVC never lets lonely folks pass away uncared for or not remembered, even those buried away from the town. They make sure everyone has a happy death whoever they are, or as happy as a death can be, and they are not ignored later – the CVC see to the flowers, tidy the graves and so on.'

'I find that very encouraging, Mr Farewell.'

'Well, you're very fortunate in having Mrs Pluke. She's an excellent carer, always helpful and sympathetic to the needs of others. She's not a boastful person, Mr Pluke, calm and pleasant, always willing to help in whatever way she can.'

'You're well acquainted with the CVC are you, Mr Farewell?'

'My work brings me into very close contact with them. I help out sometimes on those jobs that need a man about the house and so does Sooty. He'll always sweep a chimney free of charge, Mr Pluke, that shows you what sort of man he is. Lovely chap. I've known him do a chimney while I've been sorting out what trinkets the deceased wants buried with him or her. It's amazing what folks want beside them in their coffins – everything from a good book to a ready-meal. All these deaths have kept us busy and they say it's due to the mild winter, Mr Pluke, but I don't think so. I think that when your time is up, you've got to prepare to go to meet your maker, irrespective of the weather or the time of year. Me, Sooty and Rolly all help folks do that in whatever way we can.'

'Who's Rolly?'

'You must have come across him, Mr Pluke. He's an out-of-work builder. When the firm he worked for went bust he got himself work doing odd jobs around town. There's always somebody who needs a job doing, anything from cleaning spouts to fixing loose tiles. Rolly Parkinson can turn his hand to any job and he'll deal with anything. He does jobs for the CVC without wanting pay. Good chap to have around, Mr Pluke, he's on our list of volunteers. We've a good team of carers in this town.'

'You're right, Mr Farewell, we are very fortunate. But have you noticed that when the winter is mild, the graveyards fill up quickly, not just here in Yorkshire but all over Britain?'

'I don't dispute that, Mr Pluke, and I must be honest by saying I'm most grateful for the extra income. We all need extra money in winter what with heating costs, petrol and food.'

'So do your wages as groundsman include gravedigging?'

'No, the parish pays for me as groundsman, to look after the churchyard but the undertakers pay for my gravedigging and most of Sooty's work here, it's all very welcome bits of income, Mr Pluke.'

'You're very fortunate, Mr Farewell and it is a wise and very Christian attitude by your employer.'

'It is but I would never dig a grave on a Sunday, Mr Pluke, that wouldn't seem right, nor would I come here on a bank holiday unless it was an emergency. But that has never happened. Me and Sooty work well as a team, helping each other, doing extra jobs here, trimming the hedges, cutting the lawns, getting rid of dead flowers and so on.'

'You do keep the place nice, Mr Farewell.'

'I do my best. Well, it's been nice to talk, Mr Pluke, call again if I can help in any way but now I must be off. I'm not allowed an extended break and have to get this job finished before I knock off.'

As Linton Farewell headed for the little shed behind the church to enjoy his break, Pluke walked along every aisle in the churchyard, noting all the new graves. They were easily identified because they all sported vases of fresh flowers, except for Mrs Langneb's empty space, but some did not yet bear the names of their occupants. He could always double-check on the graveyard plan in the porch or get official access to the names of the recently deceased, should that prove necessary.

Counting the forthcoming tomb of Mrs Langneb, he counted the eight fairly new graves. Nine recent deaths. A lot. Millicent was right, but it was worrying that it had escaped the attention of the town's constabulary, himself included.

But, he tried to reassure himself, that situation was absolutely normal because the police had no official interest in natural deaths, and all had been without suspicion. As he prepared to leave with his professional instincts making the situation rather unclear, he felt his chat with Linton Farewell had been useful but there was nothing more he could do without the necessary support from official files.

It was time to return to the office to see what Wayne Wain had discovered.

Chapter 3

WAYNE ENTERED PLUKE'S office clutching a file and announced, 'I've remembered a case with something odd about it.'

He was followed by Mrs Plumpton bearing a tray with two coffee mugs and some biscuits. Stooping to give her charms maximum exposure, she placed one mug on Pluke's coaster and handed the other to Wayne, then departed in a cloud of perfume as Pluke sneezed.

'Bless you,' she called.

As he recovered from both the vision and the sneeze, Pluke noticed that Wayne's file didn't relate to an undetected crime because it had string around it; that indicated the case was closed and papers had been placed in the Dead Section.

'Sit down, Wayne, you look very dangerous, hovering with hot coffee.'

'As you say, sir.' He settled at the other side of Pluke's spacious desk and made good use of a pile of papers as a stand for his coffee. 'This'll interest you, with your specialist knowledge.'

'Horse troughs, you mean?'

'No, I was thinking of local folklore and superstitious practices.'

'Really?' Pluke was now settled and the coffee was perfect. 'But Wayne, from where I'm sitting that file appears to have come from the Dead Section. It means the matter has been finalized. We're looking for an *undetected* crime, an unsolved case that's suitable for a cold-case review.'

'I know, but listen to this. An elderly woman was found dead on the floor of the former pantry in her cottage. She was called Adelaide Croucher . . .'

Pluke interrupted. 'I don't recall that name, Wayne.'

'Then I'll refresh your memory. Miss Croucher used her former pantry as a utility room, a cool store for food and vegetables. It was also big enough to store her cleaning materials and the vacuum cleaner.'

'That may be so, but I still can't recall the case,' muttered Pluke. 'Or her name.'

Wayne ploughed on. 'When the doctor examined Miss Croucher, he certified her death and his brief examination suggested there were no suspicious circumstances and no sign of an attack upon her. However, he had previously visited her and treated her on fairly regular occasions so he was familiar with her medical record. He stated he had no doubt her death was from natural causes – in simple terms, old age. The coroner didn't order a post mortem or an inquest, and consequently neither the CID nor the uniform branch investigated the death. The file was therefore closed. That is absolutely normal in those circumstances. It was the end of the matter.'

'So why are you trying to resurrect this case?' asked Pluke.

'I think it was peculiar because she was lying on the floor of her pantry face-up with all the windows open and doors unlocked. Anyone could have entered her house and it was never established how she reached that ground-floor room from her bed. She was in her nightclothes but her bedroom was upstairs.'

'Is that all, Wayne? You've nothing more sinister than that?'

'What is not apparent from this file is that the police *did* attend the scene – it was me. I was there, that's how I remember it. Her neighbour had reported her lying dead and suspected an attack upon Miss Croucher so she called Crickledale police. PC Carey was on town duty patrol and was directed to the scene.'

'Are you suggesting there *were* suspicious circumstances, Wayne?'

'I'm saying there was something odd about this case.'

'Can you explain, Wayne? I need to be convinced.'

'At first sight, it did look as if she had been attacked by an intruder and it was pure chance that I happened to be there. Taking everything into account, I believe there was, and still is, an element of suspicion about the case.'

'You've not explained things very clearly, Wayne. If you say you nursed an element of suspicion, why wasn't her death categorized as suspicious? Why wasn't it investigated?'

'There was an investigation but it was a normal and very routine sudden-death enquiry which determined she had died from natural causes. It meant there was no police interest from that point. And that's all that was done.'

'So when did this death occur? I still can't understand why I wasn't aware of it.'

'It was about three years ago, you were on annual leave, sir. You went to Siena and later found the missing Golden Horse Trough that was associated with that big horse race around the market square, the *Palio*. I think you were away for nearly three weeks. It was all over by the time you returned. In any case, there was no reason why you should have known about Miss Croucher's death.'

'That must explain it, Wayne. If you had been concerned, you would have talked it over with me. But, as you say, I was in Italy. It was quite wonderful, a holiday to treasure. So Miss Croucher's death, even though you found it puzzling, was not considered a matter I should have been made aware of upon my return to duty?'

'No. The duty town inspector decided no further action should be taken. The file was closed. It's stuck in my memory because one of the funeral directors also thought it was odd . . .'

'Which director? Can you remember?'

'Not off the top of my head, no. But I expect his name will be in the file.'

'We'll find it if we need it. So in what way did he mean *odd*?'

'I think he was talking about all those open windows and unlocked doors and the fact she was lying on her back in her nightie on the pantry floor with no sign of an attack or break-in. It was probably a combination of those factors but the funeral director never explained what he meant by *odd*. He couldn't explain – I think he was relying on his instinct. Perhaps it was nothing more than a passing comment? Something said spontaneously without much thought? But I couldn't forget it had come from a person who was very experienced in dealing with dead bodies. In spite of all that, Miss Croucher's death was treated like any other routine sudden death, with no suspicious attached. The undertaker's men removed her body to their chapel of rest and she was eventually buried in Crickledale churchyard. Her cousins who lived in Suffolk came to the funeral but she had never married and had no local dependants. She wasn't wealthy even if she owned her own cottage; I doubt if there was anything in her house of interest to thieves.'

'You said she was elderly?'

'Yes. 89 and very frail although not suffering from any serious illness. Her funeral was a quiet affair. The house was willed to her neighbours, the folks living at Weaver's Cottage next door. West was their name. They've now knocked both cottages into one large property.'

'You said you were involved, Wayne? Why was that? It seems an unlikely case for a CID officer to deal with. Uniform deal with routine sudden deaths.'

'Sergeant Cockfield-pronounced-Cofield received a call to say a woman was lying dead on the ground floor of her cottage with all the doors and windows open. He despatched PC Grant Carey to make an immediate investigation because the address was on his beat.'

'And then what?'

'By chance, I was walking past Tiler's Cottage when PC Carey arrived. It was about 10 am. I stopped for a chat and he told me a neighbour had rung to say Miss Croucher had been attacked in her own home. Because it had all the signs of a suspicious death, I asked if I could help him. There was no need to break in. Both the back door and front door were standing open as they were when the neighbour found her.'

'Unlocked doors wouldn't be unusual in Crickledale at that time of day, would they? You said it was around ten in the morning.'

'It was, on a nice warm day. But those doors weren't merely unlocked, they were standing open. I could also smell smoke or soot and thought she'd been cleaning or airing the house . . . anyway, PC Carey asked if I could help him by having a look at the scene – in case it was a crime scene.'

'Did he say why he wanted help?'

'He was a young constable. He felt he needed support in case there was something suspicious or evidence he might not notice. After all, he had been told the woman had been attacked and it was the first time he'd dealt with a suspicious death so I agreed. In any case, scenes of death are always of interest to a detective.'

'One is never off duty, Wayne, one is always alert to the possibility of serious crime even in the most innocent of cir-cumstances. You did the right thing.'

'I had a good look around. She was lying on the old pantry floor in her nightdress. She was on her back with her hands crossed over her stomach with her legs straight out.'

'Very neat – folks who collapse and die don't normally arrange themselves so neatly, do they? And neither do victims of murderous attacks.'

'They don't. I didn't think she'd collapsed or tripped, she was far too tidy for that. It was just as if she'd been arranged for burial. Then I realized all the windows were open around the house, upstairs and downstairs – the pantry had no windows.'

'And you said the doors were wide open?'

'Standing open, yes. My first examination showed there were no signs of forcible entry or attacks on either Miss Croucher or the house. I told PC Carey that I saw nothing suspicious even if the circumstances were extremely peculiar and I advised him to call a doctor. After all, she could have opened her own doors and windows. I explained to PC Carey what he should do next and once I was satisfied that he could deal with the matter, I left him and took no further part in that investigation. So far as I'm aware, it was never established how she managed to get downstairs – she had had one of those stair-lift chairs and I noticed it was at the top of the stairs, not the bottom as you'd have expected.'

'So PC Carey dealt with it as a routine sudden death?'

'Yes but he was supervised throughout by the town's duty sergeant. Being such a young constable, he wouldn't have been left entirely alone to deal with that.'

'Hmm,' frowned Pluke. 'I agree there's something odd about this one. I'll need to study the file.'

'Some time ago, sir, you explained about the ritual opening of windows and doors when death occurs, but at that time I couldn't recall the full implications. Sadly you weren't there to have a look at the scene.'

'I would have wanted a lot more questions answered.'

'There were several I asked myself. How had she got down-stairs with her stair-lift left at the top? Her bed had the covers in place if she had never slept in it. Her breakfast things were on the kitchen table, untouched, as if she'd put them out the previous evening but not used them. And when, exactly, had she come downstairs? Was it in the dark? The lights were not on in the house when I entered.'

'This gets more intriguing . . .' muttered Pluke.

'My thoughts exactly. And there's more. How did she come to be lying there so sedately – at peace, in fact? Those were the sort of things a detective would – and should – notice. The sort of things that needed answers. I did wonder whether a villain had attacked her and sent her stair-lift back upstairs, then straightened the bed covers to give the impression she'd never been in bed.'

'Thanks, Wayne. That's a neat summary and I think this is perfect for a cold-case review. Now I need to know more about it.'

'This will put my mind at rest, I've often worried that a killer might have got through the net.'

'Then let's not waste any more time. Do you want to con-tinue in here or shall we find somewhere more private?'

'I would suggest somewhere more private,' Wayne was thinking of Mrs Plumpton's flapping ears but she was on the phone, something to do with a query from Headquarters about a shotgun certificate.

'Right, follow me and bring that file.' Pluke rose to his feet but did not don either his hat or his coat as he led the way downstairs to the interview room. It was part of the cell block. Without any prisoners or recently arrested persons, it would be quiet in there.

When passing the Control Room doorway, Pluke addressed Sergeant Cockfield-pronounced-Cofield.

'DS Wain and myself will be in the interview room for half an hour or so, nicely away from flapping ears, Sergeant. I mention that in case someone needs to know our whereabouts – but we shall be discussing confidential matters so kindly do not disturb us unless it is an emergency.'

'Very good, sir.'

When they were settled at the small table with the thick door closed, like an interrogator and his victim, Pluke invited Wayne to proceed.

'I've taken a photocopy of the file, sir, so you can examine the original drawings, statements and house-plans. There are copies of official photographs taken at the time, Dr Simpson's certificate and a resume of the scientific investigation of the house interior.'

'Scientific investigation? So there *was* an official enquiry?'

'Only because at the time, it was thought the death was suspicious. The examination, done by Scenes of Crime officers, was nothing more than preparation of the file for the coroner. He accepted Dr Simpson's opinion that death was from natural causes, so no further action was necessary. There was no post mortem or inquest and the coroner issued a burial certificate.' He handed Pluke the secondary file.

'In spite of our procedures failing to confirm there was suspicion, Wayne, I agree there's cause for concern. It was never established how the poor woman had come to be on the cold floor of her pantry or why her windows and doors were wide open. Every detail is vital, so can you please outline the entire case once more? I need to know all the facts before I decide how to tackle our cold case review.'

Wayne Wain reminded Pluke that Miss Adelaide Croucher, a spinster aged 89, had lived all her life at Tiler's Cottage, March Street, Crickledale; the cottage had belonged to her parents and she had inherited it. There were no other members of the family and Miss Croucher had worked in the local printers in the town centre, mainly with secretarial work interspaced with some proof reading and editing. She had no mortgage and existed on her old-age pension, her savings and a tiny pension from her former employer. She was not wealthy and hardly a target for burglars and thieves.

Throughout her long life she had never suffered a serious illness, but in recent years had become increasingly frail and unable to cope with stairs or the walk into town to do her shopping. She had had a chair-lift fitted to her staircase. She didn't own a car or invalid carriage and depended heavily on the support of carers from Crickledale Volunteer Carers (CVC), one of whom was Mrs Pluke. Their volunteers and her neighbour – also a CVC volunteer carer – called regularly to ensure she was never without food or essentials such as firewood and coal. The carers also did her washing, ironing and household cleaning. Miss Croucher could cope with routine and less-demanding work. It was the more strenuous activities that defeated her – such as taking a bath, making her bed or changing a light bulb.

'The Carers in CVC are very good, as you know,' confirmed Wayne. 'The organisation is run under the auspices of Crickledale District Council with a chairman, secretary and two full-time professional Carers who actually run the organisation and make assessments of those who may be in need of care. The chairman is a fairly recent arrival – within the last five years or so – and he seems to have got it functioning very successfully.'

'He's called Mr Furnival, according to my wife,' smiled Pluke.

'I know nothing about Mr Furnival, but most of the active

carers are volunteers and much of their care is of a routine nature – helping with meals, shopping, cleaning, making beds. Furnival arranges and supervises their duties. The volunteers are unpaid and live locally so they become known to the person in their care. In addition, of course, the professional carers tend minor injuries and sickness, help the patients to get bathed or showered, or simply washed and dressed. It's a two-tier system that works well as I'm sure you understand from Mrs Pluke's involvement.'

'She enjoys the work, Wayne,' smiled Pluke. 'She feels she is putting something back into the community. Thanks to her, I know a good deal about the carers and their work. There are plenty of them to share the load. There's a call-out system too – if a client needs urgent help, they can press a button on a bleeper worn around the neck and also on their telephone. The bleeper alerts the CVC duty member of staff either in the CVC office or at home out-of-hours. The duty controller can then alert one of the volunteers who will respond. The carers also carry official mobile phones when on duty, with a free telephone link with the CVC office – just a matter of pressing one of the red buttons. Mrs Pluke assured me it has become very well run and highly professional, thanks to Mr Furnival.'

'Perhaps I should point out that when Miss Croucher died, sir, Mrs Pluke was in Italy with you. She may know very little about Miss Croucher's death.'

'That explains why she has never mentioned it,' affirmed Pluke.

'Right, that's about all. It's the background to the case and full details are in the file.'

'One minor point, Wayne. You said that after seeing Miss Croucher's body, you found that her bed was made? As if she hadn't slept in it?'

'Yes. I wondered if she had never been upstairs to bed. Got ready perhaps, then collapsed. Or had a visitor.'

'It does seem likely someone deliberately established a decoy situation to mislead an investigator. She was in her nightdress when you found her?'

'No doubt about it, sir.'

'I'm not surprised that you've nursed concerns about this case. So, Wayne, the first question we must ask is whether this death is linked to others. Remember a ninth body in only three months is destined for the grave tomorrow.'

'And not one has come to the official notice of CID! Either the killers are very clever or there were no suspicious circumstances in any of them.'

'There's another factor, Wayne. Looking at things from a detective's point of view, I'd remind us that all have been neatly buried with the minimum of fuss. No suspicions. No police involvement. No publicity. All neatly erased from our memories. It's time we got busy with this enquiry, Wayne. We need to talk to Dr Simpson first.'

'Are you suggesting our cold-case review will include all the deaths?'

'In view of what we have learned and what we suspect, we can't ignore that, Wayne. Let's begin immediately to see what comes to light, then we can decide whether to investigate all or just some of those deaths. So tell me again, Wayne, exactly what the witness said, I'm referring to the neighbour who found Miss Croucher. How did she know Mrs Croucher was lying on her utility room floor if that room has no windows?'

Chapter 4

'SHE EXPLAINS THAT in her statement. She's Miss Rachel West who lived next door at Weaver's Cottage to the right of Tiler's Cottage when facing from the street. . . .'

'And she one of the CVC Carers, you said?'

'She is, yes.'

'Then we must interview her. She inherited Tiler's Cottage from Miss Croucher, didn't she? And had it converted to make Weaver's Cottage and Tiler's Cottage into one large house?'

'Yes, that's true.'

'Then there is your motive, Wayne. A reason to speed up the death of Miss Croucher.'

'That possibility was never investigated.'

'It should have been! We need to question Miss West and examine her background, Wayne. Please continue.'

'She had keys for both the back and front doors of Miss Croucher's house and had always been a good neighbour and close friend. She was always popping in over and above her carer's duties.'

'Was it during one of those visits that she found Miss Croucher dead?'

'Yes it was. She called in as usual after breakfast. The back door was standing open. The kitchen window was also wide open and once she was inside she noticed Miss Croucher's feet sticking out of the doorway of the former pantry.'

'A genuine account of her discovery, you think?'

'There was no reason to doubt her version of events.'

'So where exactly was Miss West when she first saw Miss Croucher's body?'

'It was when she entered the kitchen. She could haven't have seen Miss Croucher from outside the house. As you said, the former pantry has no windows.'

'We need to be absolutely certain about that sequence of events, Wayne.'

'It's not going to be easy, the house has been radically altered so we can't check her movements with any precision.'

'How very convenient, Wayne! Please continue.'

'Miss Croucher was lying on her back wearing her nightie, most of her body being inside the old pantry with its door standing open. Miss West thought her friend must have collapsed or fallen so she touched her, but found her stone cold and stiff. There was no sign of any blood, but thinking she might have been attacked she rang the police. She spoke to Sergeant Cockfield-pronounced-Cofield.'

'Where did she ring from?'

'Miss Croucher's own landline phone. She knew the house very well.'

'That call would have been recorded?'

'Yes, it was. I've listened to it. The sergeant advised her to remain where she was until his officer arrived within a few minutes. The sergeant would not know that I was going to be there too, but I turned up with PC Carey.'

'You had ample time to make your own professional observations, Wayne?'

'Yes, I was in the house for some time. Maybe as long as half an hour.'

'What was your first impression?'

'I thought it was a crime scene and said so to PC Carey. I advised him how to proceed. For a while we stood in the front doorway, visually examining the scene like good detectives, not touching or disturbing anything.'

'So there would have been a minimal disturbance of evidence despite Miss West's presence?'

'Right. When Miss West went to attend Miss Croucher, she may have unwittingly disturbed something of significance but as things transpired, it was of little consequence. It was not a crime scene. Apart from testing Miss Croucher for signs of life, she handled the telephone. Nothing else.'

'Can you be sure of that?'

'Not a hundred per cent, no. Probably eighty per cent. The front door was standing open when I arrived with PC Carey, Miss West was waiting in the hall having already found Miss Croucher. She said the inner door was standing open too when she arrived, and that puzzled her.'

'So what did you do at that stage?'

'I remained awhile to help PC Carey because this had the appearance of a crime scene. He called Control Room to request a police photographer, a Scenes of Crime officer and the police doctor, then before they arrived, I invited him to examine the corpse. After all, this was his case so that was his job. At that stage he became the coroner's officer and he'd have to identify the deceased to the coroner. It was essential he viewed the body. He touched her face and tested her pulse. She was, of course, in a state of *rigor mortis*. Undoubtedly dead.'

'Good training for the constable. Then what?'

'Due to the odd position of Miss Croucher, perhaps due to attack, I advised PC Carey to search the house in case an intruder was hiding on the premises.'

'And?'

'He carried out the search with the least possible distur-bance of evidence, but found nothing and no one.'

'Was it thorough?'

'I'd say it was more of a cursory search, bearing in mind that we did not wish to disturb any possible evidence. I made sure he searched the loft, then while we were awaiting the doctor and photographer, we made further careful searches for evidence of a physical attack or a break-in but found nothing.'

'And after that?'

'Dr Simpson arrived, he's one of the partners in Crickledale surgery as I'm sure you know. He was on the scene very quickly, confirmed the death and, knowing Miss Croucher's medical history, said she'd died from natural causes – old age. He was prepared to certify that.'

'So this was all very routine police work? In many respects a perfectly ordinary sudden death investigation?'

'It was. I left PC Carey to cope and took no further part. I was not there when SOCO and the photographer arrived but by then, of course, their presence was not necessary although the photographer took a few photographs, merely for the record. In transpired that that was a sensible thing to do – the position of Miss Croucher was somewhat unusual, the photographs explained a lot.'

'So when you left the house, you continued your normal duties?'

'Yes I did. I had to interview a witness for a statement about a crime in Manchester. However before leaving Miss Croucher's house I advised PC Carey not to forget that the deceased had been found in that rather strange position, along with all the other attendant circumstances such as the open doors and windows. I suggested he recorded those facts in his official notebook, just in case the information was needed in the future. And I advised him to obtain a statement from Dr Simpson to record his decision that death was from natural causes. He did so.'

'Now, Wayne, from your own recollections can you tell me whether Miss Croucher was wearing bedroom slippers as she lay on the floor?'

Wayne frowned. 'Slippers? To be honest, I'm not sure. Certainly she was in her nightdress and nothing else – no cardigan or dressing gown – and at first she looked as though she was asleep. But bedroom slippers? I can't be sure.'

'I would have thought that if she had come downstairs for something – a drink of cocoa or warm milk – she might have risked walking down if only to test her own abilities but surely she would have worn slippers? Especially with such a cold stone floor.'

'That's the sort of thing the photographs might show us,'

suggested Wayne.

Pluke opened the file and located the collection of official photographs – he found several depicting the body of Miss Croucher lying on the floor. Her feet were bare with no discarded slippers in sight.

'There we are, Wayne. Bare feet. I think that's another indication she didn't walk downstairs. I'm beginning to think someone carried her down, but if that happened, was she alive or dead at the time? It wouldn't be easy even for a very strong man to carry her on his own but there were no signs of her being dragged down the stairs, were there? Dead bodies are notoriously difficult to carry even if there are two or three carriers – living people of all shapes and sizes are much easier.'

'The stair carpet wasn't ruffled and her body bore no signs of rough treatment before death. No bruises or abrasions. The doctor's report confirms that.'

'We've learned a good deal already, Wayne but the question remains – how did she get downstairs? And was she dead or alive at that time? Now, when all the experts had had their say, what was PC Carey's attitude?'

'I saw him later. I think he did very well, sir, but he did explain that he felt sorry he had not found any explanation for Miss Croucher's curious death. He felt he had let her down by leaving so many unanswered questions.'

'He is speaking like a true detective, Wayne, who wants to find answers to every question, however difficult and obscure the answers might be. So where is PC Carey? We should talk to him, he might have had more recollections of the case.'

'He's been away for a few weeks on a residential police driving course but I believe he's now back in Crickledale. I think Miss Croucher's case upset him, he felt there was something not right about it but couldn't convince his superiors. I think her sad death has been forgotten by most of us.'

'Except you, Wayne. You said Miss Croucher is buried in Crickledale? In the Anglican churchyard?'

'She is. You're not thinking of an exhumation are you?'

'Not at this stage but if our cold-case review suggests a crime was committed and covered up, that's something I'll have to consider.'

'It won't be easy establishing the truth after all this time, will it? I'll find PC Carey and will have a chat with him but reconstructing events in a house that no longer exists, tracing witnesses, obtaining scientific and forensic evidence will make things difficult.'

'Nothing is impossible, Wayne. Where there's a will, there's a way, as the saying goes. You've certainly provided food for thought and there's one fortunate aspect to this. It is that Miss Croucher had lots of people caring for her, official and unofficial. They're our witnesses, Wayne, so we must interview every one of them.'

'Including Mrs Pluke?'

'She was in Italy at the time, Wayne. I can vouch for that!'

'I still think she must be interviewed if she attended Miss Croucher. She may have observed something relevant that occurred at other times.'

'Then you must interview her, Wayne, it would not be ethical for me to do so.'

'She will not be alone, we're not picking on her! All the carers had access to Miss Croucher's house so all must be interviewed. They wouldn't be interviewed at the time because it wasn't considered a suspicious death.'

'If I had been on duty at that time, Wayne, and if the suspicions surrounding this death had been made known to me, I would have spoken to every carer and every visitor who had been to her house before her death and even on the day of her death. Neighbours and friends too. I would have interviewed the undertaker – you've indicated he felt the circumstances were odd. I would want to know if anyone had noticed anything unusual about the comings and goings at Miss Croucher's. And what about her relationships with other people?'

'You make me feel I should have done more, sir, but it was out of my hands.'

'Experts and senior police officers can be wrong, Wayne. So let's re-investigate this death as if it was a case of homicide or even murder. It will make a splendid cold-case review.'

'Won't it spark off a panic in town and attract journalists? Surely we don't want rumours of a serial murderer at large in Crickledale with all the official carers being considered suspects!'

'As I said earlier, we must adopt some subterfuge to conceal our true purpose. What we must remember as police officers, Wayne, is that crimes cannot go unpunished even if our activities do alarm the general public. We must undertake our duties without fear or favour.'

'You're admitting it's a crime then?'

'I'm saying there are suspicious circumstances, Wayne, nothing more than that at this stage. However, it means we must strike whilst the subject is hot in our minds.'

'Aren't we spending too much time and effort on Miss Croucher's case, sir? Searching for motives and crimes when none might exist?'

'If we are to investigate possible cases of multiple murders, Wayne, we need a yardstick by which to judge future enquiries. Serial killers work to a pattern, and if that pattern has been formed in the case of Miss Croucher, it will have been used in other cases. Now we shall recognize it.'

'Ah, thank you. Yes, I understand.'

'If this was a case of murder, Wayne, it was achieved in such a way that it did not raise suspicion in the minds of our experts. That suggests the killer or killers are very skilled and very clever, well able to conceal evidence of their activities. Just suppose they are committing, or have committed, more crimes? Are they committing murder right under our noses without a hint of suspicion arising?'

'This does seem possible, sir, and I find that very frightening.'

'If they are as clever as that, Wayne, they will never be detected. They have perfected secret murder. Not perfect murder. Secret murder. Our job, therefore, is to work out when and how they will commit the next murder, then set a trap to catch them. With live bait! So subterfuge, with a little help from Miss Croucher, is vital.'

'You'll tell me what you have in mind?'

'I will indeed. But now it's lunchtime and Mrs Pluke will be expecting me. We're having an early meal because Mrs Pluke has an afternoon engagement; she's helping to prepare Mrs Langneb's funeral tea for tomorrow.'

'You might learn a little more from her?'

'Nothing is impossible, Wayne. I shall discuss this further with you in my office upon my return at two o'clock. In the meantime, perhaps you could establish the name of the undertaker who buried Miss Croucher, the one who thought there was something odd about her death? We must establish exactly what he thought was odd.'

Chapter 5

'HERE'S YOUR BEEF casserole, Montague,' beamed Millicent. 'I'm sorry it's an early lunch but I have to dash off. Several ladies have hair appointments for tomorrow's funeral and I promised to help by doing some of their work.'

'It's no problem,' smiled Montague. 'Glad to help.'

'I hope I'm not a nuisance but you're not very busy just now, are you?'

'Things are rather quiet,' he admitted before adding, 'But we're considering the re-opening of some old unsolved cases, Millicent, perhaps committed by serial offenders. We're going to conduct a cold-case review.'

'Serial offenders? I didn't think you had any unsolved cases, Montague? I thought you had a 100% clear-up rate for serious crime.'

'Our department does have a full detection rate, Millicent, but that doesn't include Crickledale Police Station as a whole. The uniform section has some undetected minor crimes on its books and there are always cases and procedures that need to be re-examined if and when new evidence arises. We never rest, Millicent, we are eternally vigilant and we in Crickledale CID take our responsibilities very seriously. But I would not wish my duties to impinge upon your work with the CVC.'

'As you know, Crickledale Volunteer Carers – amateurs and part-timers – work very hard alongside professionals and it's always interesting to make comparisons. We learn from one another and recently I was most impressed at the way our members rallied around to help Mrs Langneb in her final hours. She needed help and we made sure she got it, but we said we would never make the same mistakes as we did with poor Miss Hullott.'

'Miss Hullott? So what happened to Miss Hullott?' he asked.

'It was nothing really, not the sort of carelessness that would interest the police or even the newspapers. You'll remember she died last December? Just before Christmas?'

'Did she? I had no idea.'

'The police weren't involved, Montague, otherwise you'd have known. She had been ill, poor thing, for quite a long time and we all took turns caring for her. She insisted on cleanliness and hated smoke; she had her chimney swept every month. One morning when one of our ladies went to make her breakfast, she found poor Miss Hullott lying on the bedroom floor. She was quite dead with all the windows and doors open. It was quite a shock, I can tell you. Some of us were in tears. We felt we'd let her down.'

Montague did not know how to react. 'Is this true, Millicent? All the doors and windows were open? And she was lying on the bedroom floor?'

'Yes, just as if she'd been laid out for her coffin.'

'So the police weren't called? Not even the uniform branch?'

'No, it was just a routine natural death with no police enquiries and no post mortem or inquest.'

'Well, I must say I'm very surprised, Millicent. Clearly the doctor must have been confident about certifying the cause of death.'

'He'd treated her for several weeks before she died so he was familiar with her condition and had no doubts about her cause of death. It was Dr Simpson, a partner in Crickledale Surgery, I'm sure you know him. The CVC use him where possible. The police weren't involved, Montague, but I must admit I thought it all rather peculiar. I suppose that's because I am a policeman's wife, we tend to be aware of such things.'

'But you never told me, Millicent.'

'We have a duty of confidentiality towards all our patients, Montague and besides, I didn't think you'd be interested. Her death was entirely from natural causes and in no way suspicious. That was the official medical conclusion.'

'So how or why had the windows and doors come to be open, Millicent? And why was she lying on the bedroom floor? Was it carpeted?'

'No, it was bare wooden floorboards, it's an old house and she was rather old fashioned.'

'Didn't that cause the doctor some concern?'

'We never knew, Montague, there were no enquiries about it. No one tried to establish what she'd been doing before she was discovered. I think it was put down to nothing more than old age. Old people do some funny things at times. The CVC and Dr Simpson both agreed with that diagnosis.'

'So, Millicent, within your knowledge did that sort of thing happen to any other people in the care of Crickledale Volunteer Carers?'

'So far as I recall, the only other one I heard about was Miss Croucher but she had managed to get downstairs somehow.'

'We were away at that time, Millicent, in Italy.'

'Yes, I know, you *do* know about her?'

'Just a little,' he admitted. 'Detective Sergeant Wain has been going through some old files and came across Miss Croucher's death – he recalled it because he had attended the house at the time. At first, it seemed she had been attacked but tests revealed the death was due to natural causes. There was no police investigation.'

'I hope you are not snooping, Montague Pluke! Dredging up old cases that have nothing to do with you and your criminal investigations!'

'We are clearing out old files to make more space, Millicent, and this one happened to be right in front of us! We chatted about it because Detective Sergeant Wain had attended the incident – by chance he was passing when the local patrolling constable was investigating and so he stopped to give assistance. You mentioned Miss Hullott. Was there something odd about her death?'

'She was upstairs and lying on the floor beside her bed. She had been checked by Mrs Jarvis at bedtime on the Wednesday and found by one of our volunteers next morning.'

'Mrs Jarvis is efficient, is she?'

'Of course she is, Montague! Juliet Jarvis is a fine professional! I believe all our other casualties died in their beds although I can't be a 100 per cent sure. I am not privy to all such circumstances. Now, I don't want you delving into CVC practices, Montague, I don't want you snooping. I am telling you this in confidence, this is between you and I as man and wife.'

'I get the feeling that you are concerned in some way, Millicent,' was his response. 'Is something troubling you?'

'You are very perceptive, Montague. I must admit things are not quite as I would have hoped . . . little things . . . lost papers, carers not turning up on time or not at all, relatives reporting things missing when an old person dies . . . matters of that kind. No one seems to check such things . . . not like the police who check everything. But these are trivial internal matters, Montague. Such things going on in every kind of office and there is nothing to concern you. Most certainly you should not be worried about old folks who have died. All those in our care have died naturally. And that's official, just ask Dr Simpson.'

'I'm concerned because you are concerned . . .' he began.

'Then don't be! Our duty is to put our clients at peace, Montague! That is our skill, even among amateurs like me. So I don't want you poking your official nose into our affairs. We've nothing to hide from the police or anyone else.'

He finished his meal in something of a hurry, completely astonished at the phrase she had just used, 'Our duty is to put our patients at peace. . .' but he pretended he wanted Millicent to be free to leave home as soon as possible to meet her obligations. From her brief chat, it did seem things were not all running smoothly within Crickledale Voluntary Carers. Perhaps the new chief executive wasn't as efficient as many believed? So did she know more than she was admitting? But if that was the case, why would she keep her knowledge secret?

His strategy of deploying some kind of subterfuge in his investigations now seemed infinitely more important and due to Millicent's slip of the tongue, there was a new urgency. Surely she – or the entire CVC staff – wasn't involved in actually helping old folks to die? Were they? Was CVC involved in mercy killings? That would he barely credible, although due to his knowledge of old customs, practices and superstitions, Detective Inspector Pluke was seriously concerned that someone *could* be helping those old folks to die in the manner of times past ... putting patients at their ease.... That had been a fairly common practice even within living memory but was it being practised in the 21st century? In Crickledale? If so, it could mean that many unsolved and hitherto unknown murders had been committed. But how many and over what number of years? The truth could radically affect his crime detection figures but worse than that, was he right to suspect his own wife of complicity in serial killings?

Detective Inspector Pluke left home with a lot to think about.

The deaths of which he was already aware had appeared to involve a fairly ancient superstitious practice with which he was not particularly familiar. His specialities were modern customs and beliefs, most of which involved luck-enhancing rituals. He needed to refresh his understanding of those older activities and so before returning to his office, he decided to visit Crickledale library to expand his knowledge about those old beliefs and practices. As he strode purposefully through the town, his active mind recalled that even in his grandparents' time there had been parts of England, mainly remote rural areas, where superstitious rituals and actions had been practised as a prelude to the moment of death. More interestingly, there were tales of such practices continuing into the middle years of the 20th century so could they still occur in Crickledale, right under his nose? Was there a culture of assisting death? And if so, was the Crickledale Volunteer Carers service involved? So did Millicent know something he did not? Something she dare not speak about?

During his walk he recalled that when a person in the fairly recent past was enduring a 'hard death', a term that would describe a difficult transition to the spiritual world, it had been customary for friends and relations to help the sufferer to die peacefully. Their actions would reduce the agony of those final moments and produce a happy death.

It wasn't just a case of saying prayers or uttering comforting words with the family gathered around. The helpers actually took a physical part in assisting the person to die and it was done quite openly with never a thought they might be committing murder or manslaughter. One method was called 'drawing the pillow' and others included freeing all the bolts or undoing locks in the house, opening doors or windows wide or moving the bed so that it stood parallel with the floorboards and not crosswise over them.

The deaths of both Miss Hullott and Miss Croucher appeared to have such a link because their doors and windows had been opened wide. Those facts alone were insufficient to be considered evidence of a criminal offence, but they might be an indication that further enquiries were necessary to establish what other customs had been used. As he approached the library, he recalled other methods of assisting death. A very simple one was to place a soft feathery pillow over the patient's face and press gently until he or she could not breathe. In that way, they died peacefully and painlessly with the doctors of the time not noticing anything suspicious whilst undoubtedly being aware that the person was already at the point of death. It was no surprise to anyone, family or officials, when such a person slipped easily and calmly into the next world.

However, there were methods Pluke had only vaguely heard about in his role as a modern detective. Now, he realized, someone in Crickledale appeared to be using those methods to help people to die. If he was to embark upon an official investigation he must familiarize himself with all the methods. Details would be in *The Encyclopaedia of Superstitions* by E. and

M.A. Radford, as revised by Christina Hole in 1961.

He had not lost sight of the fact that the crime of murder had long required malice aforethought as an essential ingredient. In thinking about assisted death, it was always questionable whether malice was present if a person was kindly helping someone to overcome a difficult death. Surely that was not malice? It was kindness and consideration, a supreme act of compassion or love. *Malice* suggested ill-will or an intention to harm someone. Pluke pondered those questions and told himself he must be impartial in this cold-case review, whatever his enquiries revealed.

Mrs Bentham, the duty librarian and a studious lady with half-moon spectacles, watched him arrive and thought he appeared to be wearing an intense but thoughtful expression.

'Good afternoon, Mr Pluke, what a tremendous surprise, seeing you at this time of day, and during mid-week too. So how can I help you?'

'Good afternoon, Mrs Bentham. I'm here on a matter of police interest and am sure your shelves will provide the answer. I'm seeking that famous *Encyclopaedia of Superstitions* in your reference section.'

'It should be there, Mr Pluke, we don't allow scarce reference books to be taken from the premises. You can study it in there. You know the way?'

He refrained from telling her the purpose of his research because he did not want the people of Crickledale knowing that their detective inspector was possibly hot on the trail of a clever serial killer or killers who may have been active for years and who may still be operating. Such a revelation could prompt wholesale panic and wild stories in red-top newspapers. Detectives must be discreet, especially when gathering compelling and sensitive evidence, he reminded himself.

He found the book and took it to his sanctuary in the corner near the window. He quickly found the heading *Easing Death* but was surprised that that particular section was very well-thumbed with its page corners turned over, pencil marks in the margins and dirty fingerprints around the borders. Clearly, it was a popular subject. With whom? Suspicious or assisted deaths were not common in Crickledale – or were they? Were they more common that he realized? So who had left those dirty fingerprints? Could Scenes of Crime Officers produce acceptable images from them, he wondered? He would bear the possibility in mind but he did not wish to seize the book as evidence, not at this early stage of his enquiries. That would prompt rumours!

As he concentrated, his research reinforced his knowledge that, in the past, there had been a widespread desire to help people to die if their passage from life was difficult. Invariably, that help was of the practical kind with no prayers. In all cases the house where the dying person lay was prepared for the exit from life by having all its doors and windows opened to permit the soul to depart without hindrance. In some cases, the dying person was lifted out of bed and laid on the floor to ensure he or she lay parallel to the floorboards.

This was also designed to ease the departure of the soul and it was known that in the days before fitted carpets and comfortable rugs, and when bedrooms were on the ground floor, the shock of a very weak person being lifted from a warm bed and laid on a cold floor, especially one of stone, was enough to terminate the sufferer's precariously slender hold on life. It was also believed that a person could never die if their pillow contained the feathers of pigeons, doves or game birds and so there had developed a custom known as 'Drawing the Pillow'. To hasten death, any pillow thought to contain such feathers – as most did – was suddenly and rapidly withdrawn from beneath the head in such a way that it hastened death of a person already terminally weak. To enable the person to survive, however, such a pillow was left alone and indeed, others might be added by packing them around the head or close to the body beneath the bedclothes. Friends and family would always help an ailing person to live – or to die.

Even as late as 1902 in the Isle of Ely, if a person was on the point of death but struggling to die, the village nurse was asked to bring a certain pillow with a black lace edging. Reputedly made years earlier and handed down through the years from one nurse to another, it was used to speed the death by being pressed on the face of the sufferer.

Sometimes this treatment was aided by a concoction of opium pills mixed with gin – but it was all done out of kindness towards the sufferer.

Following the death, there were practices to help the soul leave the bodily remains and the home of the deceased. The opening of all doors and windows was vital to help the soul leave the premises without hindering its journey to heaven. Mirrors were turned to the wall or covered so that the departing soul would not catch sight of itself on that final journey and become confused about its purpose and direction. Wandering souls did not understand the impact of seeing their own image so they must be protected against themselves. Clocks were stopped at the time of death, animals were not permitted in the house of death and all perishable foods were thrown out. Sometimes a bucket containing earth, or perhaps water and salt, was placed under the dead person's bed, ostensibly to prevent the body swelling in death but probably to thwart the attention of the devil. Candles may be lit in the dead person's room for the same purpose – apparently the devil did not like bright lights.

One important fact was that a dead body should never be left alone in the house – someone should watch it until the funeral. This led to the practice of carrying out wakes or even having a meal with the dead person in attendance. Sometimes people would sit around drinking and eating with the coffin in the centre being used as a table. In this way, it was felt the spirit of the deceased was participating. Refreshed by his revision and satisfied he had gleaned sufficient information to further his enquiries, Pluke went to thank Mrs Bentham.

'Did you find what you wanted, Mr Pluke?'

'Thank you, I did. But I did notice that the encyclopaedia appears to have been used a lot. Do you get many people using it?'

'Superstitions are always a popular subject for research, Mr

Pluke, and we do frequently get a number of people wanting to check things. We could really do with another copy of that book but they are difficult to find.'

'Do they show interest in any particular subject?'

'I never know precisely what they are looking for, although beliefs about weddings are always popular – all brides worry about what they should wear at their wedding to ensure good luck. They never wear green, for example, but grooms don't appear to be concerned about such things.'

'So we are still a superstitious nation? Well thank you once again. I'm sure I'll return.'

He returned to his office, his head buzzing with ideas and theories. As he passed the ever-open doorway of the Control Room, he poked his head around the door to address Sergeant Cockfield-pronounced-Cofield,

'Any developments, Sergeant?'

'No messages, sir, except that Detective Sergeant Wain has gone out. He asked me to let you know. He has gone to the Registrar's Office in connection with your current investigation and suggested you join him.'

'Didn't he give any other reason? A specific area of enquiry perhaps?'

'No, sir.'

'All right, Sergeant, I'll join him. You can always contact me there if an emergency arises. Then I'll come back to my office.'

He told Mrs Plumpton where he was heading, explaining it was part of his cold-case review. Crickledale's office of the Registrar of Births, Deaths and Marriages was within the Town Hall, a five-minute walk away.

He was greeted in reception by a pleasant young woman, whose name-badge said she was Miss Joy Colman, the Assistant Registrar. She was a smartly dressed with dark hair, dark eyes and a smile full of white teeth. It seemed Miss Ledger, the registrar, was away.

'You must be Detective Inspector Pluke,' her warm greeting produced a glow of contentment within Pluke's system. Pretty women had that effect upon him but he had never met Miss

Colman before. He deduced she must be a new member of staff.

'Yes, I'm Detective Inspector Pluke and I'm very pleased to meet you, Miss Colman. You're new here?'

'Yes, I've been here six months, it's a nice place to work. One meets someone from almost every family in the town, it's an ideal way of making friends.'

'I am sure it is. Now, I'm seeking Detective Sergeant Wain.'

'Yes, he's waiting in the small conference room whilst doing some research for a survey requested by the Home Office. He said you would probably join him. If it's Mrs Ledger you wish to speak to, then I'm afraid she is at a meeting in York. She is not expected back this afternoon.'

'I am here merely because my sergeant is expecting me.'

'Thank you, so if you go through that green door, you'll find him.'

And so he did. They did not begin discussions about the purpose of their visit partly because Pluke had little idea why his sergeant had decided to come here but also because the reason for their visit might be very confidential. He liked Wayne's explanation that it was for a survey being requested by the Home Office. Even though the registrar's work was confidential and invariably of a highly personal nature, they would always co-operate with a police investigation.

'So what brings you here, Wayne?' Pluke took a seat. The room was quiet and discreet as one would expect.

'I've been thinking about those peculiar deaths, sir. I didn't want to spark off a wave of alarm nor did I want newspaper reporters discovering what we're up to. That would happen if we started quizzing folks in Crickledale or poking around in local newspaper files. So I came here where our initial enquiries can be confidential.'

'What initial enquiries? Exactly what are you trying to find out?'

'I want a list of everyone who has died in Crickledale during the past ten years. I want to establish whether there's a pattern or trend of any kind. I'll need very little information to start with – names, ages, addresses, next-of-kin, date of death, cause of death and date of funeral. Oh, and whether they were buried or cremated here or elsewhere. Most importantly I want to know which deaths were reported to the coroner.'

'You need to establish whether or not the police were involved at any stage and which deaths attracted a post mortem or an inquest. That information can be obtained from our files, Wayne. We would have investigated all suspicious deaths. You know that.'

'Yes but we haven't investigated those where there was no official suspicion. That's the point I'm making. I told Miss Colman that the Home Office is having an audit on all sudden deaths that have been reported to the police. I said I needed to find out how long we took to investigate each case, that's a good way of highlighting the depth of our enquiries. I added I was anxious to check our figures against those officially listed here. Every death in town is recorded here, suspicious or otherwise. It's a useful back-up to our own system and important if some deaths occurred in peculiar circumstances but were *not* reported to the police or coroner.'

'You could stir up nasty rumours so be very careful, Wayne. Have you found anything yet?'

'I haven't checked the statistics that show the *average* number of deaths in Crickledale in any year or even any month – that's for later but what has already emerged is that there have been more deaths in Crickledale during the last nine months than in the same period last year.'

'It could be due to the mild winter, Wayne. As I've already reminded you, it's well known that a green winter heralds a full churchyard.'

'With due respect to you, sir, I don't place much reliability on folklore theories but I do believe the number of recorded deaths gives cause for concern.'

'But *suspicious* deaths reported to the police haven't increased, have they Wayne?'

'No they haven't. That's exactly the point I'm making. I need a print-out of this information so we can compare it with our files. I'm increasingly convinced we should examine the backgrounds of all recent Crickledale deaths.'

'You're echoing my own worries and concerns, Wayne. Suppose, for a start, we examine reports of deaths in Crickledale over just one year? Last year in fact. Would that provide an accurate picture?'

'It's a good starting point but we'd need more information and it's doubtful whether a single year would produce an accurate picture. You've already indicated your own suspicions based on recent deaths. So shall I continue here and bring the result to your office? Or do we let sleeping dogs lie?'

'We do not let sleeping dogs lie, Wayne, we are dedicated police officers determined to find the truth. All right, go back ten years and in the meantime I'll return to my office to begin research into our own files.'

'Do you know something you're not telling me, sir?'

'I don't want to plant ideas in your head, Wayne, or influence your research. What we need are facts, not theories.'

'Shall I speak to the town's undertakers? They enter houses in the course of their work and may have noticed some inconsistencies, like the one who thought Miss Croucher's death was odd in some way.'

'You were going to talk to him, weren't you? You've not followed up that line of enquiry, have you?'

'No, but I haven't forgotten. It would be useful if other undertakers expressed their opinion before I quiz him.'

'By all means speak to them, Wayne, but make it an informal chat rather than an official enquiry. We need to keep the lid on all this at the moment. Remember if someone is killing vulnerable people, it could be an undertaker – after all, they have a lot to gain from death. Death provides their living, Wayne.'

'Including the gravedigger and his side-kick?' put in Wayne.

'We should include everyone associated with deaths and funerals, including the doctors. Exercise the same caution throughout and make sure you include the carers. Any one of those people could have a motive and lots will have had an opportunity to expedite a death.'

'Mrs Pluke is a carer. Might she be able to help discreetly?'

'I don't relish the idea that my wife may be a suspect in a case of multiple murder, Wayne, but she might prove to be a good witness. However, as a reputable police officer, I have to put my personal feelings aside as I investigate this matter without fear or favour. Remember we are treating everyone as witnesses at this early stage, not suspects.'

'So at the moment we have no known murder victims and no official crimes, but lots of suspects?' Wayne smiled at the thought.

'Witnesses, Wayne. Witnesses, not suspects. We must clearly identify cases where the deaths could be the result of murder and then we might interview suspects, hopefully without exhumations.'

'We've set ourselves a major task and in the meantime I'm looking for a common factor but haven't found anything apart from the apparent involvement of Crickledale Carers. That's one mighty common factor to conjure with!'

'It is indeed, and I must say the name of Dr Simpson is cropping up regularly too. I must say the entire matter weighs heavily on my shoulders. I hate to think that a serial killer could have been at work in Crickledale over several years without raising the tiniest hint of suspicion.'

'If there is someone at work, we'll find him or her or them.'

'So do you need me here, Wayne, or can you cope alone?'

'I'll be fine, working alone.'

'Exactly what sort of common factor are you looking for, Wayne? I doubt if things like open windows or deaths on cold floors will be recorded in registry files.'

'I don't know what I'm looking for until I find it. Serial killers work in odd ways.'

'Then I shall leave you to your research, Wayne, and go back in my office. If you can give me a print-out of all these official records over ten years, I'll go through them as well, just to see if I can find some common factors.'

'No sooner said than done, sir. I've already printed a duplicate set. You can take them with you now. I haven't examined them but I hope you come across something!'

'Thanks, Wayne. We do seem to be going around in rather tight circles right now, we need a breakthrough if we're to make any progress.' Pluke reached out to touch the wood of the desk upon which Wayne was working. 'Touch wood,' he smiled. 'That's a really good means of obtaining good fortune and great success, Wayne. You should try it.'

And with his mind full of new information, Pluke left.

Chapter 6

MRS PLUMPTON HEARD Detective Inspector Pluke settling down at his desk and allowed him a few moments to compose himself. Walking in with her arms full of files, she smiled and stooped low to place them before him.

'Whilst you were out, Mr Pluke, and in view of your decision to carry out a cold-case review, I've checked via our computer all our CID crime files over the past year to see if there are any major undetected cases of serious crime. I've also included minor crimes dealt with by the uniform branch but which remain undetected.'

'That's very commendable, let's hope your initiative leads to a breakthrough. So have you found anything of interest?'

'I agree that our CID office has no unsolved major crimes,' she beamed. 'That's an enviable record. However, there are many minor reported crimes that are more of a matter of record without having precious time spent on them as fruitless investigations. Inspector Horsley considered the matters too minor to involve expensive police investigations. As we are aware, some small crimes are reported merely to obtain a crime number so that the loser's insurance companies will compensate the loss; those are also listed as undetected.'

'Surely those are the concern of the town duty inspector, not me?'

'Of course but among all those unsolved minor crimes, I've found one of considerable interest!'

'Really? I must hear this but do you think we should wait until Detective Sergeant Wain returns? I'd like him to hear what you have to say.'

'Yes, of course, Mr Pluke,' and there was a hint of disappointment on her face as she placed the file in his in-tray. She had expected more interest from him.

'Thank you, Mrs Plumpton. We will deal with it as soon as we can, I assure you. Right now I need you to retrieve all files dealing with sudden deaths that have been dealt with at this station during the past ten years. I need cases that have been subjected to normal "sudden death" enquiries by the uniform branch whether or not they were followed by a post mortem or an inquest. And of course, I need the files of any deaths that were investigated by CID officers on the grounds they were initially considered suspicious, even if they were later proved not to be so.'

'Yes, of course, Mr Pluke,' and she drifted from his office to carry out his instructions. She thought he was being very masterful at the moment but she was determined to explain her own successful detection work. She regarded it as important.

Alone for a few minutes, Pluke flicked through the pile of forty or so files she had left in his in-tray. Although these cases appeared in the statistics of Crickledale Police Station, they had not been dealt with by CID officers – they included reports of thefts of sweets from shops, handbags and purses stolen from parks, gardens and supermarket trolleys, tools taken from open garden sheds, thefts from cars left unlocked while parked, thefts of garden gnomes – all minor crimes that would be recorded but not necessarily investigated.

However, the additional file that Mrs Plumpton had left had been highlighted by her. He picked it up to read. It concerned a reported theft from a dwelling house. He was surprised that this had not been recorded as burglary although a quick glance through the papers showed some official uncertainty about its category. The stolen object was a gent's gold watch on a gold bracelet, and the victim was Mr Edgar Lindsey who, at the time of the crime, had been 89 years old. He lived alone, his wife having died some years earlier.

His son had reported the crime because his father's watch had vanished from the house but the precise time and manner of its disappearance could not be ascertained due to the old man's poor memory and delicate state of mind. There was a possibility he had lost it in his garden or perhaps whilst pottering around town or doing his shopping. The report had been dealt with some eight months ago during the summer – last June in fact – when the old man might have spent some time out of doors. The town's uniform branch had made enquiries and the disappearance of the watch had been recorded as a crime in case it reappeared in a car-boot sale, flea-market or antique dealer's shop. An entry had also been made in the Lost Property Register in case the watch was found in the street or elsewhere, and handed in at a police station. Pluke was somewhat amazed that this should be recorded as a crime when to all intents and purposes it was a watch that had been lost or misplaced by its elderly owner.

No doubt the town inspector had had his reason for recording it as a crime rather than lost property. Pluke was angry as he realized this was why the crime figures appeared to be so high – most of the alleged 'stolen' property actually consisted of lost items. He was fully aware of the desirability to record lost objects as 'stolen' because they were then allocated a crime reference number so that claims could be made from insurance companies. On the other hand, stolen goods that were recorded as lost property meant the crime statistics were maintained at a reduced level and that made the police look efficient.

But why did Mrs Plumpton think he would be particularly interested in this case? She hadn't explained so he put it on one side. He'd discuss it later. Before doing anything else, Pluke settled down to take another closer look at the file on the death of Miss Adelaide Croucher.

It contained transcripts of the original messages but no sound recordings or computer print-outs. He read them carefully. The initial alarm had not been raised via a 999 emergency call, he noted. The caller had used Miss Croucher's own household telephone. The transcript read:

'Hello, this is Rachel West from Weaver's Cottage, that's in March Street, can you come quickly, please, my neighbour has been attacked. I'm calling from her house.'

'How serious is the attack?'

'The worst, she's dead.'

'Can you be sure of that?'

'She's stiff and cold and didn't respond in any way. . . .'

'Have you called the doctor?'

'No, I couldn't see the point. As I said, she's dead.'

'Where is she now?'

'Where I found her, in her utility room. Lying on the floor in her nightdress. That's Tiler's Cottage in March Street. I live next door.'

'You're at the victim's house now?'

'Yes, I thought I should stay here, the doors are all open. I have a key but didn't need to use it.'

'All right. Don't touch anything. I'll have an officer with you within a very few minutes. PC Grant Carey is patrolling that area. Could you wait outside the front door to show him what you have found? Can he gain entry to the house? We need everything to be exactly as you found it and don't let anyone else in.'

'I haven't touched anything but all the doors and window are open.'

'So is there any indication of a forced entry?'

'No, none.'

'And signs of an intruder – drawers hauled out, smashed windows, wrecked property, any other damage, blood on the victim . . . that sort of thing?'

'No, nothing like that. Nothing at all.'

'So it may be a natural death? Perhaps she collapsed? We will call a doctor and we will attend within a very few minutes.'

There was nothing more of interest in the file, but he spotted something in the background of the police photograph of her bedroom. A bath towel was hanging over the dressing table mirror, obscuring the glass. So had she placed it there to be convenient? Perhaps to dry it after washing her hair or face? He now scanned the other internal photographs of the house – and in the front lounge he saw that the mirror over the fireplace had been turned around to face the wall.

What a blessing Wayne had recognized the irregularities in Miss Croucher's supposed 'natural' death, otherwise crucial evidence would have been lost. As he scrutinized the remaining photographs, they emphasized the well-kept and clean condition of her house but also confirmed that when the body was found, all doors and windows had been standing wide open. Not merely unlocked but standing open. To some observers that would have been perfectly natural if someone had been cleaning or airing the premises, or it might have indicated a very hot day with attempts to gain some fresh air. But *all* the windows? Upstairs and down? In winter? There were only two doors – one at the back and one at the front – and they were standing open too.

Pluke was becoming more convinced that this was not a natural death. But how could he prove his theory? One way was to discover more about what had happened to Miss Hullott and compare the circumstances.

From what Millicent had told him, there had been remarkable similarities between her death and that of Miss Croucher, although the critical difference had been that Miss Hullott's death had not been subjected to a police investigation. There would be no police file, no photographs, no evidence. Then Pluke recalled the undertaker who had expressed an opinion that Miss Croucher's death was, in his words, *odd*. Wayne hadn't had an opportunity to interview him yet but that task was now becoming very important.

Who was that undertaker? Could it have been someone from a distant town? If the fellow was local, had he also dealt with Miss Hullott's funeral? Could that be a common factor? There were several undertakers in Crickledale, but it wouldn't be too difficult interviewing them all without spreading alarm around the town. And could Linton Farewell, the gravedigger, have been involved? Or his chimney-sweeping colleague,

Sooty Black? As Pluke pondered the best way of interviewing them without raising the spectre of a serial killer at large in the town, Wayne returned from the Registrar of Births, Deaths and Marriages. He strode into the office and announced, 'Sir, I've found that common factor!'

'Well done, Wayne? So what is it?'

'When I checked the days – not dates – of death of the nine people who have died within the last few months, five were on a Thursday. So I checked further back and discovered that over the past two years, twelve occurred on Thursdays out of the twenty deaths recorded in Crickledale.'

'Do you think that's significant?'

'It could be, and there's more. Most were elderly women, although one or two men were on the list. And there were a couple of teenagers who were killed in a traffic accident.'

'Did your friend at the Registrar's office give any indication of why so many are linked to a particular day of the week?'

'I didn't ask, sir, I didn't want to spark off rumours. I reasoned it was up to us to find out.'

'A wise decision. So how many of those twenty deaths were reported to the police? How many were thought to be suspicious?'

'It's very difficult to determine merely from the Registrar's files but at a rough estimate, I'd say half of them. That's the impression I've gained after considering the delay between the dates of the deaths and the dates of the funerals.'

'In other words, you're speaking of the time that's necessary to organize a post mortem or a police investigation?'

'I am, yes. It means we must go through all our old files very carefully. From the Registrar's files, I've noted the names of those likely to be of interest so it's merely a case of checking one name against another.'

'That seems simple enough. I agree. This revelation might be just what we need to justify our investigations. Well done. Your common factor theory has borne fruit.'

'Why do I get the feeling we are about to uncover one of the worst cases of serial murder since Jack the Ripper?'

'Because we are efficient police officers, Wayne. We form a good team.'

'Like the killers, perhaps?'

'Now that is a possibility! Indeed it is! I am so pleased you said that. I've been wondering how poor old Miss Croucher was man-handled downstairs. That would require a feat of considerable strength, probably impossible for a person working alone. So perhaps you're right. A *team* of killers is operating?'

'On Thursdays?'

Chapter 7

THE WORK OF locating and checking the relevant old files in the dusty loft would be time-consuming and dirty but, fired with determination to secure an answer to their suspicions, Pluke's small team set about their task. Even with the enthusiasm of Pluke, Wayne and Mrs Plumpton, it would take several hours, probably extending into tomorrow but they worked with a will until today's home-going time.

Before leaving, however, Pluke addressed them.

'Sergeant,' he said to Wayne in his most serious voice. 'I think you and I should attend Mrs Langneb's funeral tomorrow. It will be interesting to see who the mourners are, and who turns up for the funeral tea. We might become privy to local gossip about the spate of recent deaths. Unguarded gossip can be a good indicator of the genuine situation. And you might locate the undertaker you need to interview. It's important we chat with Rachel West to see how much she can recall about Miss Croucher's death – that might provide valuable guidelines as we assess other cases.'

'Is there something particular you want to check?'

'I'd like to get a list of tomorrow's mourners – that should be printed in the *Gazette* afterwards if the local correspondent proves efficient, and we shall be able to make enquiries from the undertaker who is dealing with Mrs Langneb. He could prove useful. On top of that, funerals do attract interested crowds, Wayne, not necessarily people who are closely associated with the deceased. There is a certain rather morbid curiosity on such occasions, not to mention a free meal afterwards.'

'What about a photographer, sir? Shall I ask one to attend? A police photographer, I mean.'

'I think that would be intrusive especially as this is not a murder enquiry.'

'Nonetheless, photographers are always useful.'

'I couldn't agree more. But in this instance, I think it would prompt suspicion about our presence, along with the inevitable silence as people become too frightened to speak openly. We are merely gathering intelligence at this stage . . . snooping as Mrs Pluke would describe it. I think we need to adopt a low profile.'

'I could take my own digital camera, I can hide it in the palm of my hand and take pictures without anyone realizing.'

'Your persistence wears me down, Wayne! But that could be useful.'

'Will you require me at the funeral?' asked Mrs Plumpton who had been listening keenly to this rather curious conversation. Pluke realized he had slipped up a little by speaking in her presence but she rarely missed anything of note!

'With your local knowledge, it would be very useful to have you there, Mrs Plumpton, the files can wait a while,' enthused Pluke. 'By all means join us. You can be our unofficial detective. Perhaps you could listen to conversations, get a feeling from the mourners about reasons for, or gossip about, the high local death rate. If you need to provide an explanation about the heavy police presence you can say that the Home Office is becoming increasingly interested in the part played by local police officers in cases of sudden or accidental death, or even deaths from natural causes. You could say we are looking into it. In some ways, I suppose, we are role playing and so it will be interesting to receive your honest observations on today's events.'

'I'd love to help, Mr Pluke. I've often thought I would make a good detective and am willing to use up some of those extra hours on my overtime card. I knew Mrs Langneb very slightly so that will help. She used to work in the shop where my mother bought her fruit and vegetables. She knew an awful lot about pomegranates. I was a very little girl at the time.'

'An extra pair of eyes and ears will be very useful, Mrs Plumpton. If Detective Sergeant Wain and I can attend during work hours, then so can you. There is no reason to use your accumulated overtime,' agreed Pluke. 'You may consider this as work.'

'Thank you, that is most kind.'

'If things are quiet, and if we get all those files sorted out before lunch tomorrow, we can celebrate at Mrs Langneb's funeral tea. You truly deserve an outing, Mrs Plumpton.'

'You are so thoughtful, Mr Pluke. I really am looking forward to doing some real detective work. . . .'

And so it was agreed as they set about their dust-laden task. When he returned home that night after work, Montague Pluke was smothered in dark sooty dust; even his distinctive suit was sullied by its presence.

'My goodness me, Montague, what on earth have you been doing?' shrieked Millicent. 'Get those filthy clothes off and take a shower before you dispense all that dust around the house. I don't want you sitting on my best furniture in that mess. I cleaned the brasses only last Friday . . . really, you are the limit.'

'Yes, sorry, Millicent. I've been in the police station loft looking for old files. I can leave my things here to be shaken and vacuumed or whatever you do to remove dust because tomorrow I shall require my dark suit. I have decided to attend Mrs Langneb's funeral, and will proceed there directly from work. I will see you there, I am sure.'

'Mrs Langneb's funeral? You never knew her, Montague, so why are you going to her funeral? It's not just for a free tea and a few glasses of sherry, is it?'

'No, it's more than that, Millicent. I felt it my duty, as a leading public figure in the town, to add my support,' he lied smoothly. 'And she was a very good donor to police charities. Once long ago, we found a purse she had lost and she thanked us with frequent donations to the Police Widows'

Supplementary Pension Fund.'

'Rubbish!' she retorted. 'You're up to something, Montague.'

'I am simply attending a local funeral, Millicent, nothing more than that!'

'You don't fool me, Montague Pluke. Is it something to do with all these deaths in town? I do hope you are not investigating Miss Langneb's death or indeed any other that's occurred recently. You're not snooping on the lives of private citizens, I hope?'

'I never snoop. . . .'

'You do, you are always snooping but you call it detective work. Look, Montague, her death is not in the least suspicious and neither are any of the others that have occurred recently. I don't know why you are wasting precious police time on such things.'

'Millicent, I have my duty to perform. . . .'

'Let me finish, Montague. I have already said you should not snoop on private individuals. I know you're worried that there have been so many deaths in Crickledale but that's your nasty suspicious mind at work. I'm aware of the deaths too, they were all old people who died naturally for no other reason than their age. For heaven's sake don't get it into your head that there are murderers galore at large in this town. People die when they get old, but with so many of them in CVC care, I am worried too. In the minds of some people, it could reflect badly upon the CVC, but murder is not on my mind! It's more to do with poor administration and natural circumstances.'

'I'm a senior detective, Millicent, I must do my duty as I see it. . . .'

'People die, Montague, it's part of life. And don't you dare take that filthy suit off upstairs. Go out into the backyard and do it there.'

He obeyed, thankful the neighbours couldn't see him removing his dirty clothes and hanging them over the washing line. Then he went inside to change into his gardening clothes and returned outside to thrash his work-suit with a carpet beater that looked something like an antique tennis racquet.

That would soon dispense with the dust and he hoped the neighbours wouldn't complain about the clouds of filth. As it was a fine, dry evening, he left it there as he went in once more and changed into a casual shirt and slacks. Then he made for the lounge where Millicent would have poured him a nice glass of apple juice to relax him before their evening meal. As he settled in his favourite chair, she joined him.

'Montague, I am sorry for that outburst, it was most unlike me. I know you have a very demanding job with never-ending responsibility and you become aware of matters that ordinary people never encounter. There are times the pressure must be intolerable. I don't have your calm approach to problems. Please forgive me.'

'The spouses of police officers never have an easy time,' he smiled weakly. 'You were right to chide me if your fears were genuine, but I fear my actions are connected with my duty. I can say no more at this stage.'

'Good heavens, Montague, do you actually mean that detectives will be at poor Mrs Langneb's funeral? I can't believe it! Not in Crickledale. You realize that your mere presence will get the people talking; gossip and rumour will be rife in the supermarket aisles and tea-rooms. I can't really see why you're doing this! The town can do without that kind of rumpus – the CVC has enough to think about without its carers being regarded as criminals. . . .'

'I can't avoid people making ill-informed comments about our presence, Millicent, so I'll maintain a discreet silence. Detective Sergeant Wain and Mrs Plumpton will accompany me – Mrs Plumpton knew Mrs Langneb fairly well. If anyone tries to extract information, tell them we're conducting a survey for the Home Office concerning the role of local police officers at funerals and weddings. You can add that the precise nature of our survey is highly confidential but that members of the public have absolutely nothing to fear.'

'That's a load of political gobbledegook, Montague, and you know it. You are investigating Mrs Langneb's death for no other reason than there have been so many others . . . you are making a mountain out of a mole hill, Montague, and spreading suspicion where there is none. There's no wonder people get upset!'

'We are merely doing our duty. . . .'

'You and your colleagues should be ashamed of yourselves, Montague, doing such things at a funeral. . . .'

'You've expressed yourself forcibly, Millicent, so we must let the matter rest and say no more about it.'

'But you still intend going to the funeral?'

'Of course.'

And so began Pluke's evening with him now not daring to mention Mrs Langneb's death or indeed any other. He wondered why she was so tetchy about this subject and her comment at lunch about the CVC putting their clients at peace before death was still troubling him.

But tomorrow was another day. The funeral was not until 2 p.m.

Next morning, Tuesday, was fine and dry. Fortified by his early morning good luck rituals, Montague Pluke decided not to trim his fingernails whilst preparing for the funeral even though it was safe to do so on a Tuesday without incurring ill fortune. Likewise, he could trim his hair, especially those bits that stuck out from beneath his hat, because that was considered also safe on a Tuesday. Fortified by his good luck and success-making rituals and beginning his day's work by leading with his right foot, Detective Inspector Pluke walked to work through the town centre, but this time his progress was markedly different. Although he followed his usual route, he was now dressed in a funereal black suit with black shoes, black bowler hat and black tie. In his right hand, he carried a black umbrella and in his left, a pair of black leather gloves. Such was his transformation that some of his regular encounters did not recognize him, despite him raising his black bowler to all the ladies.

However, it was to the credit of the townspeople that some did recognize his heavy black-framed spectacles, long dark hair now neatly trimmed and hat-lifting movements as he moved through the town and its people. But despite his care, his progress did lead to whispers along the route some of which were loud enough for him to hear – 'I think Mr Pluke must be going to Mrs Langneb's funeral but can't think why. Why would our most senior detective want to attend her funeral? Isn't that what detectives do when they're looking for a killer? They attend funerals of murder victims and there has been a large number of deaths recently in Crickledale . . . I said to my husband there was something fishy about them . . . doors and windows open, folks lying dead on the floor. . . .'

And so the gossip circulated and indeed intensified, as Detective Inspector Pluke strode purposefully towards his office. Some might have suggested that his remarkable appearance may have been a ploy to get people talking and gossiping – which was precisely what he needed. And precisely what was happening. Upon arrival at the police station and after checking with Sergeant Cockfield-pronounced-Cofield that there had been no dramas overnight, no murders, rapes, burglaries, sudden deaths, kidnappings of wealthy businessmen, train crashes or helicopters making urgent landings on Crickledale cricket field, he announced he would be in his office all morning where he would be continuing his research in old files. He added he would be out this afternoon attending a funeral along with Detective Sergeant Wain and Mrs Plumpton. The sergeant nodded his understanding and so Pluke ascended the stairs to his office, fully confident that his day would be a success. As usual when he entered, he flung his bowler onto the hat stand and scored a hit, then Mrs Plumpton allowed him time to rearrange his desk before delivering his coffee.

'Good morning, Mr Pluke,' she oozed as she wafted in upon clouds of powerful sneeze-making perfume. As he sneezed, he saw she was dressed in what looked like the dress worn by Queen Victoria at Albert's funeral, except that it was cut low enough to reveal parts that would never have been viewed by the most ardent of royal observers. 'Your coffee.'

'Thank you, Mrs Plumpton, and may I say how smart you

look this morning. Black does suit you, if I may be so bold as to compliment you.'

'Oh, Mr Pluke, how thoughtful and kind, that is really nice of you. And I must return the compliment. It is not often we see you in such splendid and apt clothing. And you've had your hair trimmed! My goodness, it does like nice and I must say it also makes you look extremely dignified.'

'One must respect the occasion, Mrs Plumpton, and if I wish to make myself inconspicuous at Mrs Langneb's funeral, then my appearance must allow me to mingle unnoticed among the mourners. Seasoned detectives with my long experience are able to merge into almost any background on such occasions, almost to the extent of becoming invisible to the casual observer. However, before going to the funeral, have we any urgent matters to deal with before I continue yesterday's research?'

'Just the routine mail, I will bring it in a moment but I can say there is nothing to concern us. It means we can concentrate upon your research this morning. In fact, Detective Sergeant Wain and myself arrived early so as to get a good start on those files before the funeral – I felt I owed you something as you are allowing me time off this afternoon.'

'That was not what I intended, Mrs Plumpton, I wanted to reward you in some small way for your continued attention to my needs.'

'Oh, what a lovely thought, Mr Pluke,' and she fluttered away to bring in the mail and a few acknowledgement letters she had already typed for his signature. When she returned, she brought in a list of names from the files she had already examined.

'These are some of the names we have already uncovered but we haven't finished yet.'

'You have been busy!'

'I feel it is such a worthwhile task, Mr Pluke. All the people mentioned in these files suffered a sudden or unexpected death and their cases were handled by officers based at this station. All these deaths resulted in a post mortem examination but a high percentage was determined as "natural causes" so there were no further police enquiries or inquests.'

'There seem to be a lot of names on this list.'

'Twenty-seven so far, Mr Pluke. And Detective Sergeant Wain has found more, he will bring them to you shortly.'

'And over what period of time are we talking about?'

'Twenty-five in the last four years, Mr Pluke. Not counting the current nine. As we are going back over ten years we'll surely discover more.'

'That's more than six a year not counting the current nine . . . that must be an unusually high figure for Crickledale?'

'It is, but remember these are not the total number of deaths for Crickledale; they are merely those reported to the police because they were originally classed as sudden and unexplained. In all cases, post mortems followed but, as I said earlier, all were found to have died from natural causes so no further enquiries were made. Their files were closed.'

'I'm surprised there were no wild rumours and speculative talk in the town about all this? I must confess I had no idea that we had lost such a high number of Crickledale residents and the newspapers didn't highlight the inexplicable rise in funerals and neither did the town police or anyone else.'

'It's a delicate topic, Mr Pluke, people don't like reading newspaper reports that suggest their beloved died mysteriously. And all the deceased were old people, by the way, most of them in their eighties. Men and women. Many lived alone too.'

'It is a well-known fact that people are living longer in modern times so do we know whether any of these people were attended by carers?'

'No, these files don't say so but we can check that. But surely this is merely a natural phenomenon, Mr Pluke, a blip in the statistics? And not at all suspicious.'

'You are looking at this as a non-police citizen in spite of your work with us, Mrs Plumpton, whilst I am seeing things through the official eyes of Her Majesty's Constabulary as the officer in charge of the Criminal Investigation Department in Crickledale, no less.'

'Maybe so, Mr Pluke but we've had no complaints about these deaths, have we? No requests for investigations. And no information other than they were from natural causes? From the files we have examined already, not one family questioned the doctors' diagnoses as natural causes, nor the outcome of the post mortems or the pathologists' decisions. That suggests there has never been the slightest concern about any of the deaths. However, Detective Sergeant Wain said he would speak to you before we go to the funeral, to explain some important information he has discovered.'

'And exactly what is that?' asked Pluke.

Chapter 8

'SOME INTERESTING FACTS have come to light,' Wayne announced. 'I've not had time to read the files in great detail but there are brief summaries on the outer covers. These files are past "Sudden Death" records stored in our loft. As agreed, I've checked back over the past ten years.'

'We can't rely on summaries, Wayne. We must read the entire file wherever there's suspicion, however slight,' Pluke pointed out. 'We must be very precise in this cold-case review. The data we uncover has to be reliable and truthful. Remember we could be seeking a team of clever killers, but if such a team is at work, a pattern should reveal itself as we delve deeper. Serial killers tend to repeat their successes. So what have you learned so far?'

'The total number of "natural" deaths *reported to the police* over the last ten years is sixty – far more than first thought. That's approximately a third of all deaths in the town. All were Crickledale residents, male and female, and in all cases the deaths were reported to the police because they were sudden and unexplained, even though the deceased were elderly. In all cases, the doctors, including Dr Simpson, certified the cause of death – natural causes in all cases. It meant there were no post mortems, no inquests, no police enquiries, no detailed investigations and no scientific examinations of the bodies or the scenes. In short, the police had no responsibility for investigating those deaths apart from responding to the initial report.'

'That's quite normal,' commented Pluke. 'That's the way that most sudden deaths are dealt with.'

'I realize that but in some cases I have noticed recurring aspects that might be important. For example, all were elderly, many were widows or unmarried women, some were bachelors or widowers. And all lived alone.'

'So already we can identify several common factors in addition to Thursdays,' smiled Pluke. 'But *living alone* could prove significant. And do we know how many were under the care of Crickledale Volunteer Carers? And how many were examined by Dr Simpson? We need to check those areas but I feel that already we are progressing positively, Wayne. It does seem we could be investigating serial killers.'

'My feelings too. I wondered if the same undertaker had dealt with all the funerals so I checked. The answer is no. Several were involved, some from outside Crickledale, those being selected by relatives living away from here. In fact, some funerals were not held in Crickledale. Some of the deceased were buried in the towns and villages where they had been born or close to relatives who had moved away.'

'Again, all absolutely normal. So what relevance can we place upon the undertakers?'

'I was looking for a motive. In these tough times due to Government cuts and so forth, I wondered if someone was making money from those deaths – either illicit money or a higher personal income. I thought that a particular undertaker might have a way of hastening deaths simply to earn more fees. After checking these files, I think not. The deceased were not wealthy people either, just ordinary Crickledale citizens. I think we can eliminate the undertakers from our enquiries.'

'We'll bear that in mind but it's a valid point, Wayne, and quite feasible. So do you think there's a strong link between the deaths? Perhaps money that could be made from funeral extras? Teas, memorials, floral tributes, tombstones?'

'It's always possible and we can't ignore such possibilities, but I think we should end speculation until we have more facts at our disposal. If someone is hastening deaths on a large scale, there has to be a powerful motive. I can't see they're all done out of love or compassion.'

'So are you ruling out actions that are triggered by friends and relatives through kindness or some other powerful emotion? Assisting a loved one to die in peace and without pain is not a new idea, Wayne. Love is a powerful emotion but one person, or a team would not kill lots of people for that reason. If we prove there are multiple suspicious deaths here, we're talking commercial killers, not love. Just reflect for a moment on Miss Croucher – she could never have got downstairs alone and it would take more than one person to carry her down. It suggests a team at work, Wayne. And that alone indicates very sinister motives.'

'Money, you mean? Valuable objects? Antiques? Greed?'

'That's the direction of my current thinking, Wayne.'

'I can understand that. So does this lead us to any particular suspect or suspects? Is there anyone within our sights who has a desperate need for money, strong enough to commit murder and steal from the dead? Then there's jealousy, anger, frustration with old folks and their ways – and lots of other reasons.'

'Some people can be very brutal with the elderly, Wayne, especially within their own family.'

'I realize that, but I've not uncovered any evidence that makes me believe that money or vindictiveness were motives – not that we know a great deal about any of the cases at this stage.'

'I think this realization at such an early stage of our cold-case review heralds a need to delve much deeper, Wayne. If we can prove that just one of those deaths was suspicious, then we need to seek suspects and that could lead us to other deaths and other suspects. So is there anything else we need to know at this stage, apart from the fact that several died on a Thursday?'

'Do you still think Thursday is significant?'

'It can't be dismissed or overlooked but we do need to be more precise about the exact times of all deaths. Calculating the time of death is never an exact science. Do we know whether they were *found dead* on a Thursday? Did they die the previous night, Wednesday? Or in the very early hours of a Thursday morning? I hardly need point out that the time of being found dead is not necessarily the same as the actual time of death. That distinction is important to our investigation.'

'The simple fact is that many of the deaths were discovered on a Thursday and reported to the police the same day as sudden and unexplained.'

'You mean all sixty or so?'

'More like half of them.'

'So those figures include deaths not reported to us in those ten years?'

'Yes, I've included all Crickledale deaths. I got details from the Registrar of Births, Deaths and Marriages. We can rely on those figures.'

'They make disturbing reading, Wayne. It's an average of about one death every two months, half of them suspicious. That is very ominous indeed.'

'It's important we don't forget we're talking about elderly people who are ill and perhaps on the point of death anyway. Despite the large number, I've never heard rumours or whispers that a multiple killer is at large in Crickledale. If there were worries, I'm sure rumours would have reached us before now.'

'I am keenly aware of that, Wayne, but I believe we're already in possession of sufficient data to confirm that some deaths were criminally assisted even if they were not reported to the police.'

'Mercy killings, you mean?'

'Not mercy, Wayne. I doubt if mercy enters into this.'

'You really think these are cold-blooded murders?'

'The short answer is yes. I'm coming to believe that you and I are on the threshold of identifying multiple murders in Crickledale! There is much work to be done, Wayne. We need to determine a single motive that might have been present in all the deaths. We need to determine if all or most occurred on a Thursday. We need to find out if anyone had access on

Thursdays to homes of elderly folk living alone – and then killed them without raising any suspicion. Killing them not out of compassion or love, but to acquire something valuable.'

'Like a house?'

'Probably something smaller and less valuable than a house, Wayne. He, she or they could strike at any moment, so we must maintain a close watch on all local deaths especially those not reported to the police. In dealing with such clever, secret killers, Wayne, I fear we must set a trap to catch them in the act. That is the only way we shall get the necessary evidence. It means we must work out where they will strike next. And next Thursday isn't far away!'

'Could the killer or killers be someone pretending to be a CVC carer? Even a volunteer who has joined simply to seek opportunities to steal by easing the death of an elderly client?'

'That is something to consider, but we must never presume that all CVC volunteers are killers, Wayne.' Pluke was thinking of Millicent.

'But we do know that many of the lately deceased were attended by CVC volunteers. I do find that very worrying.'

'Yes, and some were attended by carers from their own family or friends.'

'I appreciate that, but I do feel we should investigate all the CVC members. As a group, but also individually.'

'Then we shall do that.'

'We can begin by attending Mrs Langneb's funeral to pick up gossip, listen to rumours, chat to mourners. So do we know anything about Mrs Langneb?'

'Not officially, no, but Mrs Pluke has told me a little, although she feels bound by the laws of confidentiality. However, she did tell me Mrs Langneb had been found dead on the floor with her windows open. That is a key point.'

'It must add considerable strength to your theories. It means we must find out more about the death of Mrs Langneb. Her death will not be in our files but we must be extremely discreet and must act quickly without halting or disrupting the funeral.'

'I have no wish to resort to an exhumation, Wayne, or a late post mortem. So let's take things carefully today, let's not be stampeded into doing something rash.'

'Mrs Plumpton should be a great help. She's a local person and well acquainted with the daily life of Crickledale. She knew the family and I'm sure she's capable to gleaning valuable snippets of information from the mourners. She's also well acquainted with our requirements. She could prove to be a good member of our team!'

'I agree, Wayne. Let's call her in.'

Mrs Plumpton expressed her pleasure at the prospect of carrying out detective work during Mrs Langneb's funeral. Even though the old lady had been almost ninety years old, Mrs Plumpton told them she had already heard, via gossip in the town, that some strange elements had been associated with her death. At the time she had not been sure what those elements could have been but, having knowledge of the reasons for Detective Inspector Pluke's cold-case review, she felt she might be able to revive those moments and tease some useful information from the mourners. There was no finer place than a funeral for gossip!

'You should attend as a family friend,' advised Pluke. 'If you appear to be too closely associated with me or Detective Sergeant Wain, people might not confide in you. So make your own way there, behave as you would normally at such a funeral and don't appear to be asking pointed questions. Detective Sergeant Wain and I shall express our deepest sympathy in our own way but will not remain close to you.'

'My neighbour will be attending, she was a good friend of Mrs Langneb so I shall accompany her. There will not be a problem I can assure you, even if it is rather like being a member of the Secret Service!'

'Well, we wish you luck in your endeavours, Mrs Plumpton. I see rain is forecast although it is fair at the moment. There is an old saying *Happy is the corpse that the rain falls on* so it seems all will be well.'

'Oh, we don't want rain, Mr Pluke. Just imagine what it would do to our smart clothes and hair-dos, to say nothing of our hats and best black shoes!'

'Then I shall cross my fingers and take a twig of rowan wood, just to ensure success in everything,' smiled Pluke. 'Now, Detective Sergeant Wain and I will brief you about our specific requirements and the general direction of your enquiries.'

Before leaving for the funeral, Pluke found time to telephone an old colleague, Doctor Derek Page who worked in the Pathology Department at York Hospital. He and Dr Page had worked together on cases that required the skills of a pathologist.

'Ah, Derek, glad I caught you,' he began. 'It's Pluke at Crickledale. Can you spare me a moment?'

'Of course, Montague. How can I help?'

Pluke related the details of some deaths of elderly people in Crickledale and followed with his knowledge of how deaths in the past were hastened or made easier.

'Mine is a simple enquiry, Derek,' Pluke continued. 'If a weak, sick or elderly person was removed from a warm bed and laid with their back flat on a cold floor, concrete or wood, would the shock be enough to kill them? And make the death appear to be from natural causes?'

'The effect of shock upon a human body is a huge topic, Montague, and it is open to lots of interpretations and opinions with many forms of shock. It's not helped by there being so many different forms, some decidedly dangerous and lethal. I don't think it would be possible to summarize the effects of all types of shock in a brief phone call.'

'But I understand shock can kill a weak person?' persisted Pluke.

'Yes it can. That is not in doubt and I would suspect that if a frail person was placed suddenly upon a very cold floor, the shock would be enough to disrupt the functions of the heart and so lead to death. In short, such a shock could kill – but some people might survive that treatment. A fit person might not be affected. You have opened up many possibilities!'

'And would a pathologist or doctor realize that shock was the cause of death in such a case?'

'I doubt if a GP would be able to make such a diagnosis and I would even venture an opinion that a pathologist might decide that such a death was due to natural causes, unless there were other factors such as injury or bruising. I have to say, Montague, that a myriad of external factors could be involved if death followed. . . .'

'I understand that, but am I right in thinking it could happen?'

'It could – I would agree that it is a fact that people can die from shock.'

'It was a common occurrence in our forefathers' time, Derek. People were helped to die by being laid on cold floors or smothered with soft pillows. . . .'

'If it happened at that time it could happen now, Montague. Perhaps smothering would be detectable, but don't quote me! This is merely my opinion.'

'And mine!' smiled Montague Pluke, ringing off.

When Detective Inspector Pluke and Detective Sergeant Wain arrived at Crickledale's Anglican Parish Church, people were already gathering outside the lych-gate. Some smiled brief acknowledgements to the plain-clothes police officers as they joined a small group of mourners waiting outside the church door. No one questioned their presence or commented upon it. The people appeared to be gathering in silent tribute to Mrs Langneb, but neither Pluke nor Wain recognized anyone. Most were from the anonymous population of Crickledale but Pluke guessed that relatives and friends may have travelled from elsewhere.

Inside the church, through the open door, they could hear the organist playing appropriate music and then, as the clock showed it was 1.50 p.m., the people dispersed and began to shuffle inside the rather plain unadorned and uninspiring church. Each seemed unwilling to be first to enter or first to select a pew.

Pluke had no such inhibitions. He strode manfully forward followed by Wayne Wain and they selected a pew towards the rear of the nave, from which they could observe everyone sitting in front of them. Hymn books and Orders of Service were already in place on the pews. And so the handful of mourners gradually filled a few rows of seats in front of the detectives, as Pluke and Wain tried to identify each one of them. Mrs Plumpton arrived in black, accompanied by a small, elderly lady who needed to be helped into her seat, and then Millicent came forward and also selected a pew, not beside her husband but at the side of Mrs Plumpton's friend. Millicent did not acknowledge Pluke but he felt she was sullenly aware of his presence.

The bier was already in place to accommodate the coffin and Pluke was pleased that the first three pews at each side of the aisle had been left unoccupied for relatives and friends of Mrs Langneb. There was ample space for them.

Then a man's voice called, 'Please be upstanding' and the organ music ceased. A plump grey-haired lady vicar appeared and took her place close to the bier to receive the deceased. In the hushed silence, the rather small coffin with a modest arrangement of flowers on top was carried in by four bearers. It was followed by the local undertaker, Joshua Carpenter, in his usual black suit and carrying a black top hat. A small group of family and friends followed and Pluke instinctively counted them. Fourteen. They were guided to their seats and as the coffin was placed upon the bier, the people opened their hymn books and selected the one that headed the list of numbers on the hymn board.

The organist then struck up with the familiar chords of the hymn that begins *O Lord my God! When I in awesome wonder. . . .* perhaps better known as *How Great Thou Art.* At the conclusion of the short service, which revealed a total lack of emotion, sorrow or sacred atmosphere, the vicar announced that the interment would take place immediately in the churchyard surrounding the church.

Afterwards, everyone was invited to join family and friends in the church hall for refreshments. Pluke noticed it was not yet 2.30 p.m. with the interment taking a further ten minutes or so. As family and friends moved towards the graveside, Pluke and Wain headed for the refreshments but would wait politely outside until the interment was complete; he had no place at the graveside. Wayne Wain joined him whilst Mrs Plumpton and her companion joined the others at the graveside. Millicent, still not acknowledging the presence of her husband, also went to the graveside.

Then an elderly man known to Pluke and Wain as Awd Ezra appeared and joined them. He was one of the elderly charac-ters of Crickledale; he was not a criminal or a down-and-out but eked a meagre living on his pension, part of which came from military service long ago with another part from his past employment.

He had been a highway operative, perhaps more widely known as a road sweeper.

'Now then, Mr Pluke,' he displayed a wide toothless smile. 'It's not often we see you and your pal at local funerals.'

Pluke knew he must take full advantage of this man's local knowledge. A conversation initiated by this man would not appear to be a case of prying by the detectives.

'It's not often my sergeant and I have the time to attend funerals, Ezra. Our heavy workload and continuing responsi-bility for defending the people of Crickledale against ruthless criminals must take priority. But we have made an exception for Mrs Langneb, she was a good friend of my wife and she donated to police charities.'

'Aye, well, I was asked to sit with her the night she died. No relations living nearby you see, nobody to sit overnight. So I volunteered.'

'Sit where?' asked Wayne who was unaccustomed to the protocol that surrounded a local death.

'In t'house, Mr Wain. I was downstairs in t'living room and she was lying on her death-bed upstairs.'

'So she wasn't in a chapel of rest?'

'No need, there wasn't anybody else living in her house, Mr Wain, so she could be left in her own bed till t'very last minute. But we never like folks lying dead all by themselves, not 'ere in

Crickledale. So we keep 'em company by watching.'

'Watching? Watching what?'

'Sitting with 'em, keeping 'em company. We call it watching.'

'Really? Does everyone do that?'

'I expect so, it's allus been t'custom in these parts.'

'So why is it done? There must be a reason,' said Wayne.

'Search me, I've no idea. It's done because it's allus been done.'

'She died peacefully, didn't she?' put in Pluke.

'Oh, aye. Passed away overnight in her sleep. Lovely way to go. She was found next day by one of t'carers who called Doctor Simpson. I've watched since Friday night, it's all we could do for her.'

'Found, you say? Found where?' asked Pluke.

'Somewhere in t'house I would imagine.'

'Which carer was that? Any idea?'

'Search me, Mr Pluke, there's that many of 'em I never know one from t'other. But they allus took good care of Mrs Langneb and all t'other old folks.'

'So you're not one of the volunteer carers?'

'Not me, Mr Pluke. I'd be no good looking after living folks.'

'Have you watched at other deaths, Ezra?'

'Oh, aye. Lots of 'em over t'years. When folks died in their beds and there were no relations to come and watch, then I did it. Everybody needs somebody to watch over 'em in their final hours on earth.'

'And when does the watch end?' asked Wayne.

'When t'undertaker comes to take t'body away, then afterwards I come to t'funeral, like today, and I get a free meal once in a while. It's a big thing for a chap living on his own to get a meal, so I've never minded watching. We don't get paid, you know, it's a voluntary thing. I wouldn't want money anyway.'

'So are you there the whole time the deceased is lying in the house?' asked Wayne.

'No, just at night. Others come and go during t'day, friends, neighbours and such. Bringing flowers, cards, saying their farewells, that sort o' thing.'

'It's a very noble thing to do,' commented Pluke.

'Nights are different from days, I think some folks would be scared stiff about watching at night.'

'That's not surprising,' agreed Pluke.

'It doesn't bother me!'

But Wayne wanted to know more. 'But you wouldn't do this in a chapel of rest, would you? Watch all night there? It's only done in the homes of people who've died.'

'Right, Mr Wain. By t'time a body's gone to a chapel of rest, its soul will have departed.'

'What's a soul got to do with all this?' puzzled Wain.

'Well, when somebody dies in their bed, their soul needs time to find its way out of t'body without getting lost, so it would be baffled in a dark and empty house, with mirrors about and so on, not knowing which was t'way out. So whenever I watch over Anglicans or them with no religion, I allus put t'lights on, all over t'house and I turn mirrors to face t'wall or else cover 'em up with a sheet or summat, to stop souls getting confused. Catholics look after their own.'

'So what happens if a body is moved to a chapel of rest before the funeral?'

'Well, it's gone to t'right place, hasn't it? A churchy place. Souls know how to cope with churches and they'd never leave bodies that were moving around . . . so there we are.'

'I don't know what to make of all this,' admitted Wayne Wain.

'Don't try,' advised Pluke. 'Well, Ezra, I think I hear people moving from the graveside, so we can go in and help ourselves to something to eat, and have a nice cup of tea.'

'Nice talking to you both. Funny about Miss Croucher, wasn't it?'

'Was it?' asked Pluke.

'Yes, that business of putting her on t'cold floor to help her on her way. Mrs Langneb was on t'floor too, when she was found. Mebbe there were others, but it's an old custom. Opening doors and windows is one thing, but lying folks on cold floors doesn't sound very pleasant to me. But if it makes 'em pass away peacefully, then I suppose it's all right. Ah, here they come, some just turning up for a free tea. I'm going in first otherwise there'll be queues and no sandwiches left. Proper gannets some folks are, Mr Pluke. Come along both of you, don't get stuck behind a queue! First come first served, I say.'

They allowed Ezra to rush ahead to secure a full plate of goodies, but waited until the first flush of mourners were approaching, and then Pluke, acting as a leader, walked steadily towards the entrance and led the way inside. Wayne followed as everyone queued for the toilets or mingled over the table that was full of buffet food. As Pluke entered, Ezra had already piled his plate high with savouries, which he would demolish with relish before returning for a second helping. And then there were trifles and cakes. . . .

When Pluke and Wayne had helped themselves, they refrained from sitting down at one of the tables – that was a sure way of isolating themselves from the other mourners.

'Did you hear Ezra say Mrs Langneb had been found on the floor, Wayne?'

'I did. What do you make of that?'

'I'd say it was another notch in our gun, Wayne.'

'It certainly makes me think. . . .'

Millicent and other helpers were in the kitchen preparing food, washing pots and making tea so he never saw her or talked to her. Rather than seek Millicent when she was busy, Pluke felt it important that he and Wayne moved among the mourners, mingling as only an experienced mingler can do. Both would strike up conversations about Mrs Langneb, whilst referring to the fact that Ezra had kindly sat with her corpse overnight. That should persuade people to talk informally to the team of police officers.

Then Pluke spotted Jacob Carpenter, today's undertaker. He was heading for the tea urn but with one of his swift moves, Pluke reached him as he settled down to fill his cup.

'Jacob,' he asked. 'Could Sergeant Wain and I have a quick chat with you? Somewhere quiet? Out of earshot? Bring your tea.'

'Aye, of course, Mr Pluke. It's not often we see you fellows at funerals, so is there summat wrong?'

'Not that I'm aware of. It's just that I'm intrigued by some of the local funeral customs here in Crickledale, things that have escaped me in all the years I've lived and worked here,' smiled Pluke. And so, with Wayne Wain following, they made their way to a small table in a corner away from flapping ears.

'Sit down, Jacob,' invited Pluke making rare use of someone's first name. 'There's something we'd like to ask you.'

Chapter 9

'Is it summat to do with your research into ancient superstitions, Mr Pluke?' asked the undertaker. 'I do remember that talk you gave to t'annual conference of t'District Association of Funeral Directors, Undertakers and Embalmers – *Times of Death in the Yorkshire Coastal Region* it was called, if my memory serves me right. Dying as t'tide went out and getting born as t'tide came in, that sort o' thing. Very interesting stuff, Mr Pluke.'

'Thank you, Jacob,' Pluke rarely if ever used a person's Christian name in formal discussions unless he was extremely well acquainted with the other person. His occasional exceptions might include those times he interviewed people of a certain class in circumstances where he did not wish the discussion to appear like an interrogation. He continued, 'It's pleasing to note your interest and, of course, we must heed such things – we can't dismiss those beliefs as erroneous even if they do date from the Middle Ages. Many of us continue to follow ancient beliefs, perhaps in different ways, so yes, my enquiry does embrace old customs.'

'Well, I allus touch wood if I've got a tricky job to do and I spit if I see a magpie on its own. Touching wood isn't very difficult when I'm making coffins, but it's nice that I can help you to keep up to date on such things, Mr Pluke. So what do you want to know? You're not planning your own funeral, are you? Some folks do that, you know. Plan it years in advance, reserve a plot and pay up front.'

'I hope I have many more years of hunting horse-troughs ahead of me, Jacob. I have no intention of departing this life just yet. But down to serious business. Can you remember the death of Miss Croucher? Adelaide Croucher.'

'I'll never forget it, Mr Pluke. A rum do if you ask me.'

'Were you her undertaker?'

'I was. I'll never forget it, a very odd affair, Mr Pluke.'

'In what way?'

'Well, her being found lying on t'pantry floor like that, in her nightie, laid out as if waiting for me to deal with her.'

'It must have been very strange and something of a surprise, finding her like that.'

'Aye, it was, Mr Pluke. I could see she'd not tripped up or fallen or owt like that, she was just laid there. Neat and tidy. Ready for t'box. Most peaceful she was. You can tell from folks' faces whether they died in peace or not. She was at peace, there was no doubt about that, but I thought what a funny spot to end her days. I still think she was put there, she could never have laid herself out so well and so neatly. I couldn't have done a better job myself.'

'So what was your reaction?'

'Well, I thought about her only this week when I had to deal with Mrs Langneb. She was on t'floor an' all, just like poor old Miss Croucher, just lying there as if she'd been placed ready for t'box.'

'Have there been others like that? Either those you've heard about or those you've seen for yourself?'

'Aye, one or two, Mr Pluke, but I don't do all t'Crickledale funerals, you understand. I've had to cope with old folks lying on t'floor, and I know other funeral men have done t'same in this town. Don't ask for names, I can't remember much these days. Old age, you know. It gets you like that. Miss Croucher was a bit different because t'police were called in and they thought she'd been attacked. That was my reaction an' all, Mr Pluke. I thought she'd been assaulted and left there. It was a shock, believe me, you don't expect such things in Crickledale.'

'But by the time you were called in, all the preliminary work would have been done?'

'It was, but I had to deal with her remains, Mr Pluke. Anyone seeing her lying where she was would have thought somebody had broken in and attacked her. But it wasn't like that. No injuries, no bruising . . . she was just lying there at peace. Mind you, I don't know how she got herself downstairs, she could hardly walk and allus used that lift on t'staircase. It goes up and down at t'touch of a button. Marvellous contraption, Mr Pluke, for old folks who are a bit lame.'

'And where was the lift when you arrived?'

'Top o' t'stairs in its resting place, Mr Pluke. I know that because I wondered how it had got there. If she'd come down on it to get herself a drink of milk or summat, it would have come downstairs with Miss Croucher on board.'

'So what were your thoughts?'

'Well, I thought somebody must 'ave replaced it, sent it back upstairs – mebbe it was t'person who laid her out, that's what I thought. But I never asked, it was nowt to do with me, was it? I was curious, that's all.'

'So that made you think the entire situation was rather odd?'

'It did. Things didn't add up, Mr Pluke. She had no slippers on, I noticed that, undertakers do notice what their customers wear at t'time of death in case there was some request for bits and pieces to go into t'coffin with 'em. Folks still believe in that you know, they want to take their precious bits and pieces with 'em into eternity. Some want 'em beside 'em in t'coffin, and others are happy for 'em to go into t'grave at their side. Linton Farewell and his Sooty mate see to all the stuff that goes into t'grave, I see to what goes into t'coffin.'

'I'm still surprised that people want that kind of thing, Jacob. Quite fascinating.'

'I knew one fellow who wanted his Hornby train set buried with him, it had been a Christmas present from his dad when the chap was a kid o' three years old. Very touching, Mr Pluke. And we did what he wanted. Then there was that chap who wanted a bell buried with him, with a pull-string, just in case they buried him alive and he woke up under six feet of soil. Some just settle for a keepsake, a present mebbe, their wedding dress or summat. Some folks get very attached to their belongings, Mr Pluke.'

'I'll bet you can tell a few stories! Anyway, back to Miss Croucher. You think she hadn't been moved before you arrived?'

'No, Dr Simpson had certified her dead but she'd been left until t'police had come and done whatever they do in such cases. Examine t'scene, take photographs, look for fingerprints and so on. Nothing must be touched at what they think is the scene of a crime. That's summat I've learned in this trade.'

'Absolutely right. And were you there as the police started their work?'

'I got there towards the tail-end of their examination, Mr Pluke. They took photos and tested for fingerprints and such before I arrived. I think they thought there was summat odd about it all. I got there after I'd been rung up by t'police to ask me to take her off to t'hospital for a post mortem which I did, then afterwards I took her to our Chapel of Rest to await t'funeral.'

'A perfectly normal task for you?'

'Oh, aye. Nowt odd about all those routine bits and bobs. Because there were no suspicious circumstances, her funeral could go ahead. Even though t'police found nowt suspicious I still think there was summat very odd about it.'

'You're something of an expert in these matters?'

'I wouldn't say I was an expert, Mr Pluke. Let's just say I'm very experienced.'

'Were the doors and windows open whilst you were in the house?'

'Oh aye, folks often do that when there's a dead person lying there. Some say it's to let fresh air into t'place and others say it's an old fashioned belief that allows t'soul or t'spirit to depart in peace. Round here, it's more likely it's because Sooty Black will have been to sweep the chimney – that's his way of helping folks, a clean sweep for no charge, even if t'spot smells of soot afterwards. He helps out with the carers, they know when chimneys need sweeping, Mr Pluke. Some around here smoke a lot.'

'It's mainly the old folk who still have coal fires, isn't it, Jacob.'

'Aye, younger folks have central heating – folks often open their windows because that makes it too hot.'

'Opening windows after death is a very old belief, Jacob.'

'Aye, and it's still going strong, Mr Pluke. Mind you, while t'police were doing their examination, with t'body still on t'floor, they closed t'ground floor doors leading outside. For privacy, you understand. Crowds do gather to gawp at such goings-on.'

'Do you often come across that sort of thing?' asked Wain.

'Oh aye, quite often. If t'deceased is upstairs in bed, await-ing us to turn up and carry 'em off to t'Chapel of Rest, all t'windows will generally be open upstairs. . . .'

'Upstairs?' queried Pluke.

'Nowadays just upstairs but sometimes on t'landing. Downstairs there might be a door standing open but with t'windows shut and curtains drawn. To be private. But with t'mirrors turned to face t'wall, fires put out, food taken away – folks still have all kind of customs when loved ones die, Mr Pluke.'

'Similar customs, are they?'

'Aye, broadly similar although they vary from family to family. We never comment, we just let 'em get on with such things and do what they feel necessary. It helps with t'mourning process, so they tell me.'

'So can you recall anything else that was unusual or odd whilst you were in Miss Croucher's house?' asked Pluke.

'I didn't go upstairs to her bedroom, Mr Pluke, there was no need. So that's all I can tell you.'

'And was there any local gossip about the manner of her death, Jacob?'

'Oh aye, there's allus gossip, Mr Pluke.'

'Such as?' pressed Wayne.

'Normal stuff with some saying she'd been helped to die. . . .'

'Helped to die?' queried Pluke.

'Aye, it used to be done in t'olden days, Mr Pluke, when somebody was suffering. Relatives or friends would give a helping hand; there's a tale here in Crickledale where a woman's husband was having a tough time dying so she helped him on his way by cutting off his breathing with his own best tie knotted tightly around his neck. They said he went off like a lamb.'

'And such cases were never regarded as murder?'

'Good heavens no, Mr Pluke, they were done out o'love and kindness. Folks reckon it was a great act of generosity to help someone over t'final threshold, from life into death in t'easiest possible way. It goes on, Mr Pluke. It allus will in my opinion.'

'Even today you mean?'

'Oh aye, not that t'authorities will ever know. Doctors know about it and I reckon Miss Croucher was given a helping hand.'

'And that didn't puzzle you? Or trouble you?' asked Wayne.

'Nay, not in t'least. What puzzled me was how she'd got herself downstairs without using her stairlift. I wondered if she'd managed to get down and lie on her back on that cold floor to help herself to die. . . .'

'If she was desperate she might have been able to achieve that,' offered Wayne. 'She might have got herself downstairs without using the chair lift.'

'I don't think so,' ventured Pluke. 'I think she was aided in her death and that the helper accompanied her downstairs as she used her lift, and then laid her gently on the floor to die in peace – and the helper then restored the lift to the top of the stairs.'

'Why would they do that?' asked Wayne.

'To give the impression that Miss Croucher had struggled downstairs alone, perhaps to get herself a drink or something to eat, and once downstairs, the appearance would suggest her effort had been so great that she had collapsed.'

'Onto a cold stone floor? That would finish her off, sure as shot,' said Jacob. 'They reckon it's the sudden shock that does it.'

'I can believe that, Jacob. And so she died at peace,' suggested Pluke. 'Or, of course, the killer might have sent the lift back to the top of the stairs so that Miss Croucher could not make use of it to return to the warmth of her bed.'

'Aye, well, I heard she couldn't climb stairs on her own,' put in Jacob Carpenter. 'She wasn't very good on her legs.'

'You said killer, sir?' Wayne Wain was alarmed by Pluke's apparent carelessness. After all, Pluke had stressed he did not want the townspeople to be terrified by lurid stories of a killer at large. So why had he used that word, even just between the three of them? It might have been overheard.

'I think you meant helper?' suggested Jacob. 'These cases aren't murder, Mr Pluke, these folks aren't killers. It's a case of helping suffering folks to find peace in death. I'm sure you don't want to alarm the population of Crickledale by suggesting there is a sadistic killer on the rampage hereabouts.'

'That's the last thing I want to do, Jacob. But within the world of criminal law, the term killer can be applied to those who commit various degrees of homicide – murder, manslaughter, infanticide, assisting suicide, causing death by dangerous or by careless driving whilst under the influence of alcohol or drugs, self-defence and even misadventure. If someone helped people like Miss Croucher to die, then such a person is a killer – but I accept that not all killers are criminals and not all are murderers.'

'We need to be careful with our phraseology,' suggested Wayne Wain. 'I'm sure Jacob doesn't believe there's a murderer at large in the town. So, Jacob, if we think someone *has* helped Miss Croucher to die in peace, can you tell me whether similar occurrences have come to your notice?'

'On and off over t'years, yes. Mrs Langneb was found lying on her floor, Dr Simpson told me that. And with doors and window open. There was talk she'd taken a tumble but Dr Simpson found nowt wrong with her, except she was dead.'

'Any more similar cases?'

'There was a few but I can't remember t'details. Anyroad, I wouldn't want you chaps digging up my past customers to have their remains examined by forensic scientists,' protested Mr Carpenter. 'That *would* set t'alarm bells ringing.'

'I don't think that will ever happen,' Pluke tried to reassure him. 'If the causes of death of some of our recently deceased Crickledonians were considered natural by doctors and other experts, then it is doubtful whether such causes would be revealed in post mortems carried out after exhumation. To all intents and purposes, these deaths were all from natural causes. And that's the official result.'

'Well if they do decide to have exhumations, somebody would have to re-bury 'em all, Mr Pluke. I might earn myself a few good jobs, paid for by the Home Office. I wouldn't complain about that and publicity is always good for business.'

'Very true indeed, but back to my question, Jacob. So the outcome of our chat is that we think other Crickledale residents have been helped into their graves?'

'There's no doubt about it, Mr Pluke. Folks of Crickledale are a caring lot, they never want friends or loved ones to die in pain or mental agony or merely spend a long time dying when things can be made easier or speeded up a bit. But if you're going to ask me who those folks were, those who did the helping, then I can't tell you that because I've no way of knowing. And I can't remember.'

'I realize that. . .'

'I'm not privy to confidential knowledge among families or officials. It's not my job to pry into things once t'professionals have given t'all-clear for a burial. I just let things be as I get on with my job.'

'But you do visit the interiors of many homes where people have died, don't you?' pointed out Wayne.

'I do, Sergeant Wain, yes I do. And I've seen windows open and mirrors turned to face the wall and such like, but that doesn't mean the deceased was helped to die. Such things happen *after* death which is when I turn up.'

'That is a good point, Jacob,' smiled Pluke. 'You're part of the process that follows death, you seldom precede it. Well, I think we have taken up too much of your time. It has been a pleasure talking and you've been most helpful.'

'Right but think on this, Mr Pluke. Don't go round suggesting there's murderers at large in Crickledale, 'cos there isn't. This is a kindly place, not given to cruelty and so on. Helping a friend to die is a kindness, Mr Pluke, never forget that.' He rose and left them. Sipping their cold tea, they watched him leave.

'He bears out what I've been thinking, Wayne. Someone – a person working alone or perhaps as a member of a team – is helping to despatch the good people of Crickledale into the hereafter. It's done as an act of kindness, so it would seem, but I believe that is a clever cover story. Say what you like, and in spite of what Mr Carpenter thinks, I'm convinced we have a killer or killers in town, Wayne. As I've pointed out already, I doubt if they are doing it out of kindness, so we must look into the question of missing property. And as we say in major incidents, there is already a large body-count.'

'I agree with all you've said,' nodded Wayne. 'So where do we go from here? We seem to be going around in circles.'

'It's vital that we establish links with all these deaths, Wayne. Common factors we can identify – and we must establish the motives surrounding all the assisted deaths. Stealing from the deceased, for example, promising to ensure treasured items accompany them to the grave whereas they never get there . . . there is ample scope for crimes here, Wayne.'

'So it's back to our files?'

'It is, but before we go, we should make our presence known to the vicar – she's new here – and I think we should have words with any members of Mrs Langneb's family who have come to bid her farewell.'

'Why, sir? We were not friends of Mrs Langneb?'

'No but polite and considerate behaviour will be expected of senior police officers in such circumstances.'

And so they moved from their seats and joined the small group of mourners standing around with plates of food in their hands. Pluke headed for the vicar who seemed to be temporarily alone. He knew her name from chats at home with Millicent although he had never met her. She was a recent arrival and would not know details of past deaths or funerals.

'Ah, Ms Williams. So nice to meet you at last.'

'You must be Detective Inspector Pluke?' she had a winning smile, he decided. Warm and friendly but business-like. A woman in her mid-fifties, he estimated, with well-tended fair hair and a good skin. 'I am Susan Williams.'

'And I am Detective Inspector Pluke. This is my deputy, Detective Sergeant Wain.'

As they shook hands, Wayne managed to produce his most charming smile as he gazed into the blue eyes of the vicar, and she in turn thought he was wonderful . . . if only she'd been younger. . . .

'It's good of you to come to Mrs Langneb's funeral,' she said. 'She has few relations and most of her close friends have died but I know she was never alone. In the short time I've been here, I've grown to learn that Crickledale has an enviable reputation for caring for its elderly and ailing.'

'That's why we're here,' smiled Pluke. 'As the two most senior detectives in Crickledale, we feel it is our duty to be part of a caring society. After all, we are public servants with a great responsibility to the community. But work calls, Miss Williams. We must return to the office.'

'It's good of you to make yourself known.'

'That is our pleasure. I just wanted to ask if you knew whether any of Mrs Langneb's relations are here?'

'No, Mr Pluke. She has a nephew and a niece, both of whom live in the south of England, but they called me to say they are not able to attend her funeral.'

'Oh dear, such a pity.'

'I think they were hugely disappointed she did not leave her cottage to them in her will. Their absence is a protest, I feel, Mr Pluke, but Mrs Langneb did tell me, during one of my visits to her, that they had never been to visit her in her entire life. Not even following the death of her husband.'

'It's a bit early to be thinking of wills and legacies, surely?'

'It is, Mr Pluke, but I am sure you, as a policeman, know what some people are like. For some, that is their only thought after the death of a member of the family.'

'So who has inherited her house? Do we know?'

'Not yet and I have no idea who might be, Mr Pluke. If that's all her family can think about, it makes me very sad.'

'I think it is true that the love of money is the root of all evil. Please excuse us leaving now but we must hurry back to our office, Ms Williams, we have work to do.'

And so they left.

As always, when Pluke entered the police station with his right foot first, he checked with Sergeant Cockfield-pronounced-Cofield of the Control Room to see whether his presence was needed at any major crime, but there was nothing.

'It remains the quietest time I have ever known, sir,' confirmed the Sergeant. 'Something usually happens even if it's only a small crime or a tiny incident of some kind but right now there's nothing happening, absolutely nothing! I fear it might be the calm before the storm. Mrs Plumpton has left a message to say she has returned to her office after the funeral, and that she told me she would take any of your calls in your absence. But there have not been any.'

'Thank you. So if that storm does come, we shall be in our offices, Sergeant.'

Once in his office, Pluke invited Wayne to join him but at that moment, Mrs Plumpton burst in.

'I left the funeral before you,' she oozed. 'I thought you both would like a cup of tea and a chocolate biscuit. Funerals are always so testing. Shall I make one?'

'Yes please, Mrs Plumpton,' smiled Pluke. 'Then come and join us with your own tea and biscuit. We shall discuss the usefulness or otherwise of our presence at Mrs Langneb's funeral to see what valuable information we have gleaned.'

'Oh, good,' beamed Mrs Plumpton. 'I was going to suggest a meeting as soon as possible because I have something very interesting to tell you both.'

Chapter 10

'I̶T̶ ̶W̶A̶S̶ ̶S̶O̶ exciting, being a real detective, Mr Pluke. After years of working in your office, I've discovered I'd like to become a dedicated solver of crimes. It's so fascinating listening to people tell their stories and then following up with enquiries that provide answers. . . .'

'That's one of the great appeals of our work,' agreed Pluke.

'And such important work it is too. So necessary for the good of our entire society. . . .'

Pluke was now sitting at his desk with Wayne at his side whilst Mrs Plumpton settled opposite. Her black and frothy funereal dress was a shade more modest than most of her working outfits, but it did reveal lots of curious wobbles and chesty flesh.

'So what have you discovered that makes you so excited?' Montague asked her, before immediately wishing he'd never used that phrase.

'You'd be surprised,' was her anticipated response at which Wayne grinned widely. 'But it was something to do with your cold-case review.'

'I can't wait, Mrs Plumpton. It seems your detective acumen has been very well exercised.'

'I think it has, definitely. Now, you'll recall that when you decided to look for suitable subjects for your cold-case reviews, I found all those files in the uniform branch's cabinets. They related to minor crimes in the town and included all our undetected crimes, some having been committed long ago.'

'I remember it well, Mrs Plumpton. After all, it was only yesterday afternoon but I must confess I have not yet had an opportunity to examine them in detail.'

'Well, Mr Pluke, this is the interesting bit. One of them relates to a theft from an old gentleman's house, his gold watch.'

'An interesting case but sadly undetected. That's surprising because it was recorded in both the Lost Property Register as well as a Crime Report. Surely there can be little doubt the old man had mislaid it . . . we don't really want lost objects being recorded as stolen, it distorts the crime figures. If we did that with every item of lost property, our crime figures would rise to alarming proportions . . . I must speak to the town inspector about this. Inspector Horsley must be made aware of the implications of such actions.'

'Oh, it wasn't lost, Mr Pluke,' and Mrs Plumpton was quite strong in her rejection of his assessment of the case. 'It was definitely stolen. That's what I learned today.'

'Really? And who provided that information?'

'Mrs Frankland, she was next-door neighbour of Mr Lindsey, the old man whose watch was stolen. He was 89 years old and his son, Stephen, reported the crime. Mrs Frankland has always kept in touch with Stephen Lindsey who lives in the south now. . . .'

'The watch disappeared and the old man couldn't remember where he'd put it so when Stephen became aware of the loss he reported it stolen . . . am I right?'

'Yes, and he told Mrs Frankland what he'd done, just in case the watch turned up. He felt she should know about it, being his next-door neighbour and a regular visitor to his home.'

'So they were good friends?'

'Yes, and she was always on hand in case he needed anything day and night.'

'Where would the old folks be without good neighbours, Mrs Plumpton, we owe such a lot to them. And to the carers . . . we should not be afraid of growing old in Crickledale, should we?'

'You're absolutely right, Mr Pluke. Anyway, as I was saying, Mr Lindsey's watch was definitely stolen. It wasn't the case of an old man not remembering where he'd put it. He never took it off his wrist, according to Mrs Frankland. It was waterproof, shock proof and self-winding ... the very best, a present for his 75th birthday. There was no need to remove it from his wrist so he never did so. That's what she told me today. Apart from that, old Mr Lindsey never went out of the house alone, he couldn't walk or pop into town to do his shopping, there was nowhere he could lose his watch except in the house or garden and both were very carefully searched by his son, Mrs Frankland, and the police. If it had been lost, there it would have been found. And, of course, after Mr Lindsey died, the house was sold – the watch was never found when the house was cleared after the funeral.'

'Well done, Mrs Plumpton. I think I should send a memo to the duty inspector downstairs and instruct him to delete references to that watch from our lost property register. In view of what you say, it was properly recorded as a crime – and if it was taken from his house, then the crime should be burglary, not simple theft. Perhaps you could draft a memo for my signature?'

'Yes, of course, Mr Pluke. But there is something else.'

'Really, you have been busy! I must say I am impressed and grateful. There is no doubt you are a very good detective, Mrs Plumpton. We must use your talents again. So what else did you discover?'

'Mr Lindsey is one of those people whose deaths you are investigating,' she said quietly.

'Is he? I haven't reached his file yet. . . .'

'It's in my office,' chipped in Wayne. 'I'll fetch it. Give me a minute.'

He rushed from the discussion to return with a file jacket which he opened as he returned to his seat. He flicked through and said, 'You're right, Mrs Plumpton, a Mr Edgar Lindsey of 14, Normandy Terrace is on this list. His death was reported seven months ago.'

'His watch was reported stolen about the same time, Mr Pluke. Its absence was noted by his son when he came to the house. He reported it to the police here in Crickledale the same day his father's death was reported.' Mrs Plumpton had clearly delved into his death, because she added, 'I managed to spend a few minutes researching this. The death was reported as being sudden and unexpected despite Mr Lindsey's great age and it was investigated by the uniform branch as a routine sudden death. The doctor could not certify the *cause* of death which occurred in Mr Lindsey's own home, and so the coroner ordered a post mortem.'

'Absolutely routine,' nodded Pluke.

'It was. Despite the circumstances, the pathologist decided the death was from natural causes. There was no inquest and no further police investigation. The CID was never notified.'

'All that appears to be very satisfactory and is a perfectly normal situation, Mrs Plumpton, but clearly you have spotted something else?'

'Perhaps I would not have thought it unusual until I knew about your cold-case reviews and some of the interesting deaths you have already highlighted. In this case, Mr Pluke, Mr Lindsey was found lying dead on the stone floor of his cottage, in the front entrance hall. His neighbour, Mrs Frankland, found him, she entered by the back door because it was standing open. He was dressed only in the trouser-bottoms of his pyjamas and was lying on his back. He wore no other clothes, not even his slippers.'

'He was dead, you say?'

'Yes he was. It was because of that odd situation that the police were called in – the uniform branch, that is. In the file, it says there were no injuries upon Mr Lindsey's body although all the windows of his house were standing open. The front door was closed, he was lying against it but it was unlocked. There was no sign of a break-in and his bed had not been slept in.'

'The open window syndrome again! So do we know how Mr Lindsey managed to get from his bed to be found lying on his back behind the front door and in the front entrance hall? On a cold stone floor? Was he trying to get out, I wonder? To call help?'

'I doubt it, Mr Pluke. He had no need to leave the house to seek help. He had a bleeper that would have summoned Crickledale Carers if they were needed. All he had to do was press it – it was always hanging around his neck, even when in bed or in the shower. The reason for him going into the hall was never determined, except that he slept downstairs in what had formerly been the dining room. He was very frail and had difficulty walking, but his mental capabilities were quite normal. He was fully aware of what was going on around him.'

'So how did he reach the hall if he was so frail, and even on the point of death?'

'He used a Zimmer frame. The dining room had been equipped as a bedroom with a shower and toilet downstairs; that was done several years ago. Everything he needed was on the ground floor.'

'So where was the Zimmer frame when he was found in the hall? Did the police check that?'

'They did, Mr Pluke. It was still in his bedroom.'

'So either he had managed to reach the passage without his Zimmer frame, or else he had used it to get there and someone had replaced it in his bedroom?'

'According to the file, Mr Pluke, that fact was noted but the matter was never determined. It remained a mystery.'

'You've done a remarkable job, Mrs Plumpton, I am most impressed. This means we have another odd death that was recorded as being due to natural causes. But there is an impor-tant element to this one, isn't there? The gold watch. I've some thoughts about that. I wonder if my thoughts correspond with yours, Mrs Plumpton?'

'I am sure your thoughts often correspond with mine, Mr Pluke, but in this case I wondered whether the missing watch had any connection with Mr Lindsey's death? It was certainly valuable – worth several hundred pounds, according to our file.'

'This raises a very important question that could be the key to all these deaths. Tell me what you think about all this, Mrs Plumpton. I appreciate your views.'

'I want to hear this,' added Wayne who had been sitting quietly through this conversation, but not overlooking a single detail. 'I find the whole matter most intriguing – and it gets more so by the hour. Are we missing something that should be very clear to us?'

'I wouldn't like to suggest that,' she smiled diplomatically. 'But I've heard Mr Pluke and yourself saying in a case of serious crime, it can be the tiniest of details that opens the way to the truth.'

'That's very profound and very true, Mrs Plumpton,' and Pluke actually smiled. 'Did I say that? So what have we missed? I am finding our cold-case review much more difficult than the investigation of a current crime. Or perhaps I am getting too old for this sort of thing?'

'Rubbish, sir!' snapped Wayne. 'Your brain is as active as ever, but surely the purpose of interviewing witnesses is to gather information that we'd never normally have access to. And Mrs Plumpton is fulfilling that role right now. She's a witness, and a particularly good one. She is not competing against you or me.'

'Then pray proceed, Mrs Plumpton.'

'It's that theft, Mr Pluke, the gold watch taken from Mr Lindsey's house. Could that have been the *real* motive for someone being on the premises? To steal it from a vulnerable old man?'

'And covering up the crime by staging a "natural" death. . . .' whispered Pluke. 'My goodness me, Mrs Plumpton, you might have stumbled upon the missing link! If the watch was valuable – as indeed any gold watch is – then how tempting for someone to steal it if its owner would never realize it had gone! And more especially if the owner died – the crime would never be reported, no one would know about it. Relatives might believe it had been buried with the deceased.'

Wayne added his views, 'Things went wrong with that

theory because an alert son noticed the watch was missing – and reported it. And we – the police – failed to appreciate the importance of that fact, recording it as lost. People do steal from the dead, don't they? In hospitals and mortuaries? So, Mrs Plumpton, is it now your belief that elderly people have been helped to die because someone stole something from them? On a regular basis. . . . The rogues were causing the old folk to die in what appeared to be completely natural circumstances even though their deaths were hastened somewhat? What a dreadful means of committing a crime and then covering it up. If this is what they are doing, then all those deaths are murders of old or vulnerable people . . . my goodness, sir, what a dreadful thought. I'm quite shocked by this. I think we suspected something of this kind but lacked the necessary proof.'

Pluke remained silent for a few minutes with the enormity of Mrs Plumpton's suggestion making him wonder how the police could have failed to notice those possibilities.

'The only way to prevent a recurrence, Wayne, is to anticipate the next death and set a trap for the killers. We need to research all previous deaths that you have unearthed, reading the statements, checking any photographs, checking every fact before we reach any firm conclusions. It will take time, but it is most necessary.'

'I can help,' offered Mrs Plumpton.

'Your contribution could be vital,' smiled Pluke.

'The truth could still remain concealed,' cautioned Wayne. 'If a visitor did take a valuable object from the home of one of these deceased persons, the thief could always say it had been a gift from the householder before death. How could anyone prove otherwise? We would never succeed in a prosecution of such a case.'

'Remember, Wayne, that we are conducting a cold-case review and that means examining past cases that have never been detected. In other words, our initiative is already proving successful.'

Wayne replied, 'And there are three of us to share the load

of the extra investigations; I think Mrs Plumpton is already proving to be an excellent addition to our strength. We must ask lots of questions – it could be that friends, neighbours, relations or care workers have reported objects missing and that no one has ever linked the reports with those deaths.'

Pluke felt a glow of pride in the ability of his secretary and said, 'All this is thanks to you, Mrs Plumpton. Without your feminine intuition we might never have noticed the connections.'

'You know, sir,' said Wayne. 'If Mrs Plumpton is going to work with us rather than for us, then I think we should be more relaxed and refer to her by her first name. *Mrs Plumpton* does sound rather formal.'

'There are matters of discipline and etiquette to be considered, Wayne and I call you Wayne because it sounds just like Wain and thus the emphasis upon formal address between ranks can be maintained. Just as I refer to Mrs Plumpton as Mrs Plumpton in order to preserve her dignity.'

'But wouldn't you like us to address you by your first name, Mrs Plumpton?' asked Wayne.

'No I would not!' she affirmed without hesitation. 'I do not know what my parents were about when they gave me my Christian name, as it was then called. It is dreadful, a most awful name for a girl. I much prefer to be called Mrs Plumpton.'

'But surely your family and friends call you something else? A pet name: Betsy, Jane, Hilda, Candice or something nice.'

'Pet names and family names are for one's intimate relations and friends, Detective Sergeant Wain. I am not going to allow you to call me by any of my personal names, nor shall I reveal my true forename. Call me Mrs Plumpton, it is by far the nicest and most suitable.'

'Well, that's put me straight!' smiled Wayne.

'It has indeed,' Pluke was delighted that his mastery of the office routine had not been challenged. 'Let's get down to work and tomorrow morning we shall go and interview the person in charge of Crickledale Volunteer Carers. We shall start at the top as we embark upon our hunt for one or more killers in Crickledale.'

'Is the boss a witness or suspect?' asked Wayne.

'Initially a witness,' replied Detective Inspector Pluke, adding, 'Softly, softly, catchy monkey, Wayne and Mrs Plumpton.'

Chapter 11

BEFORE GOING OFF duty that Tuesday evening, Detective Inspector Pluke rang the secretary of the Crickledale Volunteer Carers at their office in The Cedars, Millbank Road, Crickledale, and arranged a meeting which would include himself and Detective Sergeant Wain. It was agreed the detectives would visit the CVC at 10.30 a.m. on Wednesday morning and Pluke asked that representatives of senior management be present.

Pluke concealed the true purpose of his visit by explaining he was gathering data as part of a Home Office survey into the role of the police when investigating sudden deaths, especially those that did not result in an inquest or a criminal investigation. The secretary, Mrs Sarah Allanby, said she understood and felt sure the CVC would give as much assistance as possible. After all, she said, the carers dealt with many cases that did not involve the police – the majority of them in fact – but in some cases, the police were necessarily called and such circumstances ranged from something as nasty as sudden and unexplained deaths to more routine matters like old folks locking themselves out of their homes, getting lost or going missing in town. As she chatted, she stressed that the carers worked closely with all the emergency services, local authorities and charitable organisations to make the life for the old people in Crickledale much more pleasant than it might otherwise be.

She assured Pluke that the Chairman, John C. Furnival would be present and she hoped that, duties permitting, at least one of the full-time professional carers would also attend. She suggested that volunteers were not necessary at this meeting – after all, they took no part in the management of the CVC and did not involve themselves with policy matters. Pluke agreed.

'Good, we look forward to meeting you both,' Mrs Allanby assured him. 'And I might add, we are very aware of the help and comfort provided by Mrs Pluke. She is one of our most dependable volunteers.'

'She does a lot of charitable work in Crickledale.' Pluke was proud of Millicent and her response to a range of social necessities. 'She understands the needs and desires of elderly citizens which is probably why she is such a good wife to me.'

'Of course, Mr Pluke. You're a very lucky man.'

'Thank you. Until tomorrow then.'

Pluke suggested to Mrs Plumpton that during his forthcoming absence from the office, she should continue her research. In particular, he wanted to know as much as possible about each of the deceased, including the time and date of death, how the deceased was found, who found them, whether an ambulance or doctor was called, whether the house had an appearance of being unlawfully entered and a note of any unusual circumstances associated with the death, no matter how minor they might be. He would also like to know of any other salient factors especially the loss or theft of valuable possessions. Mrs Plumpton assured Detective Inspector Pluke that she was fully *au fait* with the direction of his investigation and knew precisely what was required.

As Detective Inspector Montague Pluke, still wearing his funeral suit, walked home after work, he was aware that his unusual attire would continue to raise questions among the people of Crickledale. Those Crickledonians who were unaware of Mrs Langneb's funeral would wonder about his dress and ask themselves what he had been doing that afternoon.

He knew that many would allow their curiosity to over-whelm their good manners and find an excuse to ask him, but in the present circumstances, he considered that to be a good omen. It was important that people did talk and discuss puzzling things, especially if they involved police officers. He hoped some would ask how the funeral of Mrs Langneb had progressed, and whether he had been representing the police at the funeral service. If he said he was, they would then want to know why he would do such a thing for someone as quiet and unobtrusive as Mrs Langneb.

And, he knew, sooner or later, someone would be brave enough to ask him, probably after a few beers in one of the pubs, whether Mrs Langneb had been a member of the Special Branch or Security Service. According to many detective novels, little old ladies were often very good detectives, especially in rural areas. Pluke knew that many townspeople would claim it was the first time such a heavy police presence had attended a local funeral – so logically there must have been a very sound reason. In that way, Pluke would persuade the people to chat to him and he would find a means of turning the conversation around to old folks who had died suddenly in odd circumstances or who had had possessions stolen from their homes.

But to his disappointment and surprise, no one questioned his mode of dress or referred to his presence at Mrs Langneb's funeral, although he felt sure that many did make a mental note of his distinctive appearance and the reason for it. Maybe they would talk to him later? As he drew closer to his own house, he wondered if the people were reticent because they did not wish to become involved. Lots of people were like that – they did not relish the responsibility of being involved in matters that concerned the police. So did that mean they knew something he didn't? Was the entire population concealing something secretive?

He congratulated himself upon realizing he might have discovered something vital. Had they not talked to him because they knew that something was going on within Crickledale society that the police should never know about? Did they not wish to spark off some kind of investigation? Then he was home.

'I'm back, Millicent.' She was not in the kitchen, but her voice came from the sitting room.

'Good, then go and get changed into something more relaxing and in view of my busy and very trying day at Mrs Langneb's funeral, I might have a sherry with you. Then before supper you can tell me about your day.'

'I might relax my rules and join you for a sherry,' he told her, thinking that he also had spent a somewhat curious day's duty. A nice drink might help to calm his busy brain as it struggled to weave a sure way through the labyrinth of confusing strands of suspicion, superstition and supposition. By this time, he had convinced himself that something untoward *was* happening in Crickledale and equally he had convinced himself that as the head of the town's Criminal Investigation Department, he must do something about it. But what? What could he do if he didn't know what had been happening? And suppose the entire population was concealing information from him? Or was his imagination racing too far ahead? What evidence of criminality was there except some open doors and windows? And old folks lying on cold floors? And what was Millicent's role in all these events – total innocence? Or something extremely secretive?

Ten minutes later, he was sitting in his favourite armchair in front of the log fire as Millicent poured two large helpings of sweet sherry. He thought she looked tense and agitated. Certainly she was unsmiling and was not her usual self.

Had the funeral upset her? Millicent was very sensitive and things such as the death of a friend or acquaintance, inevitably made a serious impact upon her sensitivities. Despite his increasing suspicion of all involved in the CVC he felt he must strive to be at ease with his wife. He would do his best to speak to her not as a potential witness or suspect, but as his ever-loving wife.

'The meal is in the oven,' she told him as she took a large sip from her glass. 'I prepared it earlier, a casserole with veg-etables all in one dish. So easy to prepare after a stressful day.

Leftovers. Easy to serve too, and to enjoy.'

'I'll enjoy it, you can be sure of that,' he said, adding, 'Your good health,' as he proposed a brief toast by raising his glass. And then silence. She remained silent as they sipped their sherry. He began to feel rather edgy because this unnerving silence wasn't like the usual charming Millicent. He bore it for a long time and then tentatively asked, 'Something wrong, Millicent? Is something bothering you?'

'Yes, Montague! You are!'

'Me? But I've done nothing, said nothing.'

'Yes you have. You went to Mrs Langneb's funeral, you and Wayne and that woman from your office, and now the town is buzzing with speculation and gossip! I said you shouldn't go, most definitely I did not want you interfering with people's lives, snooping on them.'

'I was not snooping!' he said firmly. 'I was representing Crickledale police.'

'Rubbish!' she snapped. 'There are times, Montague Pluke, when you talk utter rubbish but you can't fool me. You were snooping.'

'I was not. . . .'

'Yes you were and you should not snoop on people, Montague, but there you all were, as large as life, disguised in your funeral clothes and asking all sorts of questions while no doubt getting Mr Carpenter to tell you his secrets. . . .'

'I insist I was there in a non-investigative role, Millicent, nothing more than that. I saw you in church but had no time to talk to you . . . you disappeared so quickly afterwards. . . .'

'I was busy in the kitchen, I had work to do. That's why I was there. I'm a Crickledale Volunteer Carer with many responsibilities. After the service, I was helping to arrange plates of sandwiches and cakes, make the tea, wash up and whatever else needed to be done. But I must admit I was shocked to see you huddled in that corner with Wayne Wain and Mr Carpenter, talking in hushed tones . . . and don't think it went unnoticed! You can't fool me that you attended the funeral as a mark of respect for Mrs Langneb, Montague. You hardly knew the poor woman . . . as I've said all along, you were snooping and you know I dislike people who snoop, whoever they are. Police or nosey neighbours.'

Rarely had he seen her in such a state. Normally she accepted the difficulties of his work and duties, but in view of her open misery, he decided to tell her a little about his current activities. He hoped it would put her more at ease.

'Millicent, I am working on a cold-case review, one whose content and aims must remain confidential. I'm sorry if you dislike what I do but I cannot get permission from my wife every time I have to undertake sensitive tasks or make difficult enquiries in this town. And this case is proving to be one of the most difficult.'

'Montague, I know what you're up to and I keep insisting there is nothing suspicious about any of those recent deaths that involved the carers. You take not the slightest scrap of notice of what I say but this afternoon, you certainly stirred up some malicious and worrying gossip. You should have heard the ladies in the kitchen, Montague! Your presence was noticed and so was that of Detective Sergeant Wain – and that secretary of yours done up like a dog's dinner and flouncing all over the place, asking more questions. A band of professional snoopers if ever there was one. You may as well admit what we all know, Montague. You were snooping, all of you.'

'We were gathering intelligence. . . .'

'Intelligence? You certainly need some of that, Montague Pluke. This afternoon's debacle was totally unnecessary. Mrs Langneb died a perfectly normal and natural death. Snooping Pluke, that's what you are!'

Montague lowered his voice. 'Millicent, I tell you quite sincerely that we were there on confidential police business and Mrs Plumpton attended as a close friend of a friend of Mrs Langneb. She accompanied that friend to the funeral because the friend did not like going alone. Mrs Plumpton was due to some time off work and used it to attend the funeral with her friend. That's all there was to it. You are listening to the silly stories that circulate among people on such occasions. . . .'

'Say what you like, Montague, you made me feel very embarrassed among my friends. The ladies in the kitchen thought I was snooping too, they wouldn't talk to me. They said I was a police informer . . . they were horrid, Montague. And I thought they were my friends.'

At this point he detected moisture in her eyes. That certainly announced that she was very, very upset. Now he could see why. But, he asked himself, why would the ladies in the kitchen think she was spying on behalf of her husband?

Did it mean there *was* a very good reason to spy on Mrs Langneb's funeral – or make discreet enquiries about her death? He sensed deep undercurrents within the CVC, probably internal matters of no concern to the police but interesting nonetheless, and perhaps relevant? Certainly, some of the carers had attended the funeral and enjoyed tea afterwards.

'Were any of your critics from the CVC?' he could not miss the opportunity to ask that question. 'The kitchen workers, I mean. Or had a professional caterer been asked to provide the funeral tea?'

'Some of the helpers are carers, yes, but that's what the CVC does, it helps others in all sorts of ways and we depend on volunteers. The tea was done by a professional caterer, but it was cheaper if we provided unpaid assistance on the day. That's why we were there. I hope you don't read something sinister into their presence as well, Montague Pluke!'

'I'm not . . .'

'If you continue like this you'll be blaming all our charities for causing the very work that needs the attention of charities. . . .'

'Really?' was all he could think of saying. 'Millicent, the simple truth is I am just doing my job, for the good of society. So can you tell me which of the carers were helping in the kitchen?'

'You never stop asking questions, do you? Why do you want to know that?'

'Because of my delicate enquiries, Millicent.'

'So you were snooping! And now you want me to be a

snooper! They were right. . . .'

'I can ask elsewhere, Millicent.'

'All right, there was me, Mrs Barnett and Mrs Roseberry.'

'Thank you,' and he made a mental note to investigate those ladies. He must have met them somewhere in town, perhaps at one of Millicent's church events.

'I'm going to lay the table,' she snapped and headed for the kitchen. He watched her leave – she was certainly behaving uncharacteristically and he wondered why. She was usually so supportive of his work in Crickledale, a truly wonderful wife, partner and friend, especially during his most difficult times. So what on earth was going on within the realms of the Crickledale Carers?

He decided it would be best to say no more, especially this evening. Daringly, and in her absence whilst she worked in the kitchen, he poured himself another generous sherry but he was not looking forward to his meal in the present chilly climate. But, he told himself, he had successfully confronted some terrible situations. However, what could be worse than Millicent falling under increasing suspicion of being involved in something illegal? He found himself wondering whether she would actually help a sick person to die . . . as an act of charity?

That evening he was very much alone with his dark thoughts.

On Wednesday morning after checking at the Control Room to learn yet again there were no serious matters requiring attention, Detective Inspector Pluke and Detective Sergeant Wain walked across town to the offices of Crickledale Volunteer Carers. The office was housed in a very pleasing bungalow in Millbank Road, one that had formerly belonged to a wealthy owner of factories in Leeds and Bradford. When the owner's wife was alive, they had used it for holidays and weekends but after her death he had donated it to the CVC for their unrestricted use. It was his way of saying 'Thank You' for the care they had provided for his wife. Pluke wondered if they had helped her to die.

The bungalow was large enough to provide two offices, a conference/meetings room, a waiting area, a kitchen and even en-suite limited bedroom accommodation for those who suddenly found themselves homeless. There was a press-button security lock on the outer door and after pressing it and announcing his name and that of Wayne Wain, they pressed Buttons 2 and 6 and were admitted. A pleasant middle-aged woman met them in the foyer. She was tall and attractive with short blonde hair and an easy smile.

'Ah, Mr Pluke and Mr Wain. I am Sarah Allanby, the secretary. We spoke yesterday.'

'Pleased to meet you,' chorused both Pluke and Wayne Wain. 'It is good of you to see us.'

'Our chairman, Mr Furnival will see you in the conference room; I shall be there too and so will one of our professional carers, Mrs Juliet Jarvis. Her colleague, Mrs Frankland, is with one of our clients just now. So please follow me.'

She led them along a short corridor to what had clearly been a spacious lounge in the former bungalow; it was now a conference room with a large oval table, a dozen chairs and an open fireplace filled with flowers. Place-settings with pads, pencils and water glasses were waiting on the table and Pluke noted that the required seats were identified with name plates. The six places occupied one half of the table; the rest of it remained empty. Mrs Allanby indicated their places and they settled down, with Mrs Jarvis and John Furnival, the chairman, walking in together. Pluke noted they were smartly dressed and well groomed. Even that small point indicated a highly professional group of people.

Furnival detached himself from his companion and came over to greet Pluke and Wain who rose to their feet to meet him. They all shook hands.

'Detective Inspector Pluke, how nice to meet you. I have heard so much about you and your work for the citizens of this small town. And Detective Sergeant Wain – you too. I am John Furnival, chairman of the CVC; you have already met Mrs Allanby, our secretary and this is Juliet Jarvis one of our professional carers. Most of our carers, as I am sure you appreciate, are volunteers as indeed is your very capable wife, Millicent.'

'Have we met, Mr Furnival?' asked Pluke, shaking his hand. 'I seem to know your face but I cannot recall our paths ever crossing?'

'I am sure our paths have crossed, Mr Pluke, after all this is a very small town.'

He then shook hands with Mrs Jarvis, a tall, powerful-looking woman in her mid-forties. Dark haired and with an air of absolute efficiency about her, she gripped his hand firmly.

'Delighted to meet you, Mr Pluke,' her smile was welcoming and warm. 'We are so pleased that your wife is one of us, such a helpful and lovely lady. But I don't think you and I have ever met, have we? Except perhaps at the hospital some years ago? I used to be a nurse there but left due to all the unnecessary red-tape and filling-in of pointless forms with little boxes to tick. The NHS is being stifled by paperwork, Mr Pluke. It is so sad.' And then she turned to shake hands with Wayne.

Furnival was a tall, well-built man with barely an ounce of fat on his body. In his late fifties, judging by his appearance, he seemed fit and healthy with a good head of grey hair and rimless spectacles. Pluke felt he oozed charm and confidence.

'I am sure we have passed one another as we have walked to work through the town, Mr Pluke. Like you, I walk to work every day but unlike you, I am a fairly new resident of the town – a mere five years.'

'You'll find we are lovely people who will make you feel most welcome, Mr Furnival. I hope you found a warm welcome when you arrived.'

'Yes, I did. I soon felt very much at home. You may like to know that I am a retired senior fire officer from West Yorkshire and as you know, the Fire Service has long enjoyed a reputation for its out-of-hours care for the community. Like police officers, we have to retire at a comparatively early age and so I decided this is how I could continue my former charitable work. Firefighters are always such hard workers for those less fortunate than themselves, they do such a lot of charitable work in their spare time, much of it unknown to the wider public.'

'I am very aware of all that, Mr Furnival, many police officers do likewise. They regularly come across the poorest in society. Anyway, we're glad to meet you and your staff.'

'How can we help you?'

Chapter 12

'As I am sure you know, Mr Furnival . . .' began Pluke.
'Call me John.'

'And I'm Wayne,' chipped in Wayne Wain.

'And I am Detective Inspector Pluke.'

'Oh,' said Furnival.

Pluke never explained why he did not immediately resort to the use of forenames especially during informal situations, but Wayne knew his boss felt it was most certainly not advisable during criminal investigations or indeed in any police enquiry, nor when meeting anyone for the first time. An added factor was that within many police stations there were distinct barriers between the higher ranks and subordinates and also civilian employees. The emphasis was upon formality, correctness and mutual respect. Pluke also expected children and young people to refer to him by his full name and rank; he thought it wrong for youngsters to call him Monty. Not even Millicent used that form of address. He was always Montague to her.

'As I'm sure you know,' Pluke began to explain, 'the Government is making severe cutbacks in public services and the police are no exception.'

'We're acutely aware of that, Detective Inspector Pluke,' agreed Furnival. 'It's happening to the Fire Service too and the cuts are permeating down to our level as carers, through local and district councils. Everyone is affected.'

'From our point of view, and in common with all police forces, we've been instructed to examine the ways in which we execute our duties and responsibilities with a view to finding less expensive but equally efficient methods. I refer to all our work, not only criminal investigations.'

'That won't be easy, Detective Inspector. So how are we involved?'

'Your work rarely involves the police, Mr Furnival, but one area under scrutiny is the way that sudden deaths are dealt with. In particular, the Home Office is concerned about the police role and the time spent in dealing with deaths that do not develop into either criminal investigations or involve an inquest.'

'I wouldn't have thought the police could ever spend too much time on that sort of thing, Detective Inspector Pluke. It's vital police work, that's how criminality is uncovered and offenders detected.'

'That's true, but the top-and-bottom of it, Mr Furnival, is that the Home Office seems to believe that a lot of police time and expense is spent on unnecessary enquiries. In their view, this includes the investigation of deaths that occur from purely natural causes. My task, therefore, is to identify areas where savings can be made without jeopardizing criminal justice.'

'It's a tall order, Mr Pluke. If the police are anything like the Fire Service, their time and expenditure will already have been cut to the bone.'

'Then you can understand our dilemma. What I must do is to make our political masters feel they are doing something useful,' and Pluke produced one of his rare smiles. 'If I can be seen, in my official returns, to reduce the time and effort of my officers – CID officers that is, the uniform branch will make their own decisions on this matter – then it will please the Home Office boffins. As I am sure you know, Mr Furnival, reforms are quite alright so long as they don't change anything.'

'That's how I see things too. Well, if there's any way we can help, I shall be pleased to cooperate. So how do you think

Crickledale Volunteer Carers can contribute? Surely you should be speaking to doctors, hospitals, the ambulance service and so on. . . .'

'That will be done in due course, I assure you,' smiled Pluke. 'This is just the beginning of our struggle to conform to Home Office directives without jeopardizing our service to the public.'

'Although I understand your dilemma, Detective Inspector, I fail to see how we can help. We are a volunteer group working on the proverbial shoestring. Part charity and part officially funded.'

'But you do operate under the aegis of the local council?'

'Yes we do. We're ultimately responsible to the district council. They provide funds and help with the upkeep and running costs of this building and the agreed salaries of our permanent staff. A high proportion of our income is from charitable donations, so we don't pay wages or expenses to our volunteers.'

'Which is why I'm here, talking to you,' smiled Pluke. 'I have no doubt you will be, or have been, ordered to reduce costs?'

'It goes on all the time, Mr Pluke. We're not exempt.'

'So, Mr Furnival, I am sure you have specific procedures for particular events so can I begin by asking this – in the event of a death of a person in your care, under what circumstances would you call the police?'

'Well, the obvious answer would be if there was a break-in at the person's home, or perhaps if the person appeared to have been attacked. Or if we suspected suicide or any sort of crime. In any of those circumstances, it would be an automatic reaction by any of our volunteers to call the police before taking further action.'

'So are the police your first choice? What if there were no suspicions or if emergency treatments were not necessary? Wouldn't you call a doctor first? Or the ambulance?'

'As you know, Mr Pluke, one must interpret rules with common sense – I'm a great believer in the old saying that rules are for the obedience of fools and the guidance of wise people. What I am saying is that there is no set procedure – it all depends on the circumstances in each individual case, but I am sure you realize that the police are first considered in most of our emergency calls.'

'Surely you provide some kind of training or guidance for your volunteers?'

'We do, and my Fire Service career has helped. Like the police, fire fighters are trained in the recognition of suspicious deaths and the action that needs to be taken. I have revived that training for the benefit of my carers.'

'So what happens if one of your volunteers is first at the scene where there is a dead person? Say in the dead person's own home? They are not trained like police officers and fire fighters so what would they do?'

'I have to say again that it would depend upon the circumstances, what they saw or what they thought had happened. They'd probably call this office to seek advice and guidance. I hope our training, brief though it is, would cope with most eventualities, but we can't anticipate everything. No one can.'

'So you don't have a book of rules? A small leaflet explaining how they should react? One that is issued to all the volunteers?'

'As a matter of fact we don't. We can't anticipate every set of circumstances and can't provide guidance for all situations. There are simply too many variations so we must trust that an element of common sense among our carers would prevail. And, of course, we do encourage them to use their initiative.'

'That doesn't always work, especially in an emergency when panic can dominate one's actions.'

'That's a good point, Chief Inspector. . . .'

'Detective Inspector,' corrected Pluke. 'Not Chief Inspector.'

'Sorry.'

'The reason I'm asking all these questions, Mr Furnival, is to try and establish whether your carers instinctively first call the police as a matter of routine in *all* cases where the cause of death is unknown. This is the kernel of this discussion. Or would they think of calling a doctor before contacting any of the other agencies?'

'Oh, I think they'd call the police. . . .'

'But if a doctor was first on the scene and certified the cause of death by acknowledging it had resulted from natural causes, then the police would not need to attend. That would save a lot of time and expense. Do you agree?'

'Well, yes I do. . . .'

Pluke continued. 'That would represent a substantial saving in police time and money over the months and years. This is what the Home Office is agitating about.'

'Well, I must agree that the police aren't needed at the scene of *every* sudden death. If the casualty was examined first by a doctor who decided it was a natural death, then there would be no need for the police.'

'That's precisely the point I'm making, Mr Furnival. As things stand, the police are routinely called to the scene of almost every sudden or unexplained death, even when it is not necessary. This is where savings can be made. And you and I are aware that we never call the ambulance if the person is obviously dead. Ambulances are there to save life, not to deal with death.'

'You've raised some good points, Detective Inspector Pluke. Rest assured, I shall do my utmost to persuade our carers against calling the police to *every* death although it will be difficult to persuade them to do otherwise.'

'I'll be pleased to help you find the right type of training,' offered Pluke.

'It's more involved than that, Detective Inspector. You're asking our carers to make very important, on-the-spot decisions. We have to take account of the fact that some apparently natural deaths might be due to murder. Then there's the question of preservation of the scene and so forth. Our carers need to be aware of those matters.'

'Investigating a death is never simple, Mr Furnival and I'm aware that the action taken upon first arriving at a scene of death often presents difficulties to an untrained carer.'

'Surely that's why calling the police is the most sensible thing they can do,' said Furnival. 'It's a safe and valuable starting point. The police will know what to do next and which procedure to follow.'

'Absolutely true, but all this boils down to is that the Home Office doesn't want police officers dealing with tasks that are not police matters.'

'You've raised some interesting points, Detective Inspector Pluke. My immediate reaction is that it would be very useful if there was some kind of formal training that could be undertaken by our carers to show them the best way to deal with a whole range of emergencies. They need practical examples too.'

'Our training school has a film that shows exactly that, Mr Furnival, it explains to trainee constables – specials and regular officers – how to respond in a range of circumstances. I'll speak to our Force Training Officer to see whether he could lend a copy to the CVC.'

'That's a very good beginning.'

'Fine. We might even run a special course for your carers, to help them deal with whatever circumstances they encounter. That could be done without spending too much and in the long term it might help to save money and increase efficiency.'

'We all need to do that, so is there any way I can help further?' asked Furnival.

'Yes,' smiled Pluke. 'Would you object to me talking to all your volunteers, one by one. Not during those times they are working, of course, but in their spare time. At home, perhaps? I need their cooperation in the compilation of my report to the Home Office and it would help if I could quote actual circumstances where carers have acted instinctively and called the police when perhaps, with a little thought, they might have called a doctor first. This is not a criticism, by the way, but we must look to the future.'

'I don't want to upset my staff by apparently being critical of their work. They do a wonderful job for no money, and their clients warm to them. But if you can convince our staff to think twice before taking action, I see no reason why we can't help. I can see the logic behind Home Office thinking, so I'll give you my full support.'

'Please don't alert them in advance, Mr Furnival. I would like to speak to them cold, as it were, to get their instinctive response rather than a carefully thought-out reply. I don't want responses that have been approved by someone in higher authority.'

'Then I'll show my cooperation by offering a list of all our carers? With their addresses and personal details.'

'That would be of enormous help. And this is entirely confidential, as we can all appreciate. . . .'

'Absolutely, Detective Inspector Pluke.'

'So do your volunteers maintain work-time diaries, Mr Furnival?' Wayne Wain suddenly joined the debate. 'Or is there a master diary in Head Office? I'm thinking of a record of all cases dealt with . . . I would have thought a log of duty operations would be essential for your own security. We do live in an age when people can be sued for the most innocent of actions and for very trivial reasons.'

Mrs Jarvis had been listening intently and now responded, 'We keep very detailed records, Sergeant. Remember, we are entering peoples' homes and dealing with very personal matters, so our volunteers are advised, for legal and practical reasons, to maintain an accurate daily record of all their activities. I check them regularly to keep them on their toes!'

'A very wise and necessary procedure, Mrs Jarvis.'

'We wouldn't want to lay ourselves open to accusations of any kind from our clients or their families. I'm sure both of you realize that most of our clients are elderly and forgetful, they lose things and it is not unknown for some of our volunteers to be accused of theft or worse, Sergeant. In fact we have one old man who has an extremely valuable oil painting hanging above his fireplace . . . I do worry about it because he leaves his doors unlocked and invites all sorts of people in, just for companionship. . . .'

'That's exactly the sort of thing that needs to be recorded, for your own safety. And the old man does need some good advice too! So what is recorded in your master diary?' asked Pluke. 'And who's responsible for maintaining it?'

'I'm ultimately responsible,' said Furnival. 'But Sarah does the donkey work.'

Sarah Allanby, sitting next to him at the head of table as she took notes of this meeting, looked up and smiled.

'We keep a duty rota, Mr Pluke,' she explained. 'We need to know what our volunteers are doing, where they are and whom they are visiting. We maintain what might be called a duty sheet to ensure there are always volunteers available at short notice, and here in the office, we need to know where they are at any given moment when on duty.'

'It sounds like a police operation,' smiled Wayne.

'We're very strict about such things. Mr Furnival and both our professionals make sure we maintain very detailed records of all official activities. As the full-time secretary, I compile the duty rota and diary with help from our professionals and Mr Furnival checks it every morning. We look to see whether any of our volunteers have done something that might give rise to dissatisfaction or complaints and if they have, our professionals give them suitable advice and guidance. In addition, Mrs Jarvis covers evenings on Monday, Wednesday and Friday, with Mrs Frankland doing Tuesday, Thursday and Saturday. Mr Furnival does Sundays but they can swap with each other if necessary – that's when they give help and advice to the volunteers. I might add that it is not easy, being a volunteer carer. There is much to consider.'

'Even so, I would imagine most of their work will be innocuous stuff – helping an elderly person to get up on a morning, have a bath and breakfast, and then do a bit of shopping for them, washing and ironing, or whatever is needed.'

'It is, Mr Pluke, but we do ask that our volunteers be very specific when compiling their records – they can be tempted to write stuff like "domestic help – 8 a.m. until 10 a.m." when in fact we like them to itemize their work: *"helping Mrs So-and-So to get dressed, shopping for her at Brown's corner shop to buy groceries – £5.66p spent."* We think it is important to keep very detailed records, Mr Pluke, just in case we get complaints.'

'That's exactly why *we* keep such comprehensive records.'

'There are lots of complainers in our society, Detective Inspector, not only our old people but their friends and families.'

'Don't we know it! And do you find the volunteers reliable in compiling their records?'

'As good as possible, I feel. I know some will pop into a house if they are passing en route to the shops for their own needs; they like to check whether the occupant also needs anything . . . that kind of visit might go unrecorded. I'm sure there are many similar examples but to date nothing of that nature has given rise to concerns.'

'So how do volunteers gain entry to the clients' homes?' asked Pluke.

'We have copies of their keys,' Furnival told him. 'We have a secure key board with spares for all our clients' homes. And each house is also fitted with a key-safe for emergencies – a small secure box on an outer wall where a code will release a key if required. Mostly, we are admitted by the occupants, either by leaving doors open when they expect us or unlocking them when our carers arrive. But if our staff can't gain entry and the need is urgent, then we use keys from our stock – and each one is booked out and booked back in. Our cabinet is secured by a coded lock, the code is known only to myself, Sarah and our two professional carers.'

'Everything seems to be very well organized, Mr Furnival, you have my congratulations,' smiled Pluke.

Mr Furnival responded, 'We do our best, but I have to say that the Crickledale Volunteer Carers were up-and-running most effectively when I arrived on the scene. I'd say they are the best-run of all the groups I have been associated with, both professionally and in the voluntary sector.'

Sarah butted in now. 'Shall I print off a list of volunteers for Mr Pluke?'

'Good idea, Sarah, and include a list of our clients too. Then Detective Inspector Pluke can ask them for their observations.'

As Sarah left the room, Mr Furnival smiled at Pluke. 'I think we can come to some agreement here, Detective Inspector

Pluke. Your efforts might help also us to save money too, and reduce staff requirements. That can only be good for everyone. So what sort of things will you be asking the volunteers?'

'As I said earlier, my prime purpose is to determine the circumstances in which they would call the police. There may be times when they've wondered what to do, cases when they didn't need to call the police but did so because they couldn't think of an alternative. It's not a case of being critical, Mr Furnival, it's being objective, trying to reduce costs, avoid wasting time and establish workable procedures. And as this is a Home Office initiative, it is highly confidential at the moment.'

Mrs Jarvis now interrupted. 'So will you want to chat to me, Mr Pluke? I must say I entirely agree with what Mr Furnival has said but I must admit there are times when even I, with my long nursing experience, have been uncertain who to call first at the scene of a sudden or unexpected death.'

'I'll be interviewing all the carers in due course,' acknowledged Pluke. 'Perhaps I could interview you after I've spoken to the others? That might help. We will draft a questionnaire to ensure everyone gets the same attention.'

'Well, I'm not sure about that, Mr Pluke . . . more forms to fill in, boxes to tick.' Mrs Jarvis sounded concerned.

Furnival interrupted. 'It's very important that we cooperate, Juliet. We must make the most of our funding and this initiative from the Home Office can help us as well as the police. So yes, Detective Inspector, we're pleased to help in any way.'

'So can I ask you a question at this point, Mrs Jarvis,' asked Wayne. 'What is your personal first action at the scene of a problematical death? Sudden or unexpected?'

'I would call the police,' she shrugged her shoulders. 'They would know what to do next, who else to call and so on. But I've never thought I was wasting police time by doing that.'

'It's certainly never a waste of police time,' acknowledged Pluke. 'But things are changing and the question is whether, in view of the Government cuts, we can reduce the time the police spend on call-outs that may not be strictly necessary. It is a very important and delicate matter and any views from you and your staff would be appreciated.'

'I'll help all I can,' Mrs Jarvis assured them.

At that point, Sarah Allanby returned with the list of volunteers and another file containing a list of clients; she handed copies of each to Pluke.

'Their full names and addresses are there, Mr Pluke, along with any special skills that some might possess. I am sure you will find them – volunteers, carers and clients, past and present – all most delightful and helpful, especially Mrs Pluke. She always helps with our Thursday night rounds too, she is loved by all our patients and clients.'

'I might discover something I never knew!' he smiled. 'I hope I can persuade Mrs Pluke to help me with this initiative! But thanks, all of you. We shall get to work immediately and will keep in touch with all the CVC members through Mr Furnival. Thanks for your time.'

'A pleasure, Mr . . . er . . . Detective Inspector Pluke,' said Furnival.

'Thank you all for your help, it was most useful. So come along, Detective Sergeant Wain,' Pluke rose to his feet. 'We can't delay, there is much to do.'

Chapter 13

'So what was all that about?' asked Wayne Wain as they walked back to the police station. 'I had no idea what you were getting at Sir, you lost me in all that nonsense about cuts and wasting police time. The Home Office hasn't initiated any such policy and I've never heard those theories from anyone else. It goes without saying that ordinary citizens will call the police when they're confronted by a dead body. That applies even if they are trained volunteers working for a charity. What else can they do?'

'You'll recall I said we may have to use subterfuge, Wayne, and so I was. I was softening him up, as they say. I wanted to get him talking so I produced a sound reason for interviewing him and eventually his volunteers. I want to know more about the CVC carers without asking Millicent and, at this stage, I don't want him to think I'm suspicious of him or his staff. I've no doubt, however, that we'll have to interview them before too long to establish their movements in cases where there have been suspicious deaths. By that, I include old folks on the floor! If we get a match between a CVC visit and such a deceased person, then we shall have to delve even deeper. You can understand why I had to disguise my motives but I think he'll cooperate – and we do need his cooperation.'

'I had no idea you could be so devious but we've got what we wanted from him.'

'Exactly, Wayne. It's a very positive start. We can examine

cases where their patients or clients died even if the deaths did not come to the attention of the police. And we got something else.'

'What was that?'

'Permission to speak to volunteers and clients without any formal involvement of the police. Strictly speaking, I needn't obtain his consent to talk to his volunteers but by seeking his permission I made him feel good towards us. It was a very useful concession he thought he had made, but it means I can now discreetly ask his volunteers about some of the deaths. This could become a truly productive cold-case review, Wayne. If someone is using the CVC as a smokescreen for their activities, then we shall blow that smoke away.'

'I never thought of it like that but it does make sense.'

'We must find ways to outwit the villains, Wayne. If someone is duping the police, doctors and all the other CVC members and officials, we must find out who it is, and why. Why are these helpless old folk being targeted, Wayne? Are their deaths a cover for other crimes? Now consider what we must prove if we suspect murder – we must show the killer had the ability to carry out the crime, the opportunity and the means to do so, *and a motive for committing it*. Not kindness, Wayne, not helping a person to die out of love or compassion. If the first three requirements are present, it's vital we find the fourth – the real motive. By talking informally to the volunteers and using our disguised reason for our questions, we shall gain a very positive start. Quite suddenly, I can feel my cold-case review quickly getting warmer.'

'Furnival will alert them, surely? I know you asked him not to, but he or those women will warn their friends and colleagues, that's for sure. Somebody will let the proverbial cat out of the bag and those volunteers will rehearse their responses or say nothing at all.'

'But if he tells them what to say, I shall recognize that that is happening. If he does so, it means he'll be covering up something or someone, doesn't it?'

'That will mean he is an accomplice?'

'It will, but at no point in the early stages will we hint at deaths or murders – we must give the impression we are there to help both the CVC and the police to save money and become more efficient.'

'You're a cunning old devil, aren't you!'

'Not so much of the old, Wayne!'

'All right, I'll say you are an experienced old devil!'

'That's better. But I know, Wayne, that it takes a cunning old police officer to ferret out facts, so I'm merely doing my job. I know it is shocking and even unbelievable to suggest there is a killer among the carers, but by doing that, we might find out there isn't one, just someone using them as a cover for their own nasty work. . . .'

'So you're now saying you *don't* suspect any of the carers of murder?'

'I'm not saying that, Wayne. I'm open-minded. Our enquiries will reveal the truth.'

'So you'll be interviewing Mrs Pluke?'

'No, *you'll* be doing that, Wayne! Very discreetly. And you must do it whilst I'm nowhere near her. Try to make it appear nothing more than a chat. I want to know if she suspects anything unsavoury within the realms of the CVC. I feel sure that something is bothering her, but she won't tell me.'

'So now what are we looking for? You've confused me with all that talk of unnecessarily calling the police to sudden deaths, and then you say you don't really suspect a CVC volunteer is helping clients to die. Just what are we doing?'

'In simple terms, Wayne, we're looking for anyone who might have helped those old folks to die. That alone is murder.'

'But there's more?'

'Right. People don't commit murder without a motive and I cannot accept these deaths are done out of kindness alone. If the same team is causing all the deaths, then there must one motive – so what is it? Bearing in mind what we've already heard, could it be theft of the belongings of vulnerable people? I think that is highly likely and if so, the old folks cannot make complaints because they're dead. We, the police, are never made aware of the crime and so we cannot take appropriate action. So is someone helping victims to die simply to prevent them complaining about a lesser crime? Answers to those questions could lead us to the killer or killers.'

'Having said all that, sir, we need to eliminate the innocent from this cold-case review,' mused Wayne. 'When we achieve that, only the guilty will remain. . . .'

'Then *you* can start by proving the innocence of Mrs Pluke beyond all doubt, Wayne. And perhaps you could interview Dr Simpson to obtain his views on all this? Is he part of a criminal team or is he merely doing his job by certifying the deaths? Has he dealt with all such deaths, or merely a selection of them?'

Wayne said nothing. There was nothing he could say at that instant because their walk was over. They were entering the mighty portals of Crickledale Sub-Divisional Police Station where, as always, Pluke poked his head into the Control Room.

'Ah, Sergeant Cockfield-pronounced-Cofield, is everything peaceful and quiet?'

'All quiet, sir, nothing's changed. It doesn't mean we are heading for an earthquake, does it? Even the sparrows have stopped chirping. They say that wild creatures can sense the approach of severe storms and tempests. . . .'

'Then we can expect something nasty,' warned Pluke as he headed up the stairs to his office, making sure he touched the wooden handrail to ensure the best of fortune. Wayne went to his own office.

Once at his desk, Pluke moved the various ornaments into their correct places then settled down. At that point, Mrs Plumpton entered.

'Anything I can get you, Mr Pluke?'

'Yes please, Mrs Plumpton. Is that file about the death of Edgar Lindsey convenient or is it still in my in-tray? He was the man whose gold watch was lost or possibly stolen.'

'I can find it in a moment or two.'

'Excellent. Then perhaps you could copy this list of CVC volunteers and run a criminal record check against their names?

I want to know if any have come to the notice of the police. And there is also a list of clients/patients of the CVC, both past and present – can you check all their names against our files of sudden deaths? It's important we establish who, among these CVC patients, particularly the elderly ones, died unexpectedly or in peculiar circumstances without the police being officially notified. I don't think the CVC cares for every old person in Crickledale but we need to know the name of those who are CVC clients and who have died.'

'That shouldn't be a problem, you've done well to obtain these lists. It'll give me something useful to do.'

'You might have to search back a long way, even to the time the CVC was formed, whenever that was. And we need to check whether any CVC clients over the years, have reported any matter to the police. I'm thinking of fairly minor stuff that old folks might complain about or merely mention – thefts from their homes, items that may have been lost or stolen, prowlers in the house or the immediate vicinity.'

'I'll get Sergeant Cockfield-pronounced-Cofield to check his complaints files. He will keep such records.'

'Do that, and include strangers arriving on the doorstep trying to gain admission, even assaults by staff and generally things that go bump in the night. Anything that has alarmed them, anything out of the ordinary.'

'I'll be pleased to do that for you,' she smiled, thinking how forceful he had become now that he had something to occupy him. 'It will make me feel like a real detective.'

'You've already displayed your remarkable talents,' he smiled.

As she left his office she pondered the deeper meaning of his last remark and he settled down to examine the routine correspondence that always managed to accumulate even when he was absent for a very short time. He initialled most of it to indicate he had read it, and then placed it in the 'out' file. Mrs Plumpton would do something with it.

Sitting alone in his quiet office, he decided this was an ideal opportunity to speak to the town duty inspector about Mr

Lindsey. He could do so before Mrs Plumpton located the file and information he'd requested. He told Mrs Plumpton where he was heading and left without taking his hat, but making sure he stepped out with his right foot first. En route, he passed the open doorway of the Control Room but on this occasion did not stop to ask Sergeant Cockfield-pronounced-Cofield whether there had been any incidents.

The sergeant was very puzzled that Pluke had walked past without stopping – was he ill? He always poked his head inside to ask what had happened. So was something actually happening at this moment? Is that why he had sent Mrs Plumpton down to go through his files?

The sergeant returned to his silent console and waited for his radio to chirp or his phone to ring but they remained silent. Mrs Plumpton was in the back room but as the sergeant waited, he could hear Pluke's progress along the corridor and was astonished when he halted outside Inspector Horsley's office. So there *was* something afoot – Pluke and Horsley never seemed to get along with one another so a friendly visit was out of the question. Obviously, there was important and perhaps secret police business afoot.

Pluke tapped on the door and a voice called 'Enter'.

'Ah, Montague,' the thick-set, dark-haired figure of Inspector Horsley was seated at his desk. 'To what do I owe this rare honour? Come in and sit down.'

'May I have a word, Inspector Horsley,' as always Pluke refrained from using Christian names when conducting official police business.

'You can, I have the time right now, it's so very quiet these days. Nothing is happening. So how can I help the majesty of Crickledale CID?'

Pluke sat on a chair near the inspector's desk and opened with, 'I'm conducting a cold-case review and whilst I would normally have selected an undetected crime for detailed analysis I find we have no undetected major crimes in Crickledale's CID records.'

'That's because nothing very serious ever happens in

Crickledale, Montague. The uniform lads deal with all the minor crimes as you know, but we can't boast a 100 per cent detection rate. It means your officers don't have enough to occupy them, do they? There are times I wonder what your department does with itself all day.'

Pluke responded. 'We investigate crimes committed in other areas as well as our own, their villains might be living and operating on our patch, Inspector Horsley. And don't forget that much of our work is secret and confidential, often involving national security.'

'You can tell a good story, Montague, but our local uniformed officers work closely with the public. We accept that thieves get away with some minor crimes and we've a lot of undetected cases on our books. Criminal damage to car wing-mirrors, theft of ladies' handbags, nicking apples from displays outside fruit shops, taking spoons as souvenirs from coffee shops. You name it, we deal with it. If we are made aware of any crimes, we do our best to detect them, but most will never be detected. So how can I help?'

'You will recall a gold watch that was reported stolen last June – the owner was an elderly gentleman called Lindsey. Edgar Lindsey.'

'Yes, I remember it. It was one of those peculiar cases that one never forgets. His son reported the watch either lost or stolen. I remember it because it was distinctly odd.'

'What was odd about it?'

'I'll get the file, Montague. It's still active because we haven't traced the watch or identified the thief. We live in eternal hope that it might turn up in an antique shop or car boot sale.'

He went into his secretary's office and returned with the file, not yet tied up with string.

'As I said, there were peculiar circumstances, Montague, one of which was that the loser died within a few days of the theft coming to our notice. He was 89 years old and lived alone. His wife had died some years earlier and his only child, a son called Rupert, lived in Coventry and rarely visited his dad.'

'Neglect, was it?'

'Not really. The son did his best to visit at weekends but it was often impossible due to his own domestic commitments and work. Our local carers – the CVC – looked after the old man and so far as I was concerned, they did a good job.'

'When you said there were other peculiar circumstances, what did you mean?'

'We police officers have an instinct for such things, Montague. You know when things aren't quite right even though there seems to be no apparent reason for such thoughts. That's how I felt with this one. It smelled, as we say.'

'Was it because the watch had been lost whilst you thought it had been stolen?'

'Obviously you know something about it. We must remember, Montague, that old Mr Lindsey was in a poor state of health, his memory had gone and he was suffering from dementia.'

'That doesn't excuse a crime being committed against him.'

'Far from it, but he was vulnerable. It was just a few days before his death that his gold watch disappeared. It was valuable from a financial point of view and as a family heirloom. I can't give you a true value because I never saw it but his son Rupert insisted it was worth at least £500 and probably more.'

'Well worth stealing?'

'Certainly, but the circumstances were very strange. It was said the old man never left the house although I don't think that was ever proved – he could have wandered outside and lost it in his garden which was then overgrown, or lost it in the street or a shop. Or even in his own house. We searched but never found it. Now you're going to ask whether it was lost or stolen, aren't you?'

'It was recorded as a theft, Inspector, but also as lost property. That's how I became aware of it. I found it odd that you should record it as both. Normally it's one or the other.'

'I recorded it as both to cover all the options – if it was lost, it might have been found and handed in somewhere, even at another police station. The computers would have traced it. If it had been stolen, more extensive enquiries would have been made.'

'So did your officers investigate it as a crime?'

'We recorded it as a crime, Montague, and circulated details which is why it is in the station records. I would hesitate to say we investigated it, there were no in-depth enquiries. Mr Lindsey's fragile health and state of mind made it impossible to interview him. The truth is, we never established what had happened but his son made quite a fuss about it.'

'It wasn't buried with him, was it?'

'No, it went missing before he died.'

'So if Mr Lindsey was so old and suffering from dementia, how can you be certain it was either stolen or lost? It could have been missing for years.'

'It wasn't, Montague. His son kept an eye on it every time he visited his dad. It was a family heirloom handed down from father to eldest son, so the son had a good reason for looking after it. Although we don't know the age or value of the watch, and have only a vague description, I felt we should do our best to find it. We know it was a Tissot, a good make. We also know that Mr Lindsey never took it off his wrist, not even when having a bath or gardening – that was when he was able to do such things. His son told us this – the son did not like to take it into his own possession for safety because his dad was so attached to it.'

'I can understand your problems,' sympathized Montague.

'I think the son made a fuss because he should have inherited the watch when the old man passed away.'

'So you've discovered quite a lot about it. What intrigues me is how it came to be reported lost or stolen if the old man was not aware of what was happening around him? The crime file says the theft was reported by his son. How did that come about if he was living in Coventry?'

'One of Mr Lindsey's carers alerted the son – they had his phone number and address and their officials made a point of keeping in touch about the progress or otherwise of Mr Lindsey. Rupert is a lovely man, Montague, most genuine, caring and reliable. He really did love his old dad.'

'A nice touch, but how did he, and not the carer, come to report the loss of his father's watch?'

'The carer noticed it missing from the old man's wrist and rang the son who reported it to us by telephone. All he could recollect was that it was a Tissot make with a white face bearing Roman numerals. The old fashioned wind-up type. And it had a gold expanding bracelet. We had no further details. And as I said earlier, the value was unknown. And we don't know precisely when it disappeared.'

'Surely, there was a search for it? By someone? Family, carer?'

'There was. A very thorough search was made but it was never found. As I told you, PC Carey searched his house and garden too.'

'And did you suspect the carer? Was the carer a member of the CVC?'

'Yes, as it happens. Anyone could have stolen it, even a sneak thief. I had an open mind, Montague, I suspected everyone. The house doors were often left unlocked to permit entry by carers, neighbours and friends in an emergency.'

'So it would have been easy to enter the house and steal that watch, especially if the old fellow was asleep or if it was on show. Even on his wrist?'

'Yes, even if it was on his wrist.'

'We could be thinking of a sneak-thief here, an opportunist villain. They are always about,' acknowledged Pluke. 'But the CVC has keys to all their clients' homes and most are fitted with key-safes, so why did Mr Lindsey leave his doors open?'

'The carers' keys aren't available to friends and neighbours, Montague, and the codes to the key-safes are not generally known. People such as friends and neighbours need unlocked doors to gain access. Inevitably that puts the house and its contents at risk and the occupants too but it allows constant access to the householder. It's a case of finding the right balance and it seems to work very well in Crickledale. It's full of honest decent people. I don't think there are many sneak-thieves in the population. Such crimes are rare here, as I'm sure you know.'

'That's quite true. So did you interview the carer? Who was she? Or he?'

'We targeted the old man's regular CVC carer. One of my experienced constables went to see her and I accompanied him. She was a newcomer to the CVC, a 22-year-old called Fiona Grainger. Miss Fiona Grainger.'

'And her background?'

'She's an unemployed cleaner who lives at home with her parents in Crickledale. I interviewed her at the CVC offices with her boss present.'

'John Furnival?'

'That's him. He's got those carers licked into shape, Montague. They were somewhat disorganized until he arrived. No records maintained, a lackadaisical system of working.'

'A new broom, eh?'

'Exactly. He tightened things up admin-wise, and he keeps the staff on their toes – he often drops in unannounced, even on his days off, to check on the standard of care his volunteers are giving their clients. He takes his duties very seriously.'

'It sounds rather like the inspector or sergeant arriving unannounced to check a constable's work?'

'It's the same principle. It protects the clients and helps to prevent the carers being falsely accused of wrongdoing. You and I both know how easy it is to accuse someone of theft or worse if they regularly visit the homes of vulnerable people.'

'Sadly, they are always at risk, even from the most unexpected people.'

'Furnival will be aware of that. He's an ex-fire officer, he knows the ropes, Montague. Have you met him?'

'Briefly at his office, I can't claim to know him. So was this young woman the only one you interviewed?'

'She was, but only because she said she had noticed the absence of the watch but not alerted anyone. You know the system, Montague – the person who reports a murder is often the guilty party trying to cover up their culpability by reporting the death. It's the same with reported thefts.'

'So did you suspect her? Surely other carers visited Mr Lindsey?'

'They did, but she was the most regular, and the newest recruit. She called at the same time every day and did most of his housework and some preparation of meals in a two-hour spell of duty. Obviously she came into the frame but I felt she was innocent – if indeed there had been a theft. That is still in doubt, the old chap could have simply lost his watch. Or mislaid it.'

'So Fiona Grainger spent quite a substantial amount of time alone with him?'

'Yes. That's how the Carers build up trust with their clients. Miss Grainger had no job prior to this, Montague, she had no money. A motive for theft may have there but she does not have a criminal record. And she hasn't disposed of the watch anywhere in town – we've checked all the likely outlets, even car boot sales.'

'Did you check the other carers?'

'We did. Same result. All clear, even Mrs Pluke!'

'She never told me!'

'That's understandable. However, I must tell you that there was suspicion against one of the professional carers when she worked for a local firm. She was suspected of pilfering – Juliet Jarvis that is. Nothing was ever proved, there was a suggestion it was a malicious complaint by a subordinate who felt she'd been wronged. In addition, one of the male carers has a record. He's called Dorsey, Keith Dorsey, a 47-year old window cleaner by profession. He has one conviction as an 18 year old for fighting in the street. CVC uses men like him for fixing things like plumbing, electrical faults and so on.'

'You've checked his whereabouts at the time the watch vanished?'

'Not really, we couldn't. We were never sure when it vanished, only when it was found to be missing. He was nowhere near the premises then. He was cleaning drains for an old woman at the other side of town.'

'Any other suspects?'

'Mr Lindsey had his chimney swept about a week before his watch was reported missing. A sweep called Black, Sooty Black. He helps out at the churchyard and gives free sweeps of chimneys for CVC clients. We quizzed him about the watch, but he denied ever seeing it.'

'It sounds as though you did a thorough job, Inspector Horsley. And that young woman, Fiona Grainger has never admitted the crime?'

'No, she was very upset when we interviewed her but adamant she was innocent. Mr Furnival comforted her and assured her he had not the slightest suspicion against her, and promised she would not be dismissed. We assured her that our interview was to establish her innocence, not her guilt. I think that helped her come to terms with what was happening. So there we are, Montague, a very good cold-case review subject for you. If you can find that watch and the thief responsible, I shall be very grateful. We'll be able to record it as a crime detected.'

'At the moment I'm interested in more serious crimes.'

'Then why are you here, asking me about a missing watch?'

'Because it belonged to a man whose death was considered sudden and unexpected; the police were called but the conclusion was that Mr Lindsey died from natural causes. I'm examining all such deaths where there was a hint of suspicion.'

'Well, I can tell you there was suspicion in this one, Montague, but it was all wrapped up as a death from natural causes. The death was never investigated as a possible crime.'

'Suspicion, you say? So what was unusual about it?'

'Well, when I visited the scene to see if PC Carey was coping, all the doors and windows were standing wide open and the deceased was lying on the cold floor of the downstairs bathroom. A freezing cold stone floor.'

Chapter 14

'Is PC CAREY on duty this morning?' asked Pluke before leaving the inspector's office. 'I'd like a chat with him.'

'He's on the town centre beat. Shall I call him?'

'Thanks, that would be helpful. Ask him to come to my office. Depending on what he tells me, I may want a further chat with you.'

'I'm always pleased to help the might of the CID, Montague. Shall I sit in on your chat with young Carey? Then I'll know exactly what's going on in your exclusive world and might be able to offer more assistance. After all, I am the town duty Inspector for Crickledale.'

'You're welcome to join us. I'll be in my office when PC Carey arrives.'

And so Pluke returned to the CID suite upstairs and invited Wayne to join him for his chat with PC Carey. As they settled down, Mrs Plumpton arrived with an armful of files.

'I've examined all these, Mr Pluke,' and she placed some on his blotter and others beside them. 'Those on your blotter are sudden death reports over the last ten years where a post mortem examination *was* carried out, and the others are where there was no post mortem.'

'Very efficient of you, Mrs Plumpton. Now that we are together, another thought has occurred to me. There have been many deaths in the town with which the police were not involved. That's absolutely normal. So, Wayne, did your search at the Registry of Births, Deaths and Marriages, produce such a list?'

'Yes, it's in my office.'

'Then we must examine it to ascertain whether any of them were receiving care from the CVC. In particular, we're looking for elderly people living alone, people the police would rarely be aware of in an official capacity.'

Mrs Plumpton chipped in, 'I can do that, Mr Pluke. I'll run them through my computer as a double check. It won't take long.'

'Good, thank you.'

Inspector Horsley and PC Carey, dark haired, slim and pow-erful in appearance, arrived a quarter of an hour later to find Mrs Plumpton fussing over them with a tray of coffee cups and chocolate biscuits. As they settled down, she performed her usual bowing and ducking manoeuvres to the puzzlement of the young Constable Carey. He thought she was rather too old to be trying to attract a man as young as he and when she departed, Horsley smiled and said,

'Well, Montague, we don't all get a Folies-Bergère cabaret with our coffee and biscuits. Some of us live the high life and some of us never get a cup of coffee on a morning, do we, PC Carey?'

'No, sir,' said Carey not really understanding the undertones of Horsley's comments. Office politics among the higher ranks was not something with which he was familiar, although he was regularly offered cups of coffee or tea whilst patrolling.

'So,' said Pluke as he opened the proceedings. 'PC Carey, I'm pleased to meet you. How was the driving course?'

'Very good, sir, thank you. I had no idea there was so much to learn about driving police vehicles and so much to discover about the ways motor vehicles can be stolen and shipped over-seas. I hope to get a transfer to Traffic before too long.'

'Then I wish you luck. Now, I understand from Detective Sergeant Wain that you dealt with a rather curious sudden death some time ago. Miss Adelaide Croucher? Can you remember it?'

'Yes, sir, I can. Very clearly. It turned out to be death from natural causes.'

'There were peculiar circumstances, I believe? Can you remember your first impressions of the house interior? Detective Sergeant Wain has explained because he was at the scene too but I would like your version.'

Sipping his coffee with some nervousness in the presence of a trio of such high-ranking police officers, PC Carey explained about his attendance at Miss Croucher's house. Listening intently, neither Pluke nor Wain detected any difference from the formal version of that case. Both Pluke and Horsley asked him a few questions to clarify doubts but his story supported the known recorded facts.

'Now,' said Pluke. 'I believe you dealt with another sudden death with odd circumstances – Mr Edgar Lindsey. Can you recall that one?'

'Yes, sir, it was another death from natural causes but there was no post mortem. His doctor had treated him regularly and certified the cause of death.'

'Who was the doctor?'

'Doctor Simpson, from Crickledale Surgery.'

'Do you recall which day of the week the death occurred?'

'It was a Thursday, sir. I remember because my weekly rest days were Tuesday and Wednesday that week, it was my first day back on duty working nights.'

'So did the death actually occur on the Thursday or was that when the body was found?'

'The precise time of death was never determined, sir. I was called at two o'clock on the Friday morning. The doctor said he thought it might have happened late on the Thursday night but wasn't prepared to make a positive statement about it.'

'Thanks for that clear memory. I believe something at the scene was rather odd which was the reason why the police were called in?' persisted Pluke, wanting the constable to tell his story without any prompting.

'Mr Lindsey was found lying on the floor just inside his front door. His neighbour, Mrs Frankland, found him. He was wearing only pyjamas trousers. His bed was upstairs but was made and seemed not to have been slept in. It was assumed he had collapsed and died ... Doctor Simpson couldn't explain how he had come to be lying on the floor but thought he must have collapsed. He was not injured and there was no sign of a physical attack but all the windows and the back door were standing open.'

'So were SOCO or the police photographers called in?'

'No, sir, nothing like that. Once the doctor certified death was from natural causes, it had nothing more to do with us. The doctor organized collection of the body and the undertaker took Mr Lindsey's remains to the chapel of rest to await his funeral. I took no further part in investigating his death.'

'So his death was not associated with the theft of his gold watch?'

As PC Carey hesitated slightly, Inspector Horsley responded. 'I have read the file, Montague, and there was not the slightest evidence to suggest his death and loss of the watch were connected. His death occurred several days *after* his watch had reportedly disappeared and there was no sign of injury on the body – there was no cause to believe his watch had been forcibly or illegally removed from him whilst alive and certainly it hadn't in death.'

'But there was doubt, was there?'

'Well, it's quite possible he could have mislaid or lost his watch some time before his death.'

'So the only odd thing about his death was the circumstances in which his body was found?'

'Right, Montague. And neither the doctor, the undertaker nor our officers could offer any explanation about that.'

'So who were the undertakers?'

'It wasn't a Crickledale firm, Montague. They came from Coventry, the son wanted his dad buried in Coventry where he could visit and tend the grave. The son did not comment on the manner in which his father had been found dead.'

'Perhaps he thought it was a normal type of collapse?'

'Well, the doctor never went upstairs so he wouldn't see the undisturbed bed. We didn't have the body transferred back upstairs to be laid out, that would have been very difficult for untrained people, so we covered him with a sheet and left him.'

'Was he lying there for a long time?'

'No, he was awaiting the Coventry undertakers. They came late on the Friday afternoon.'

'So they didn't question or comment on the fact that the deceased had been found lying on the floor just inside his front door?'

'No, they accepted the doctor's opinion he had collapsed there. After all, Montague, old folks are unpredictable especially when they are ill and suffering from dementia. They do some peculiar things and get into odd situations, like leaving windows and doors open.'

'Yes, that happens. Now I must ask this question of you, Inspector Horsley. Have any of the sudden deaths that you've attended or supervised been odd in any way whilst later being attributed to natural causes? When I say odd, I mean strange either in the way of Mr Lindsey's or peculiar due to some other factor?'

'Yes, a few. I can't recall their names just now but as you appreciate, we do deal with many sudden deaths even in Crickledale, most of which turn out to be due to natural causes. And don't forget, a high percentage never come to the official notice of the police – after all, they are not our concern.'

'It means we are unaware of all those personal dramas and it's unlikely we would officially know anything about them. Is that an open door for secret murders, Inspector? So how many of the deaths that your officers have attended within the last three or four years, involved elderly folks living alone whilst under the care of Crickledale Volunteer Carers?'

'You're up to something, Montague! Are our carers up to no good?'

'Just answer my question, Inspector.'

PC Carey never said a word during the high-level interchanges but he listened very carefully as his inspector continued.

'Well, as you ask, Montague, I would think that most of the elderly folks living alone in Crickledale would be known to CVC. CVC can't compel them to accept the offer of care even if it's free, but I believe the carers are constantly aware of those old folks and always keep an eye on them without being formally called in. The people of this town are like that, Montague. Very caring. They look after one another most discreetly and will raise the alarm if and when necessary.'

'That's very comforting, but taking this a step further, can you answer this? Among the old folks living alone, how many, to your knowledge, have been victims of crime? I'm referring to minor crimes, probably of the sort your uniform patrols would deal with. In the CID, we would surely be aware of any old folks being victims of serious crime.'

'I'd have to go through our crime complaint files to answer that with any degree of accuracy, Montague, but from memory I can say there are some who have been victims of minor crime.'

'Can you give examples?'

'There was one old lady whose daughter claimed that her mum had lost a valuable necklace. She kept it in a box on her dressing table and it disappeared.'

'So what did you do about that?'

'What could we do? She was elderly and senile, there was no evidence of a break-in at her home and she'd not had any intruders during the daytime or night-time. She had never been out of the house so how could we prove theft? She could have simply lost it, Montague.'

'Are you saying you recorded it as lost property? Not stolen?'

'We couldn't record it as a crime, Montague. You know that. So yes, it was noted in the Lost Property Register.'

'And she did have CVC to care for her?'

'Yes, it was one of the carers who reported the missing necklace after the lady's daughter had noticed its absence.'

'Was it found?'

'Never. Not a sign of it.'

'And did she die?'

'Yes, she lingered longer than most people expected but died about a week after we had learned about the missing necklace.'

'Was it a normal death? Not on the kitchen floor or in the garage or anywhere like that?'

'No, quite ordinary. She died in her armchair in front of the fire. There were no suspicious circumstances. Doctor Simpson certified the death as being due to nothing but old age, natural causes in other words. She was 94.'

'Did her death occur on a Thursday by any chance?'

'You *are* up to something, Montague! Are you trying to create a drama or crisis out of nothing? If our worthy and highly trained doctors are prepared to certify these deaths are from natural causes, who are we to question their professionalism? Besides, we've enough to do without regarding every death as suspicious enough to require investigation as if it was a murder enquiry.'

'My duty, Inspector Horsley, is to protect life and property and to investigate crime without fear or favour, even if it means extra work for our officers and support staff. So I repeat my question. Did that old lady's death occur on a Thursday?'

'No it didn't. I remember hearing about it as the church bells were ringing, so it must have been a Sunday. I can check our files if necessary. But I repeat, we were not involved in any investigation into her death.'

'How much was the necklace worth?'

'The daughter said she'd had it valued a couple of years earlier and it was then worth in excess of £2,000.'

'A very valuable piece of jewellery. Did you interview any of the carers about it?'

'You've done it again, Montague. You're trying to implicate the CVC in these losses and I'm sure they are not responsible. As I said earlier, there was no evidence of a crime.'

'So you didn't interview any of the carers? Is that what you're saying?'

'Yes, I am saying we didn't interview any of them.'

'May I ask why?'

'As I've repeatedly told you, we had no reason to think a crime was involved and it's not our job to go looking for lost property unless it is something likely to cause danger to the public. We record the loss in case the property is eventually found and handed in. That's all. We did everything that was necessary. This was a very old woman, Montague, the general feeling was that she'd mislaid it. I did hear that the carers and her daughter had searched the house and all her clothing, bags and so forth, even the dustbin, but it was never found.'

'And did similar incidents involve more elderly people?'

'Yes, there were others. One old lady lost a diamond brooch and died before its lost was noticed – she was found dead on a Thursday as it happens – and another owned a valuable miniature painting which hung over the bedhead, and that vanished.'

'Who reported the loss?'

'A neighbour. Its absence was noted after the old lady had died but I can't recall the day or date without checking our files and a third died a few days before the loss of a valuable vase was noticed.'

'And none was recorded as theft?' asked Pluke.

'No, Montague. Not one of them. I've already explained why such losses were all recorded as lost property but only because I felt they should be on record.'

'And none could be associated with the death of the owner?'

'Right. There was no evidence that any of the losses were linked to the deaths, apart from the coincidence of their timing. After all, the items could have been given away by their owners – relatives come into the houses to clear up after death of an elderly parent and that's when some notice things had gone missing. Some of them tell us but not everyone does so. I do know that some old folks want precious items buried with them and the carers would arrange that with the undertakers and family.'

'Were you involved in such transactions? Making sure the undertakers actually placed the goods in the coffins or graves?'

'No, that is no part of our responsibility, Montague.'

'So all this is hearsay, Inspector Horsley? We have no facts to help us.'

'That's the way things are, Montague, but we don't keep records if the items have been given away by the owners.'

'I have that list of deaths from the Registrar,' piped up Wayne Wain. 'If we can examine just a few entries about items that have been recorded lost or stolen, it might help if we can link them to the names of deceased persons. It might reveal a trend but it won't be a comprehensive record.'

'It's worth a try,' agreed Montague Pluke. 'We'll also need to check all your lost property registers, Inspector Horsley. I'll be in touch about my findings in due course and thank you, PC Carey for your help. I order you both not to divulge what has transpired during this meeting.'

'You *are* up to something, Montague!'

'I am about to walk through the town for a nice lunch at home with my loving wife,' smiled Montague Pluke. 'It will give me time to consider what you have told me and I look forward to examining your files and registers in due course.'

'You're not thinking Crickledale Carers might be bumping off old folk to get their hands on their valuables, are you?' persisted Horsley. 'Great stuffed turtles, Montague, we don't want to panic the townspeople into thinking we have a team of mass murderers at large!'

'Then say nothing about this. It is highly confidential, top secret in fact, and I have an open mind at the moment.' Pluke rose from his desk to retrieve his panama from its hat stand. 'It is very open indeed.'

His normal light lunch with Millicent was uncharacteristically quiet. She was not in her usual ebullient mood and apart from general pleasantries she did not ask how his work had progressed that morning. That was unusual – she always showed a keen interest in his ceaseless efforts to maintain a crime-free town. Instead, she chattered aimlessly about her daily routine – she'd had coffee with Mrs Findale and Miss Crimpton in the George Hotel when they had been discussing a proposed summer flower festival at the parish church, then she'd visited an exhibition of clip rugs in the Town Hall. She talked about a new dress and possibly a new overcoat and some shoes, and said she would pop into town this afternoon to find a nice chicken for their meal tonight. It was all domestic trivia, he felt; in fact, he was sure she was deliberately avoiding any discussion about his work. He made no attempt to provide an account of his morning's activities – he felt any reference to his cold-case review might prompt her antagonism and more accusations of professional snooping.

It was whilst walking back to his office through Crickledale after lunch that something troubled him. The victims who appeared to have had their belongings stolen shortly before death had never been in a position to make formal complaints to the police or anyone else.

It was the actions of others that had brought the problem to the notice of the police. As time progressed and more facts emerged, it did appear increasingly likely they had been killed to silence them and that fact alone suggested the missing articles must have been valuable. Was any valuable thing worth a death, even one supposedly inducted out of kindness and love?

That raised another issue. As his stroll carried him back to his office with people greeting him and with much hat-raising on his part, he realized that another area of investigation had developed. It was based on the fact that only a small proportion of the people under the care of CVC had died in circumstances that involved the police. Lots had died without any involvement of either the CVC or the police. So had others died prematurely so that thieves could remove their precious belongings?

Such victims may not be elderly people in imminent danger of death but they would include widows and widowers, infirm people and blind people, people who for a variety of reasons looked after themselves and maintained their own homes. Perhaps the CVC helped some from time to time because many may need modest help such as collecting the shopping, cleaning the roof gutters or having their chimneys swept. The wide range of available assistance meant that carers were invited into many homes in Crickledale that were *not* on the CVC's official list. He wondered how many had reported either lost or stolen belongings? And how easy was it for someone to pretend to be from the CVC when in fact they were in no way connected? Did CVC volunteers carry identity cards? Had any of those people noticed thieves or burglars around their homes or been attacked during a burglary? If so, surely they would have reported the matter? Unless they had died soon afterwards. . . .

Attempting to assemble and check those facts was a huge task and Montague realized that a complete answer was impossible. Then there was the worrying question of Millicent's involvement. She was one of the carers who worked on Thursday nights and so she must be questioned. He must insist that Wayne Wain interviewed her as soon as possible, but would he absolve her of all suspicion?

Chapter 15

PLUKE RETURNED TO his office in a reflective mood, hung his hat on its stand instead of throwing it, removed his top coat and sat at his desk. Almost idly and in deep thought, he shifted the ornaments and trays to their correct locations, at which point Mrs Plumpton entered.

'I'm up to date with my work, Mr Pluke, so is there anything else I can be doing to help your cold-case review?'

'I'm interested in that information we received from the CVC. Those lists of volunteers and clients, past and present. We need to examine them very closely.'

'They're all very detailed, Mr Pluke, and I've already loaded the file into my computer. I can print the lists in seconds, any time you require copies.'

'And what about cross-referencing that information with our police computers? Is that feasible?'

'Yes, no problem, Mr Pluke. Unlike the so-called good old days, the computers do all the work. So what exactly are you looking for?'

'The list of clients includes everyone currently receiving care from CVC even if it only involves something like half-an-hour a week. It also includes those who have benefited from their care in previous years. What we have been concentrating upon are those elderly people who live alone and who require regular care. There are many others receiving attention, Mrs Plumpton and at this point I'm going to ask you to become a detective all over again. What I need to know is which of those other people in care – not necessarily the elderly – have complained about things missing from their homes, stolen in other words. And we need a list of those who have reported other matters such as lost property, prowlers, intruders, anti-social behaviour – anything that might have required action by Crickledale police.'

'So you believe the carers are abusing their position of trust?'

'I can't rule it out, Mrs Plumpton. As you and I know, dishonest and disreputable people join genuine organisations to steal or assault vulnerable people including children. I don't think all our carers are doing such things and I don't think it is institutionalized, but I fear someone – or more than one – is abusing the trust placed in them. I'm rapidly approaching the moment when I shall have to be bold enough to officially state my fears. It would not surprise me if an evil person has joined the carers to gain access to potential victims. It's rather like paedophiles working as scoutmasters, choir masters or priests to gain access to young children. Such people don't suddenly become paedophiles, Mrs Plumpton, but they will join any organization that enables them to pursue their evil ways. Such deviousness among the criminal fraternity is not unknown but it taints others working in the same profession. What I need to know, therefore, are the names of all those who have become victims of this abuse of trust, if indeed it has happened. And I need to know the day, date and time of any offending, along with the day, dates and times of any deaths. If anyone did make a formal complaint against the CVC I need to know the outcome. Do you think it is possible to obtain all that information by searching our files in tandem with those of the town police and the CVC? And, of course, we need to ensure that our enquiries are undertaken with the greatest of discretion. We must do our best to keep the proverbial lid on this enquiry for as long as possible.'

'Our computers will do most of the work,' she reminded him with confidence. 'The Control Room maintains confidential records of incoming calls or verbal reports. Sergeant Cockfield-pronounced-Cofield gave me a lesson when the system was installed so that I, as your secretary and PA, could access the station computer. It's all in there, Mr Pluke, it can all be found.'

'Good! Then you've got yourself a job! You'll probably realize I'm still seeking some kind of plan or system that's used by the criminals. Their MO, *modus operandi*, method of operating. It's usually a good means of identifying criminals.'

'I understand. I'll start straight away and can obtain the data in confidence – although, of course, I do have to provide our password before I can start.'

'Do whatever is necessary.'

'Over what period shall I search, Mr Pluke?'

'The last two or three years will be a useful starting point. It should determine whether we need further back-checks over longer periods.'

'You realize the abstracts will include the cases we already know about?'

'Yes, but that will provide a good double check on our work. Now, I trust that the list of Crickledale Carers includes Mr Furnival, Mrs Allanby and the two full-time carers in addition to all the volunteers?'

'They are all there, Mr Pluke, including volunteers and staff who have recently left.'

'Excellent. The guilty person could be someone who has left but who still knows how to work the system. And have they all been checked for convictions and police records?'

'They have, that's done before they are selected for the posts. As you already know, those on the current list are all clear except one, a Mr Dorsey, a window-cleaner. It was a juvenile conviction for assault – actual bodily harm – which has since expired but it is still shown on his record due to the vulnerability of our clients. Especially the young ones.'

'So we have no known sneak-thieves or burglars among them?'

'Not according to our records, but we all know that some thieves never get caught or prosecuted.'

'Thanks, Mrs Plumpton. It's astonishing that some thieves

and villains pass through life without being caught for their crimes. They show up on routine checks as clean and whole-some, whereas they are true villains. I have to bear in mind that we might now have people of that kind in Crickledale! Even as CVC volunteers!'

'I've always considered Crickledale to be a law-abiding community.'

'It can appear so but we never know what's bubbling beneath the surface, do we? It's like looking at the smooth and bright water of your garden pond, knowing that all manner of unsavoury creatures live and lurk down there, killing and plundering . . . but we must accept what we see and know. Anyway, Mrs Plumpton, you are doing a good job with your ventures into crime detection. Perhaps it is a blessing that we are going through a very quiet spell just now.'

'I'm really enjoying my detective work, it's such a change from routine office procedures. And I do like to be kept busy.'

'Now where is Sergeant Wain? I have a special task for him.'

'I'm not sure where he is. . . .'

'I'll find him. Well, Mrs Plumpton, I think that's all for now. It will be interesting to see what your research reveals.'

'Let's hope I can reveal all kinds of interesting things, Mr Pluke,' and with one of her large smiles, Mrs Plumpton left him.

In the solitude of his office, therefore, he decided he must re-examine and analyse yet again all the information he had gathered. He was fully aware that it was so very easy, especially when discovering something new and exciting, to overlook the obvious whilst being side-tracked or swamped with masses of new information.

So what had he missed? What had escaped his notice, he wondered? It was time to reassess his progress, so he began to jot down the positive information he had gleaned so far. He hoped it would indicate the future direction of his enquiry. For example, was he concentrating too much on the elderly when others in care might be victims? Or were there victims among other elderly people not on the CVC's formal list? Or even young people . . . all the possible combinations must not be overlooked.

Despite his reservations, he had to accept that Crickledale Volunteer Carers were strongly in the frame due to their involvement in some of those puzzling deaths, but he was acutely aware that the actions of just one rogue could so easily tarnish the others. So had the carers themselves noticed anything untoward during their ministrations? Had they noticed one of their own members falling short of their very high standards – if so, how could they make a reasoned complaint? Indeed, he realized, that might explain Millicent's recent odd behaviour. Had she noticed something that was not right whilst being nervous of becoming a whistle-blower by informing on her colleagues? And had her role as the wife of a senior detective meant she had been targeted at work?

Getting closer to home, had Millicent witnessed anyone misbehaving in the vicinity of the old folks, or indeed with any of their other clients, particularly those who had lost their belongings? And if Millicent had discovered someone misbehaving or being dishonest, what could or would she do about it? Inform her policeman husband? Would any individual carer inform against their own kind? Did peer pressure or misplaced loyalty persuade the witness from revealing the truth, however unsavoury it happened to be? Or was he, Pluke, reading far too much into the entire situation?

Was Millicent right in her condemnation of his alleged snooping? Was he obsessed with looking for a murderer when in fact no murder had been committed? Or seeking a gang of thieves when nothing had been stolen? He had to bear in mind that there had never been any official complaints about the behaviour of any of the Crickledale Carers, so perhaps he had no right to investigate them as he was doing now. In spite of his own reservations, he nursed a deep desire to uncover the truth, whatever it was; that over-ruled any sense of precaution he was experiencing.

He began to write down all the volunteers' names in pencil in one of his many notepads. He found that writing *aides-memoires* in pencil rather than keying it into a computer meant he could recall it with greater clarity and so he compiled his list which was headed:

Crickledale Volunteer Carers
The Cedars, Millbank Road,
Crickledale (Phone Crickledale 776020)

Staff List
Chairman: Mr John C. Furnival, widower in his late 50s-early 60s. Ex-fireman
Secretary: Mrs Sarah Allanby, a widow in her 50s
Professional Carers: Mrs Rebecca Frankland, 35 (776870)
Mrs Juliet Jarvis, 42 (776670)
Volunteers and their contact telephone numbers, all with a Crickledale prefix code.
Mrs Eileen Baker, 28. Ex-chambermaid. 1 child (776114)
Mrs Anne Barnett, 55. Retired nurse. Adult children (776808)
Miss Fiona Blackwell, 18. Out-of-work. No children (776272)
Mr Keith Dorsey, 47. Window cleaner. Unmarried (776007)
Miss Fiona Grainger, 22. Cleaner, out-of-work. No children (776435)
Roland Parkinson, 45. Out-of-work stonemason/builder. Single (776670)
Mrs Millicent Pluke, 47, wife of Detective Inspector Pluke (776316)
Mrs Cynthia Roseberry, 76, retired local government officer (776304)
Mrs Marie Rose Stonehouse, 32. Housewife, 2 children (776535)
Miss Rachel West, 33. Former secretary, 1 child (776270)

He added six footnotes:

1. *Miss West had inherited the house belonging to Miss Croucher, her next-door neighbour.*

2. *Miss Grainger had been carer to Mr Lindsey before his death.*

3. *Mrs Stonehouse, Mrs Barnett and Mrs Roseberry all worked on Thursdays.*

4. *Thursday evenings were set aside for extra visits.*

5. *Mrs Barnett and Mrs Roseberry had both attended Mrs Langneb's funeral.*

6. *Mobile telephone numbers are not listed here because several carers do not possess them and in any case, such conversations are not always confidential.*

As he pondered this list, he wondered who, if anyone, had inherited Mrs Langneb's house – Miss West had inherited the house belonging to Miss Croucher but, in addition to being a carer, she was a friend and neighbour of Miss Croucher. There was no evidence to suggest that Miss West had connived in any way to inherit the cottage and it was widely known that Miss Croucher had no family. Being made aware of whom had inherited houses was not the sort of information that would generally be known by the police but he knew that, in the event of a murder investigation, he must elicit such information as a possible motive. That may yet prove necessary.

In addition, the undertaker for Mrs Langneb's funeral had been a local man, Jacob Carpenter. It was he who had commented that Miss Croucher's death was rather odd and Pluke had discussed that with him. So far, however, he had not been interviewed about his role in the funerals of the other deceased clients of the CVC. Could he or Sooty Black have engineered deaths to provide themselves with extra income? It was highly likely they knew that access to the homes of those old folk was fairly easy because many left their doors unlocked for friends, neighbours and carers. And if they knew that, then so would other local undertakers. And their staff. Then there was that other old character at Mrs Langneb's funeral, Awd Ezra. He'd sat alone with bodies before the funerals – although his visits followed the deaths, they did not precede them, but they would provide opportunities for theft.

As he stared at the list of people that had so far 'come into the frame' he realized he knew very little about any of them, apart from Millicent. And now he wondered how much he really knew about her! But if he was to drive this cold-case review to a successful conclusion, he must forge ahead. If there was an answer to his concerns, he would find it!

It was now time to consider whether or not he should openly regard this as a murder investigation or even a major crime enquiry. Perhaps it was a little too early for that radical step! He was still trying to determine whether or not any crimes, other than the theft of Mr Lindsey's gold watch, had been committed.

But first he must learn more about individual carers. In so doing, he must avoid generating any alarm or any suggestion that he suspected any of them of committing crimes, even murder. Furthermore, he would have to start at the top. He then realized he knew virtually nothing about John Furnival, the director of Crickledale Volunteer Carers, except that he was a former senior fire officer.

His first task, therefore, was to learn more about that man and to determine the qualifications he had displayed in securing his post. He must do that without alarming any of the townspeople or the local council under whose auspices the carers functioned. He must not alert Furnival to the reason for his sudden personal interest.

Likewise, his knowledge of Mrs Allanby, the CVC secretary, was extremely limited. Certainly he had passed her in the street on occasions when he had invariably raised his panama and greeted her warmly – as he did with all attractive women.

It was perhaps fortuitous that the list of carers included many people known to him, albeit rather slightly in most cases. He began to realize that, deeply and truly, he did not know much about the majority of individual townspeople. He further realized there was a difference between knowing something or someone, and being totally sure that such knowledge was based on truth. As a police officer he was aware that many people operated their daily lives under some kind of personal façade – many wanted to portray themselves as successful and clever when in reality their skills and personality were contrived.

So where had Mr Furnival served as a member of the Fire Service? What rank had he held? And why had he left? Indeed, where did he live now – did he live in Crickledale or did he commute to work? And how could Pluke acquire all the necessary information without setting off alarm bells in town? But the truth must be found. He would proceed with great caution.

His mind made up, he used the secure telephone in his office to ring an old friend whose hobby was researching the medieval trods of the North York Moors. His expertise had led Pluke to many locations of hidden or forgotten horse troughs and, in return, Pluke had identified some of the ancient trods of interest to his friend.

That friend was now the manager of Rosklethorpe Fire Station in the north-east of the county and he carried the rank of Assistant Divisional Officer, ADO for short. Not surprisingly he had to endure jokes about making much ado about nothing but his real name was James Russell. Because Pluke was using a secure line, his call went direct to Russell whose handset identified the person who was calling.

'Hello there, Montague,' came the brisk response. 'Nice to hear from you. Does this mean you've found some more trods for me?'

'Not at this point, James. My explorations of the moors have been rather few recently. I really must get myself out to find more troughs.'

'I discovered a new trod only last week, Montague. It stretches for five miles from the coast towards Rosklethorpe, but there is less than three miles of stone flags left. I think the rest have been stolen for building operations or covered up during road construction. But it's a new find – it was discovered under the heather after some controlled moor burning.'

'Then I trust you will make a note of its whereabouts!'

'You know I will, Montague. It's one more for the book that I promise myself I will write one day. Fully illustrated of course, like your book on troughs. So how can I help you?'

'It's a highly confidential enquiry, James.'

'I guessed as much, with you coming through on the secure phone.'

'It's this – do you know of a former fire officer – retired or otherwise – by the name of John C. Furnival. I am not sure what the C stands for. He's around fifty give or take a few years. And he says he held a senior rank in the Fire Service. A CRO check was carried out upon his appointment and nothing was known against him.'

'His name doesn't ring any immediate fire bells, Montague! Did he serve in this county?'

'I don't know but he doesn't sound like a Yorkshireman. He has one of those featureless accents. I think he would leave the service at least five years ago, maybe earlier. I don't know whether he retired on pension or left for other reasons. I've got to be very secretive about this enquiry so I can't use established sources.'

'I understand. Can you give me an hour or so? I'll check in our official almanac and also our list of current pensioners. The almanac lists every fire station in England and Wales, with the names of all their senior personnel currently serving and what posts they occupy. We keep previous years' copies on our shelves. If he is, or has been, one of us, he will be there, Montague. And now, of course, those details are kept on our computers. It won't take long. I'll call you back later today.'

'Thanks, I appreciate it.'

When he rang off, Pluke checked the next name on his list: Mrs Sarah Allanby. A widow in her 50s, she was the secretary of Crickledale Volunteer Carers but rarely if ever went out to care for the clients. A local woman, she was purely an administrator and so Pluke wondered if Mrs Plumpton knew anything about her. He buzzed her on his intercom.

'Ah, Mrs Plumpton, you are a fountain of all local knowledge so do you know anything about Mrs Allanby who works for CVC?'

'I do know her, Mr Pluke, but only as an acquaintance rather than a friend. She is a local woman who lives in a nice terrace house along Newton Lane, her husband worked in York, something to do with one of those insurance companies in those big offices that used to be near the railway station, I believe. He travelled in every day by bus and she has always done clerical work in offices at Crickledale or nearby, sometimes on a part-time basis. She said she always wanted to share her free time with her husband. Unfortunately he died very young, cancer I think, but she has a good pension from his employment and is comfortably off. She has no children, Mr Pluke, which saddens her. She does a lot of charity work, you'll often see her collecting funds for everything from Save The Children to Yorkshire Cancer Relief. A very nice lady indeed.'

'Well, I couldn't have asked for a more comprehensive account! Thank you. And clearly, that brings me to the two professionals and all the other volunteers. All are Crickledale residents, so how about them? You've got the list.'

'Yes, it's on my screen, Mr Pluke. I've met the two professionals quite often, socially as well as in their former places of work. Mrs Frankland used to work in the Crickledale Building Society as a receptionist, and she lost her job when it was taken over by one of the big names. Halifax, I think. I know nothing against her, Mr Pluke.'

'And Mrs Jarvis?'

'She's in her early forties, I would say, and she used to work in the Brewer Brothers department store here in Crickledale, moving from counter to counter.'

'That could be where I have seen her!' remarked Pluke.

Mrs Plumpton continued, 'Quite possibly. I've always bought my clothes there, you know, she always gave me good advice on how to make myself more attractive . . . and then I once saw her on the perfume counter, then in the furniture department . . . she moved around quite a lot. Her husband left her for another woman, fortunately there were no children. Then she left Brewer Brothers very suddenly.'

'Why was that? Do you know?'

'There was talk, Mr Pluke. It began when her husband left her. Money going missing . . . cash from tills . . . nothing was ever proved and there was no court case or police involvement. She was asked to resign. Even though nothing was proved against her, word got around town as it does on these occasions. She couldn't get work and I think she's on benefits now. She rents a house on that big council estate at the West End and occupies herself with CVC. I believe she is very good in her dealings with the elderly. There is just a hint that she was entirely innocent – another employee was later caught with her hand in the till and sacked.'

'So how did Mrs Jarvis cope with that?'

'She had to live with that reputation. As they say, mud always sticks.'

'This could be relevant, Mrs Plumpton. So what about the other volunteer carers? They're all part-timers, I believe, working when they are required . . . in this case, I think you had better come into my office and we will discuss these face-to-face. I'll call Detective Sergeant Wain to join us.'

He pressed Wayne's intercom button; he was in his office from wherever he had been and Pluke asked him to join them immediately.

'Well, Mr Pluke, I can tell you something about that Mr Parkinson who is on the list.'

'Then let's get started the moment Wayne arrives.'

'Ooh, you are impetuous, Mr Pluke. . . .'

Then Pluke's secure phone rang. It was a call from James Russell.

'Hi Montague,' came his breezy voice. 'You certainly set me a right puzzle here. I've been through all our records past and present, including the national list of Fire Service pensioners, and your Mr Furnival is not shown anywhere. All I can say is that he has never been a member of the Fire Service in England and Wales. We do have links with Scotland and I did a check there – same result, Montague. He's not known to any of the Fire Service Headquarters in Britain. You could always try overseas but I have no idea where to suggest you start. Is it a false name? Can you check his passport? Immigration Office?'

'I'll have words with our Special Branch,' said Pluke. 'They might have the means of tracing such a person. But thanks very much indeed for your help.'

'It's a pleasure, Montague. Now you owe me the discovery of another trod.'

'I will do my best.' And Pluke rang off.

Wayne Wain then entered the office and noticed Pluke's rather glum expression.

'Ah, Wayne. Glad you're here. Please join us,' and so the sergeant settled on a chair near Pluke's desk. 'I have a very difficult task for you – this afternoon.'

'Something wrong, sir?'

'There are two things, Wayne. I have just been told that the man in charge of Crickledale Carers might have a secret past; that means he must be closely investigated. And the second thing is that I fear it is time for you to do something I will not be allowed to do. It is time to interview Mrs Pluke.'

'To establish her innocence?' asked Wayne.

'To establish the truth, Wayne.'

Chapter 16

'Let's start with Mr Furnival, Wayne,' began Pluke. 'The short question is that he claims to be a former senior fire officer but there is no record of his recent service in this country. Any thoughts on that?'

'If he was an auxiliary – a part-timer – he would never become a senior officer, would he? And his part-time membership wouldn't be recorded, would it?'

'It should be somewhere in the system, Wayne, probably buried very deep in some dusty old files, but not available to the public. There's an official almanac, produced annually, and back copies have been checked by my contact. It lists officers of high rank – but Mr Furnival's name is not there. It should be. In spite of that, he gave the impression he is a retired former full-time fire officer of high rank.'

'Could he have slipped through the net, sir? Was his name omitted by accident? These things can happen. Or is he one of those conmen who apply for top jobs, and often get them?'

'We've also checked the fire officers' pensioners' pay lists, Wayne, he's not there either. And that contains every paid pensioner, irrespective of rank.'

'So if he's not in any of our British lists, is it possible he could have returned to Britain after service overseas? We've got to think like that, we live in a global world now, not an island community. Anyway, couldn't we question him discreetly? Be devious – you're very good at that. Chat to him about his success in moulding Crickledale Carers into such a successful and effective organization whilst persuading him to reveal more about himself? Or has he done time in prison? You know the sort of thing – a murderer released on licence under a new identity?'

'We would have been informed if such a person was living within our area,' Pluke reminded Wayne. 'Furnival will only reveal what he wants us to know.'

'Then it means we must investigate him – initially without him being aware of what we're doing.'

'You've had experience in Special Branch, haven't you, Wayne?'

'Yes but not for very long. Two years in fact. I could arrange an interview with him as a follow-up to our chat about his carers.'

'I was thinking of any contacts you might have had in, say, the Immigration Office or the police forces of our ports and airports. I think that would be a good means of finding out his overseas past, and to check whether his identity is false.'

'I can try but I'd rather talk to him first, to establish a few known truths that we can use as key-points in our research. In talking to him, I would continue the theme about his staff not understanding when a call to the police was unnecessary. I'd refer to that Home Office initiative we talked about; I don't know how you came up with that idea, sir, but it was perfect for that occasion. And I could be wired up?'

'Wired up?'

'Yes, I could conceal a miniature voice recorder about my person so we can get everything he says on tape without me spoiling things by openly taking notes.'

'All right, if he is being devious then so can we. I agree to your plan, Wayne, at a time to suit you. And don't forget – there's nothing proven against him and so your interview might eliminate him, and his organization, from our enquiries. We'd then have to reappraise our cold-case review. Furthermore, if we do establish that he's a confidence trickster or someone operating under a false identity, it doesn't mean he's a killer. Do bear all that in mind.'

'I will and there's no time like the present. I'll start now. So was there anything else?'

'I wondered whether you have been able to cast your eyes down the list of volunteers. As the main detective on the ground, one who is out-and-about in Crickledale, you might have more local knowledge of those people than I.'

'I do know some of them, and among them are those whom I would not trust one inch let alone with my cherished belongings. Eileen Baker, for example, was a chambermaid at Crickledale Manor Hotel and I happen to know she was asked to leave because, on more than one occasion, guests reported things missing from their rooms when she was on duty. I was called in on one occasion but because there was no proof against her, she was asked to resign – which she did. She was never prosecuted. I couldn't prove the case against her. And, of course, Fiona Grainger was suspected of stealing Mr Lindsey's gold watch but no one was interviewed about that. To be honest, I doubt if any of the carers have snowy white characters. We've all got secrets, sir.'

'Except Mrs Pluke,' interjected Mrs Plumpton.

'Of course,' agreed Wayne. 'I hadn't forgotten about interviewing her, but the opportunity hasn't arisen. It's not going to be easy. . . .'

'If anyone can do it, it's you, Wayne!' smiled Pluke. 'As soon as possible.'

'I'll cope, but right now, I'm more interested in Furnival. If the barrel full of apples is rotten right to the top, it would seem a good idea to have someone within the organization who is pure and unsullied, like Mrs Pluke. Her presence as a volunteer carer must provide an air of confidence to the people of Crickledale. You'd think the behaviour of dodgy ones would have been noticed, wouldn't you? Mrs Pluke might have done so and now be bearing a mighty burden of knowledge she daren't reveal.'

'She could always discuss things with me, Wayne.'

'No she can't, you're the town's senior detective. If there

was a criminal operating within the carers, she would realize you would be duty bound to expose him or her, at the cost of massive publicity. And we can't overlook the possibility that she was recruited to give the whole organization an air of respectability.'

'You're not suggesting the entire CVC is corrupt, are you?' asked Pluke.

'Such things do happen. All you need is one charming rogue at the top and the entire system will begin to creak. A rogue boss will be operating so that he gains all the benefits from his work, often in cash or bonuses, even if that is not immediately obvious to his underlings. So it wouldn't surprise me if our very efficient and charming Mr Furnival has a dark and secret past.'

'You'll get to the truth of this?'

'I'll do my best and I can start immediately. He should be in his office because his staff will be out and about the town, doing their stuff. And, remember, we did get permission to speak to his volunteers but haven't done so yet. When we start on them, might they be interrogations rather than cosy chats?'

'In view of these new circumstances, Wayne, we should first find out more about Mr Furnival. Are we suggesting he might be running a kind of illegal operation that Dickens' Fagin would have been proud of? Using others to do his dirty work? That's what we need to find out fairly urgently, Wayne. You can talk to Mrs Pluke afterwards, you might find her shopping in town. And don't forget Dr Simpson!'

'Leave it with me. This is most intriguing. It's developing into something that could be very serious. We need to talk to all the volunteers to find out exactly what they know and perhaps a chat with some lucid patients. We've a lot of secretive work ahead. Suddenly, Crickledale CID has become very busy.'

'Don't be too heavy-handed at this stage, Wayne, we don't want to alarm the whole town, but depending upon what you learn, we could talk to the other carers. Meanwhile, Mrs Plumpton and I shall undertake essential research of our own records and CVC members. I'm beginning to feel we have barely scratched the surface.'

'I like the idea of doing more research, Mr Pluke, it sounds exciting!' beamed Mrs Plumpton. 'But if you're thinking of talking to a CVC patient or client, you could do worse than Joe Knowles of Hawkswell Street. He's listed as a client.'

'So what's the different between a client and a patient?'

'I think a client is someone who needs help with their daily routine but does not require medical care; a patient needs rather more personal attention, even to bathing and being helped to eat their food. But that's just my own rough guide!'

'Do you know anything about Mr Knowles?' Wayne asked her.

'He's got a locally famous collection of antiques, all kept in his house. I know that through being a local lass. He's always pleased to show them off and luckily, he knows the local rogues and conmen so he can keep them at bay. Now, sadly, he is a very old man and sometimes not very lucid.'

'Well I've heard of his collection but never seen it,' admitted Pluke. 'But thank you, he sounds like an important contact so I'll make sure we chat to him. Is that another job for you, Wayne?'

'I'll see to him, I like being busy and I'm getting my claws into this investigation. Leave it to me. I'll talk to Mrs Pluke, Dr Simpson and Mr Knowles.'

And so Wayne left, but first returned to his own office to collect a miniature voice recorder before heading for the offices of Crickledale Volunteer Carers. He was determined to hear Mr Furnival's life story from the man's own lips.

'Have you enough to keep you busy?' Pluke asked Mrs Plumpton, only now realizing the provocative words he had uttered.

'I would love to keep myself busy with you, Mr Pluke,' and she rippled her massive chest as she rose from the chair. It reminded him of an oncoming tsunami about to break its advance wave on shore. 'But I have yet more files to go through, checking for matches between the Control Room's records and our CID files that name the clients of CVC.'

'Good, well whilst you and Detective Sergeant Wain are usefully occupied, I shall pay a visit to the Town Hall. I want to speak to the Town Clerk.'

'It's always a good idea to check whether he is in his office and able to see you, Mr Pluke. Mr Ridgeway is a very busy man.'

'Very good thinking, Mrs Plumpton. I was getting carried away with the enthusiasm of working on my cold-case review. So can you call him and ask if it is convenient this afternoon? Tell him it is a confidential chat that I wish to have with him.'

But at that moment, Pluke's phone rang.

'Detective Inspector Pluke speaking.'

'Ah, glad I caught you, Mr Pluke. It's Wilkinson from the *Gazette.*'

'Yes, Mr Wilkinson, what can I do for you?'

'I've heard rumours you are investigating a suspicious death in town, Mr Pluke. Can you confirm that?'

'I have been conducting enquiries on behalf of the Home Office, Mr Wilkinson. They wish to reduce the time we spend in dealing with sudden deaths that occur from natural causes. I fear your contact is mistaken.'

'But that is not what I heard. . . .'

'Then you heard wrong, Mr Wilkinson. I have nothing further to say because there is nothing further to say, except for this quote: "We are facing Government cuts like every other public service and we need to make sure our time is well spent. We are discussing the actions that follow a report of a sudden death to determine whether we can save both time and money by altering our procedures." That is all. Good-bye.'

And as Pluke put down his telephone, Mrs Plumpton picked it up immediately to avoid the return call and rang the Town Hall. She spoke to Mr Ridgeway's secretary who checked with him and said it would be fine. He could accommodate Detective Inspector Pluke at 3pm.

'I fear the press may have discovered our activities, Mrs Plumpton, so do not make any comments if they call while I am out. You heard what I said to that man, and so that will have to do for the time being.'

'I understand,' she smiled as Pluke left.

As Pluke walked into the town centre, now fairly quiet because it was Wednesday afternoon and half-day closing, with several shops continuing that old fashioned custom although such shops did open all day Saturday. He had made time to stroll through the graveyard, checking whether any crows were perching on tombstones and noting that Mrs Langneb's grave now had vases of flowers upon it.

That small but very open token of respect for a woman who had in life been so alone, pleased him immensely. One reason for his walk away from the confines of his office was that he wanted to make use of yet another rather devious topic of conversation in his efforts to learn more about John Furnival. He didn't think his well-tried tale about the need for cuts in the way the police conducted themselves was feasible in this case but he did have a neat idea.

When he arrived at the Town Hall, the receptionist recognized him and asked him to wait in the ante-room whilst she checked that Mr Ridgeway was free. He was.

'Up the stairs, Mr Pluke, first left and his office is on your left. You can't miss it, his name is on the door.'

He knocked and a man's voice called, 'Come in, Montague.'

With his hat in hand, Montague Pluke entered this rather plain office and accepted the invitation to be seated. He knew Alwyn Ridgeway quite well; from time to time they both attended the same meetings and conferences and Pluke liked the Town Clerk. In his middle fifties, he was a plain-spoken Yorkshireman with a sharp brain, a head of silver-grey hair, blue eyes and a lively sense of humour.

'So, Montague, what brings you here at short notice?'

'A rather peculiar mission,' smiled Pluke. 'I don't quite know how to tackle a matter that has dropped into my lap from Police Headquarters, via the Home Office I might add. Then I thought of you and your expertise on matters relating to this little town of ours.'

'You flatter me, Montague, but fire away. If I can help, I will.'

'What I am going to mention now is highly confidential, Alwyn, not to be repeated outside these four walls.' He referred to Alwyn by his Christian name because he and Millicent had once been invited to the Ridgeways' home for dinner.

Pluke could almost classify him as a friend but even friends could not be told the entire truth in very delicate police investigations.

He went on. 'I'm referring to the drastic cuts that are facing ourselves, your council and all the public services. We all know they will cause a lot of hurt and distress, even though they are very necessary, but the Home Office Police Department has floated an idea that it believes will help us all.

'One area of concern for us, as police officers, is that we are frequently called to deal with matters that are not within our range of duties – domestic disputes, for example; sudden deaths where there is no suspicion of crime and where a doctor is prepared to certify the cause of death; rescuing cats from trees or rooftops; dealing with lost and found property; people wanting us to attend events on private property such as garden parties or weddings, looking after car parking or security for example . . . there are many unofficial tasks we are expected to undertake and the Home Office is trying to encourage us not to involve ourselves in such work.'

'I can sympathize with you, Montague. We're in a similar situation with some people expecting the town council to sort out their own private problems. So how can I help? It seems to me that it is a question of educating the people as to where your boundaries lie. The role of the police has changed dramatically over the last half century or so.'

'I couldn't have put it better myself, Alwyn. Under normal circumstances we always do our best to answer any call-out and deal with any problem, whether official police duty or not. But with cuts in manpower and finance, we may have to refuse to deal with some things, however distressful our response might be to the public.'

'You're echoing my own thoughts, Montague.'

'One of the Home Office boffins has come up with an idea that we should recruit a person, known to the community, who can span the gap between police and public. I think the idea is that people wanting help and advice that may not necessarily be within the realm of police duty could contact this person – or someone in his office – whereupon he or she would decide whether or not to call the police, ring the hospital, call a doctor or whatever needs to be done. He or she would be a type of go-between, but it would have to be a voluntary post, Alwyn – to save time and money.'

'Well, I hope you're not considering me for that job, Montague! I've enough on my plate right now.'

'No, you've no need to worry about that! As I said, this is very much a theory at the moment without any of the necessary groundwork being undertaken. Certainly there has not been a feasibility study but we are being asked for our initial opinions, along with the name of possible candidates.'

'So who have you in mind? Am I allowed to ask?'

'Yes, it's the reason I'm here. I was thinking of John Furnival, the chairman of Crickledale Volunteer Carers. He seems to have got that organization up and running in a most remarkable way. He gives the appearance of a real go-getter, he keeps in touch with his clients and his staff, he's well-known around the town and on top of all that, he seems to be very decent sort of fellow, approachable and helpful.'

'He is all those things, Montague, and I'm pleased to hear your comments because I appointed him.'

'So where did he come from?'

'He's a former senior fire officer, Montague. He served mainly in Suffolk and Lincolnshire with a short spell in Leeds City, winning promotion through the ranks and he left to take his pension about five years ago. That was when we appointed him. He told us he had done lots of charitable work whilst in the fire service – fire officers are known for their hard work for charities and the needy – and he felt that being chairman of CVC would provide him with all the stimulus he needed to keep busy in retirement, whilst his CVC salary – which is not very large – would help to eke out his pension.'

'Did he provide references?' asked Pluke.

'Oh yes, we don't make such important appointments without references. I'll get his file, Montague, then I can show you them along with his application form. This is confidential of course, but you and I are on the same side, aren't we? I must say he was by far the best out of the five candidates, and we are very happy with his work. Whether he has the time to take on additional commitments of the sort you envisage is something I cannot answer – he could, I suppose, do it through a member of my staff – but certainly he is in regular contact with the sort of people who might require help or advice from the police, or indeed any other of the public services. But I wouldn't want you to poach him from us, Montague!'

'I don't see any likelihood of that happening, Alwyn.'

He pressed his intercom and spoke to his secretary/PA. 'Jane, can you bring me Mr Furnival's file please. He's with Crickledale CVC. Thank you.'

It arrived a few moments later and as his secretary left the room, Alwyn Ridgeway opened it on his desk.

'Here we are, Montague. His application form complete with references. Take a look. You can see what a real catch he was for us. I know you'll be discreet.'

Alwyn turned the file around so that Pluke could examine the rather meagre contents but it did contain the all-important information about the life of John Clement Furnival. Pluke found his date and place of birth – fifty two years ago in Bermondsey, London; he was not married and never had been, and for a time had served in the Merchant Navy, working on cruise ships. Anxious to secure an occupation on shore, he had joined the Fire Service in Suffolk and after six years had transferred to Lincolnshire on promotion. He had risen through the ranks to become a Senior Divisional Officer in Leeds City Fire Service, compulsorily retiring on pension upon reaching the age of 50.

Attached to his application form were certificates of service and references from the Fire Services in which he had served along with more references from influential organizations with which he had been involved. All praised him for his strength of character, organizational abilities and his ability to plan ahead. One reference went so far as to say that Mr John Furnival would make a success of any enterprise for which he was responsible. The file also contained Furnival's previous home address and his current one which was a village outside Crickledale. Pluke felt he was now getting somewhere with his cold-case review.

'I can't let you have photocopies, Montague, but you can see we managed to catch a good'un, as they say.'

'It all looks very impressive,' conceded Pluke, without informing Alwyn of the several errors he had already noticed, especially in the details of Furnival's personal career. He decided not to alert Alwyn at this early stage. 'So is it your policy to check references; we always do so in the police. Always.'

'Not with a senior post such as this one, Montague. It would be most insulting if we did not believe the word of a man who has achieved so much. Mr Furnival's career is self-explanatory as you can see for yourself. I think he could be a very sound candidate for your new post. . . .'

'That's if it ever happens!' cautioned Pluke. 'You know as well as I, that many of these ambitious Government plans never reach fruition. All we can do is go along with the flow and do as we are told when the time comes.'

In reading the file, Pluke could quickly absorb the essential details and whilst he did not claim to possess a photographic memory, he did have a strong capacity for recalling the salient details. He looked through the file once again, reading it carefully before returning it to Alwyn and his filing cabinet.

'So what happens next?' asked Alwyn in all innocence.

'I will report my findings to our Force Headquarters, Alwyn, who will then notify the Police Department of the Home Office that Mr Furnival does appear to be a very positive candidate for the type of voluntary work they envisage. I would also add that I think the idea has some merit – an intermediary between police and public does seem to be a sound idea. Once I have done that, I have no idea what will happen – but I will keep you informed.'

Leaving the Town Hall, he made his way back to the police station whilst telling himself that his deceptions were necessary in this kind of undercover police work. He had much to tell Detective Sergeant Wain, particularly that Furnival appeared to be a fraudster but that could wait until the sergeant had completed his own rather delicate enquiries. Montague decided not to return to his home just yet – he wanted Millicent's ordeal to be over before he went off duty.

Chapter 17

Whilst Pluke was conducting his rather devious enquiries, Detective Sergeant Wayne Wain was on his way to the head office of Crickledale Volunteer Carers for an equally devious chat with John Furnival. He had not made an appointment because he wanted to surprise his target; Furnival would not be forewarned and would not produce rehearsed responses.

As he walked across the town centre, however, Wayne noticed Mrs Pluke making her way through the marketplace. She noticed him at the same instant. This sort of thing happened frequently in Crickledale – it could almost be guaranteed that if you wanted to meet someone, you'd eventually encounter them in the marketplace. It was ideal for chance meetings or even pretend chance meetings!

'Ah, Detective Sergeant Wain,' Millicent called as she approached, using his formal name as Montague would have done. 'Nice to see you. How are you?'

Wayne thought fast. 'I'm fine, thanks, Mrs Pluke. Look, I was just heading for a nice cup of tea before my next meeting. Would you care to join me? My treat!'

'I was heading for Tea Break café too so isn't that a pleasant coincidence! It would be nice to catch up with your news.'

Wayne selected a window table where they could talk in confidence, ordered a pot of tea with two cupcakes and prepared to be sociable with his boss's wife. After the introductory small talk, he commented, 'Work always gets in the way of socializing, Mrs Pluke. We've been busy until just now, but for the past few days things have been dreadfully quiet. But that's the way of police duty – we can never plan our workload but happily our work is rarely boring.'

'So Montague tells me. And he tells me he is making good use of the quiet time for a cold-case review. He always works so hard; I do hope he produces results.'

'If I know your husband, Mrs Pluke, he will certainly produce results. It's due to him that we have such a positive record of crime detection in this town, so I'm sure his cold-case review will prove highly satisfactory.'

'I hope he leaves the carers alone, Sergeant. He seems to have got some kind of bee in his bonnet about the way CVC goes about its business. I know there have been lots of deaths recently in Crickledale, many being under our care, but I'm sure he can't hold us responsible, especially as none of the deaths was suspicious.'

Wayne decided to try and balance things by saying, 'I'm sure he doesn't think crimes were committed, Mrs Pluke. We're aware of those deaths and I'm sure we've not the slightest reason to believe the CVC is failing in its duties. After all, the deaths were from natural causes, old age in most cases, so I am told. So is something troubling you?'

'I'll be honest with you, Wayne,' she used his Christian name now. 'I must admit I'm rather concerned. I've been aware of some odd and rather worrying things happening within the CVC. As you are aware of those deaths I feel I can speak to you in confidence. . . .'

'Of course you can. Tell me what's bothering you and perhaps I can help.'

'It may be nothing but I fear some of our carers are less than professional. Speaking personally, I've not seen such things happen but, as you might expect, there is always talk among the volunteers whenever they get together.'

'Do you want to tell me about it?'

'I need to tell someone, Wayne, someone quite independent

of the CVC. I don't think Montague is the right person. He would decide to launch an enquiry or begin an investigation which would upset everyone and I'm sure we don't need that! He's already hinted he's checking something within the CVC.'

'Has he really?'

'He won't tell me what it is but I can see he's concentrating on something important, although I've told him I have no reason to think crimes are being committed by the carers.'

'So if they're not committing crimes, what exactly is troubling you?'

'As I said, I fear there is some sloppy and careless attention to our patients and clients, Wayne. I know that's of no concern to the police, it's an internal matter but some of those who were recently found dead were lying on cold floors – someone must have helped them and then abandoned them. Heaven knows why! Also, Wayne, I know some have lost things from their homes.'

'Lost things? What sort of things?'

'Personal belongings, heirlooms, small objects that are quite valuable.'

'Has anyone done anything about them?'

'When I mentioned it to senior management, I think they felt I was nit-picking and they responded by saying old people did silly things and lost their belongings or even gave things away to friends and neighbours. They said such things were no concern of the CVC.'

'I can understand why that would worry you.'

'I've been very worried recently. In fact I am thinking of resigning, no one seems to care, and that's a bad thing to say about professional carers!'

'So to sum it up, you think there is something going on behind the scenes that is not very pleasant? Something that requires attention?'

'That's a good way of putting it, Wayne. Yes, that sums it up neatly.'

'So have you done anything to try and rectify matters?'

'I have mentioned my concerns to Mrs Jarvis and I've also

been visiting some patients and clients in my own time, occasionally in the evenings, to see if they are all right. I know I must be careful in what I do, I must not appear to be interfering. In any case, I suspect they think I'm a policeman's wife checking up on them, being nosey! And I told Montague not to go snooping on the carers; what they do by way of carelessness or slip-shod work should not concern him. I've told him that those are internal matters, Wayne, of no concern to the police.'

'Is that why you don't want him to get involved?'

'It is. It would stir up all sorts of trouble and problems and undo much of the good work the carers do. It would give them a bad reputation and lead to a crisis of confidence. I don't want that, Wayne, so I don't want a police investigation. That would be totally counterproductive. We're not criminals even if we are inefficient.'

'I understand your concern, Mrs Pluke, but I believe I should tell you this. We've been in discussion with Mr Furnival about when to call a police officer to a natural death but that doesn't mean we're suspicious or critical of the carers' work. We're trying to make our duties, and theirs, more productive with less time being wasted on non-essentials.'

'I knew something was going on but Montague doesn't reveal much. The trouble is you never know with police enquiries, Wayne! What often appears to be the very innocent beginning of something can flare up to reveal hidden secrets. I do know quite a lot about how the police operate, as you can imagine.'

Wayne decided he should continue his gentle deceit by using the cover story. He did not want Millicent to stop talking – it seemed he had gained her trust because she would never talk to Montague in this way. He smiled and said, 'All I can say is that our interest in the CVC is part of a Home Office initiative to reduce costs. It will affect other organizations such as the Fire Service and National Health Service. In our case, the police are called out to deal with deaths which, if a doctor examined them first, would be determined from the outset as occurring from natural causes. That means the police would not be involved. We are trying to persuade Mr Furnival to train his carers *not* to call the police *first* as a matter of routine – we want them to call a doctor first. That small act alone would save a lot of police time.'

'Oh, I see. Then perhaps I've misunderstood things and mis-interpreted Montague's involvement? Anyway, Wayne, you can rest assured that the carers are doing lots of good work even if they do sometimes fall from the ideal. In fact, I'm on my way to a client now. It keeps me occupied on Wednesday afternoons when the shops are shut!'

'I'm pleased we've had this chat, Mrs Pluke, it's helped enor-mously. Now I'm heading for a talk with Mr Furnival about our need to reduce costs and become more efficient whilst not dam-aging the service we, or they, give to the public.'

'You've not made an appointment, have you?' she asked.

'No, as a matter of fact, I haven't.'

'I thought not. He won't be in his office today and he isn't out visiting clients. He likes to visit a selection of our clients to see how they are faring but Wednesday afternoon after 1pm and that same evening, constitute his half-day off. He works at weekends, you see. Mind you, he does sometimes pop in to see a carer who is working late on Wednesdays in addition to our Thursday Special. He is very thorough and dedicated to his job.'

'Thursday Special? What's that?'

'Oh, well, we ensure there is one night in the week when we can help clients with special or extra needs or requests, things we rarely have time to consider during our normal visiting hours. It might be nothing more than a person-to-person chat, or painting a door and decorating a ceiling, fixing a leaking tap, getting a chimney swept, helping to clean the brasses – anything that can't be fitted into a routine visit.'

'That seems a good idea. So if Mr Furnival keeps his staff on their toes, as it were, maybe he's aware of the problems you've just highlighted? Have you discussed them with him? It's often a good idea to go right to the top. . . .'

'No, I felt I should not try to subvert the system, Wayne. . . .'

'There are times when that is a good idea. So where will Mr Furnival be now? Will I be able to talk to him at his home address?'

'That's something I can't answer, Wayne. For one thing, I don't know where he lives and for another, I don't know what he does when he's not on duty. If he's anything like police officers he'll go somewhere where he can't be found unless there's a dire emergency.'

'We all do that! My granddad used to tell of the days when policemen had to leave a holiday address at their police station whenever they went away or even on their weekly days off, just in case they were needed in an emergency. He added that many claimed they were touring whilst on holiday or enjoying their days-off and so they were out of contact!'

'Fortunately that's no longer the case, but sadly I've no idea where you'll find Mr Furnival. If it's very important you could ask his secretary.'

'I'm on my way there next so I'll do that,' he said. 'Thanks for telling me this, Mrs Pluke, it's been most useful. I'll respect your wish for confidentiality and hope your ministrations are appreciated this afternoon.'

'Thank you for listening to me, I feel better already,' she said, smiling sweetly as he prepared to leave her. 'I'm visiting Mrs Cardwell in Shipton Avenue next.'

'Fully dependent, is she?'

'Not really, no. She can do things and likes to show her skills. She may even have a cup of tea ready but has difficulty dusting, polishing and cleaning, especially her silver on high shelves. I must admit I check everything each time I call, just to see that nothing is missing.'

Wayne thought he might have time to visit the surgery in the hope of catching Dr David Simpson for a quick chat. He was lucky – the doctor did not have a patient in at that moment and invited him into his consulting room. He knew Wayne by sight and name.

'A quick chat, please,' asked Wayne the young doctor. 'Not a consultation, it's a police matter.'

'That sounds serious! What have I done?'

'Nothing, I hope, doctor!' And Wayne explained the cold-case review, with due emphasis on the doctor's role in examining most of the deceased.

'Well, Wayne, I must admit I did think some of the deaths were rather peculiar – lying on the floor, having windows open and so on, but my job was not to be a detective. It was simply to examine the deceased firstly to confirm that he or she was dead, and secondly to certify the cause of the death, if I was sure enough. In most cases, I could do so; those where I could not certify the cause of death were referred to a pathologist for a post mortem.'

'Weren't you suspicious of some of the recurring facts? Several deceased lying on a cold floor, doors and windows standing open?'

'I thought it odd, but old folks do get themselves into some strange situations. I once dealt with a man who died in his outside coalhouse and another who was found dead in a dog kennel . . . I must say, however, that in these cases when I felt things were not quite as one would expect, I did alert the policeman who had been called to the scene – but what happened thereafter was not my concern. If I could certify the cause of death, the matter was concluded very swiftly. If not, the post mortem confirmed the death was not suspicious and so there was no coroner's inquest.'

'So despite the curious scenes of death, you did not feel compelled to alert anyone in authority?'

'As I said just now, I did tell the police officer who had been called to the scene, but it was a different officer on each occasion. I had done my job, Wayne, nothing more, nothing less.'

'Thanks, that's a help,' said Wayne. 'Now I must go elsewhere. . . .'

'Sorry I couldn't help more,' said the doctor, emerging to call in his next patient.

When Wayne reached the offices of Crickledale Volunteer Carers, Wayne tapped on the door marked 'Secretary' and was invited to enter. Mrs Allanby was behind the counter, busy with her computer and a pile of files.

'Detective Sergeant Wain!' she smiled warmly. 'How can I help you?'

'I'm sorry to arrive unannounced but I was hoping to catch Mr Furnival.'

'Oh dear, he doesn't come in on Wednesday afternoons or evenings, it's his day off.'

'So where can I find him? It's rather important? Will he be at home? Or does he have a mobile phone?'

'He has one but never switches it on when he's off duty. This is his only time off; he works very hard and needs time for himself, Sergeant, just like anyone else. And I'm not at liberty to reveal his home address.'

'So how does he occupy himself off duty? Is he a golfer, does he go fishing?'

'Nothing like that. He's very keen on antiques and goes off to places like Leeds or Harrogate to look around second-hand shops, market stalls, car boot sales and the smarter antique dealers that sell items like jewellery, gold, silver, pocket watches, precious stones, artwork, trinkets, that sort of stuff. He does a spot of dealing too, buying good stuff and selling it to dealers. He's quite knowledgeable.'

'There's good money in such things, they're wise investments.'

'That's his view. He's not into larger items like furniture or grandfather clocks!'

'Any idea where he's gone today?'

'Sorry, no, except it's not in Crickledale. He always gets away from the town – his job makes him very well known so he needs to get away from those who stop him in the street to discuss personal problems. He keeps his private life very private.'

'So what happens if there is a really serious emergency that requires his immediate attention?'

'That has never happened to my knowledge, Sergeant, and I hope it never will. Sadly, deaths among our clients are not considered emergencies by this organization. . . .'

'Well, my purpose is not all that urgent. I've other visits to make. If I can't resolve my enquiry, I can always make arrangements for a formal meeting.'

'Is it anything I can deal with?' she asked. 'Or perhaps one of our professional carers could help? Both are out at the moment but Mrs Jarvis deputizes for Mr Furnival when he's away for any reason.'

'Not to worry, Mrs Allanby. Please inform Mr Furnival that I called and say that I wish to discuss something we talked about earlier; tell him I'll return when it's convenient.'

And so he left Crickledale Volunteer Carers without achieving much success – except it appeared that Furnival was a devotee of antique shops and car boot sales, places that sold small goods. That was useful information. Now he must begin his interviews with some of the carers' patients; he had a list in his pocket. He was pleased Mrs Plumpton had divided them into two sections. One group comprised those who were elderly and lived alone, and who were allocated regular care by the CVC; the second did not necessarily live alone but received occasional care when required, say after an accident or illness, or perhaps following a period in hospital. That was also arranged through the CVC office. He knew that the two professional carers ensured that all clients received as much attention as was either possible or feasible, with due emphasis on night-time care. There were times when a carer may be expected to stay overnight – that task usually fell to the professionals. He decided not to visit Mrs Cardwell because Mrs Pluke would be there, nor would he visit any of the clients who lived remotely close to Shipton Avenue.

He would select one of the elderly clients who lived alone – someone he considered vulnerable. He recalled Mrs Plumpton's suggestion of Joe Knowles and Pluke's suggestion about interviewing the old fellow. As a consequence he found himself heading for 17, Hauxwell Street. He did not know this gentleman and had no idea of his circumstances, although he hoped he would be able to communicate.

He did not want any of the carers to be present and so in

many ways this visit was something of a gamble. Hauxwell Street lay off the main road that passed the eastern outskirts of Crickledale; it was opposite the Tesco supermarket and about a five or six minute walk from the town centre. It was a terrace of brick-built houses on a large estate dating to around World War I. Each house had three rooms downstairs – a kitchen with an adjoining pantry, dining room and lounge with a toilet off the kitchen, and upstairs there may be two or three bedrooms, and a bathroom with a separate toilet. These houses were traditional, very warm and dry, quiet internally and ideal when living with good neighbours at each side. They were cool on hot days, with the pantry being ideal for the storage of food long before refrigerators had been invented. And now, it was possible for old folks to live downstairs. If they needed upstairs regularly then chair lifts could be fitted.

When he arrived at No. 17, Hauxwell Street, he found the exterior rather neglected. There was an uncut lawn the size of a doormat, a couple of unpruned rose bushes and a surplus of weeds. Wayne strode purposefully up to the front door, pressed the bell-push and walked in, shouting, 'Hello Mr Knowles, it's Wayne.'

This was a well-tried and tested tactic employed by police officers and the performance was also for the benefit of any neighbours who may be watching or listening. Inside he closed the door, stood in the entrance hall and shouted, 'Mr Knowles. It's me, Wayne.'

'Hello,' returned a weak voice.

'Where are you?'

'In here.'

The voice was downstairs.

He peered into the front lounge that overlooked the street with a bow window, but there was no one. The room contained a settee and two easy chairs. It looked very comfortable and well tended. Next to it as he headed into the kitchen, was the dining room – but he found it had been converted into Mr Knowles' bedroom. His single bed, a dressing table and wardrobe had been squeezed into the limited space, but it was comfortable.

'Hello?' called Wayne before entering. 'Is that Mr Knowles?'

'I didn't know you were with the carers now, Wayne? Have you just joined? And have you brought the tickets?' his voice was barely above a whisper.

'I'm with the carers,' he did not want to confuse the old fellow or alarm him by explaining his real purpose. 'I'm helping out today but you know my name?'

'You said it when you came in.'

'So I did! So what are tickets you're waiting for?'

He found an elderly and very frail bearded man sitting in a comfortable chair beside the bed. He looked very thin with skin like grey parchment. The bed had been made and the room was tidy, so clearly the morning carer had been here. Mr Knowles was watching television; beside his chair was a small table bearing drinks of orange squash, packets of biscuits and a paperback book. The old man had the courtesy to switch off the television, muttering, 'They put such a load of rubbish on nowadays. I don't know why we can't have wrestling like we used to. So you're the new chap, Wayne, and I'm Joe, they all call me Joe.'

'Pleased to meet you, Joe.' And they shook hands.

'I've seen you around, Wayne, not in here though, in town I mean but I'm no trouble to anybody. I can't get about very easily so I spend most of my time here. I can't do much energetic stuff, I'm 89 you know. I used to be very active, football, cricket, cross-country racing, high jump, hundred yards, all that sort o' stuff but my heart started to go wonky . . . it's not in very good shape right now. When I was younger, there wasn't much I couldn't do on a sports field but now I couldn't even walk halfway across a football pitch.'

'So is there anything I can get you whilst I'm here?'

'I wouldn't say no to a cup of tea and a chocolate biscuit, Wayne. Help yourself, you have one an' all. You'll find all the stuff in the kitchen, and milk on the pantry floor where it's cold. So did you bring the tickets?'

'Which tickets are they, Joe? I'm new, you see, I didn't know about the tickets.'

'Cup Final tickets, Wayne. Two, one for me and t'other for

my pal. Jack Vivers, you mebbe know him. That other chap promised he could get some for me and either send them on with one of the other carers or fetch 'em himself. He promised I'd have 'em later today.'

'What other chap?'

'Him off the telly, Wayne, he comes here sometimes. Nice chap. He reckons he has a pal who can get Cup Final tickets cheap.'

'It's a bit early to be thinking of the Cup Final, Joe.'

'Is it? I thought Middlesbrough was playing.'

'Not to my knowledge but they did get into the quarter-finals recently. So are you fit to go the Final, Joe?'

'Not on my own I'm not, no, but my pal said he would look after me. I'm not ill, you know, just old. We'd go on a bus, they do bus trips from Crickledale to t'Final so I'd be looked after. I hope he hasn't forgotten about them tickets. Mebbe you could ask when you see him?'

'I'll do that, Joe. Now is he the only man who comes to care for you?'

'He doesn't come to care for me, Wayne, not like getting me out of bed and washing me and all that, or tidying up and cooking. Them young lasses come and do all that, mornings and afternoons. Sometimes evenings. This feller, you know him, you must know him. He's that feller off t'telly, he comes and fixings things when they go wrong. My kettle kept blowing fuses, everything went off and he came to fettle it. Fettle my kettle, that's good, eh? Fettle my kettle. . . .'

'So when does this man come to see you?' asked Wayne.

'Not regular, not like them lasses. He'll come when they call him in, when summat goes wrong. Like t'drains getting blocked, fuses blowing, new dabs o' paint needed here and there, window catches not working properly. . . .'

'And he's one of the carers?'

'So he says.'

'So what's his name?'

'Summat to do with the telly, he is. I can't think of his name right now.'

'And the carer, the young woman. Who is she?'

'Now you've got me there, Wayne. I can't remember. Bonny young lass, very nice to me. Not Fiona, she's here a lot, nice lass. Mrs Pluke comes sometimes if other folks can get here. Of an evening usually.'

'But you've had the man before?'

'Oh, aye. He can turn his hand to anything, he can even knock a meal up for me or write a letter t'Council if I have a complaint about 'em not emptying my bins, or grumble about folks dropping rubbish on t'street outside or t'street lights not working. Good folks, them carers. Very talented and helpful.'

'So is there anything you want now, Joe?'

'No thanks, Wayne, except that cuppa. Then there's just them tickets when you can fix that. One of the lasses will be here later to see to my supper and wash up. . . .'

'I could do with a cup of tea myself,' said Wayne as he went through to find the kitchen and the tea-making necessities.

'Everything's in t'kitchen, Wayne,' Joe tried to shout but his voice was too frail. 'Help yourself then come in here and we can have a chat.'

'I'll do that.'

'I'll tell you all about my younger days when I was a top athlete . . . won cups I have, you'll see 'em on that shelf in my bedroom upstairs . . . solid silver some of 'em . . . go and have a look while t'kettle's boiling. Some are more than seventy years old, that ages me, eh?'

'You're still very fit, but thanks, Joe. I'll be back in a minute.'

Wayne left Joe for a while as he found the kitchen, filled the kettle and switched it on. He found a couple of mugs, some milk in a bottle on the cement floor, a teapot and caddy full of teabags. Whilst the kettle began to sing, he went upstairs to look at Joe's collection of trophies. On the landing, all the doors were closed and so he opened the first and peered inside – it was a small room but fitted out with shelves with glass fronted doors and on the shelves were hundreds of scent bottles arranged in neat rows. Now they had dust gathering upon them and around them despite the protection of their glass doors.

There was a single bed in the room, along with a small wardrobe and dressing table, and the pink décor with its floral theme suggested it had been a woman's room. He closed the door and tried the next – it was a bathroom with a toilet incorporated; next to it was another door, also closed. When he opened it, it was clearly a man's room, plainly decorated with magnolia paint and corresponding walls covered with emulsion of the same colour.

Another single bed stood near the far wall, with a wardrobe, dressing table and armchair nearby. But here the walls were covered with more shelves, this time full of silver cups and shields, all being sporting trophies from Joe's past. Most looked rather cheap but some were certainly hallmarked silver. There were ancient faded photographs on the walls too, all showing the young Joe in his sports gear and invariably holding a trophy of some kind.

One frame on the wall contained a page from an edition of the Crickledale Gazette showing Joe holding a huge silver cup along with a caption saying, *'Knowles Does It Again – Crickledale Joe Breaks Local Mile Record.'* But as Wayne examined each shelf, he noticed several gaps – cups had been removed and the circular clean patch in the dust that settled over the years without anyone cleaning it, revealed their former places. He counted four gaps. Wayne looked around the room to see if the missing cups had been placed elsewhere such as the window ledge or dressing table, but there was no sign of them.

However, there was a further door on the landing and so he went to find out what lay behind it, and this time there was a large double room complete with double bed, wardrobe, dressing table and chairs.

And this room also contained collectibles, row upon row of ink wells all arranged neatly along glass-fronted shelves on the western wall, whilst the eastern wall contained a similar display of snuff boxes.

He examined the interiors of those display cabinets and there were several empty spaces all identified by their dust-free places; clearly, they had been removed very recently. None of the cabinets or shelves bore any means of locking or securing them and so Wayne wondered who had removed the items – but he had no idea what exactly had been removed. The value could not be ascertained either and of course, there would be no available description unless Joe could recall the details with clarity.

He closed the door and returned to the kitchen where the kettle was boiling. He made two mugs of tea, found some chocolate biscuits in a tin and carried them all through to Joe on a tray, complete with a milk jug and sugar basin.

'By gum, Wayne lad, you're well trained in domestic matters!'

'It takes years of practice,' grinned Wayne, settling on the chair at Joe's side. Joe helped himself to two teaspoons full of sugar. Wayne did not take sugar.

'Well, Wayne, did you see my trophies? I reckon they need dusting and cleaning, but they'll take no harm up there.'

'I had no idea you'd won so many,' Wayne was honest. 'And in so many different sports. Nowadays they have pentathlons for folks like you!'

'We just did it for fun, not for money. I was good at what I did.'

'I noticed there were gaps among your cups, Joe, as if some had been removed?'

'Aye, they have. And some of my snuff boxes and my wife's scent bottles. And my ink wells.'

'You were obviously keen collectors, you and your wife,' complimented Wayne.

'My wife. Sophie that is, started it off with her scent bottles, and when she died a few years back, I kept on finding new ones so I bought 'em for her room ... we've gathered a right good collection over t'years. Folks say they'll be worth a bob or two now. That's why I always keep my doors and windows locked. I don't want thieves coming in here to help themselves to my treasures, Wayne.'

'But your door was open when I came in,' Wayne pointed

out. 'I just opened the door and shouted.'

'Aye, well, that woman who came early this morning said her friend was coming later today, this evening more than likely, to value my stuff, so I told her to leave t'door open so the chap could get in. I haven't got one of them key-safes, I don't trust 'em. You carers have keys but if he hadn't one I might not hear him knocking. My hearing's not as sharp as it used to be.'

'So what did you do?'

'I said to her I'd leave the door unlocked and he should come in, that would be OK by me. That's why I thought you were him.'

'Did she say what time he was expected?' asked Wayne.

'No, just it might be after his work tonight but before I go to bed.'

'That's a big risk, Joe. Leaving the door open for somebody you don't know.'

'Well, she's honest enough, Wayne, like all you carers. I reckoned she wouldn't send somebody in that wasn't honest so I didn't think there was a problem. I mean, Wayne. And I reckon you're honest enough, being a carer.'

'You place rather a lot of trust in your carers, Joe.'

'I do, they've always been good to me. Never a bad moment, Wayne. And besides, I always keep the back door locked and bolted, so it's just the front door that's open and not many folks know that.'

'Well, I must say the folk of Crickledale are generally honest and trustworthy, Joe. So what's happened to those items that are missing?'

'Oh, they'll come back, Wayne. They were taken away by one of those lasses from t'carers, she said she knew a chap who would give an honest valuation, that's the chap I'm expecting. Not that I want to sell 'em, of course, but it'll be nice to know how much they're worth if I ever need cash in a rush.'

'So how long ago was that?'

'I can't say, Wayne, I get a bit confused nowadays. One day just fuzzes into t'next but I'm sure she came this morning.'

'Could someone else have called? Have you a family, Joe?

Someone who might inherit these antiques?'

'No, we were never blessed with children, me and Sophie. When she died, I thought I'd give all my stuff to Crickledale Folk Museum but I've never got round to it. To be honest, I find it hard to part with any of 'em, Wayne. They've all got memories for me, me and Sophie.'

'Perhaps you should donate them to the museum, Joe? They'll be safe there. Would you like me to have a word with the curator?'

'Oh, that lass from t'carers said she'd do that, Wayne. She said she would get that chap off the telly to come round here this evening and have a look at 'em all, the lot in fact, and take everything away to be assessed by experts, then he'd give me a valuation. In fact, I thought you were him coming early, Wayne. She said he'd come on Wednesday evening after tea so he must be due any time now.'

'I'll wait.'

'What time is it now? I never know what time it is. Anyroad, mebbe you should meet him?'

'I think that would be a good idea, Joe. Do you mind if I wait here?'

But the alarm bells were already ringing in Wayne's mind. Wednesday evening was when some of the deaths must have occurred so that the casualties were found on the cold floor next morning. Thursday was not the key date for the cold-case review – it was Wednesday. Today. That was when CVC Carers called, people died and precious items went missing . . . and when Furnival had his day off. Pluke had mentioned the need to set a trap to catch the villains in action, with live bait.

'Can I use your phone, Joe? To call my boss? It's urgent. We'll pay . . .'

'Help yourself, it's in the front room.'

And so Wayne went to ring Detective Inspector Pluke.

Chapter 18

Aᶠᵀᴱᴿ ᴸᴵˢᵀᴱᴺᴵᴺᴳ ᵀᴼ Wayne's account, Pluke congratulated him upon his swift assessment of the situation. He agreed that it was the right moment to set a trap to catch those suspected of stealing from elderly people and at the same time, trap the suspected killers.

'It seems we can discount Dr Simpson as being part of the killer team. From what you say, he was merely doing his job and he did alert the police if and when he thought something was wrong. Now we know the key moment was always when he declared a death to be from natural causes – that was just what the plotters wanted. Little did the doctor realize what would follow his diagnosis.'

'I don't think he was culpable, sir.'

'Now we must consider Joe with his collection of trophies. I think he's at risk, Wayne, so you'd better remain with him tonight,' he advised Wayne. 'I'll arrange back-up from Inspector Horsley and his officers. I'll contact you again, on Mr Knowles' house telephone, the one you're using now, for an update on our precise timing and other details. The phone is secure, is it? Will he overhear you?'

'No, I'll make sure the doors are closed and his television is on. He likes it loud in the room he uses as a bedroom. The phone's quite a way from where he sleeps and eats. I bet he has a lot of unanswered phone calls!'

'I'll let you know my plans once I have sorted things out

with Inspector Horsley. There's no time to waste.'

'I hope it all goes to plan.'

'It will, Wayne. It will have to go to plan, we can't afford slip-ups at this stage!'

Having ended his call to Pluke, Wayne went to see Joe and said, 'Joe, you are far too trusting. I have a confession to make. I'm not a Crickledale Carer.'

'I know you're not! I'm not daft! You're a detective, one of Mr Pluke's men but that doesn't stop you being a carer! Mrs Pluke once pointed you out when I was walking through the market-place. I know her, she pops in here sometimes. Nice woman. We saw you crossing the square – very recognizable. But just now, when you came to see me, I thought there was nothing odd about it. I just reckoned you must be working for the carers like Mrs Pluke does. I'm not senile, you know. I keep my wits about me.'

'That's put me firmly in my place!' laughed Wayne. 'But Detective Inspector Pluke and I are working closely with the carers on a project – it's a bit complicated but we're trying to find way of cutting down the number of unnecessary calls to the police.'

'Well, Wayne, if I had an emergency, I'd just press this button,' and he opened his shirt front and pulled out a chain bearing a red button; it was rather like a jewellery pendant. 'My call goes straight into the CVC office for help. We never ring the police, Wayne, it's easier to press our red button and call the carers. Somebody always responds.'

'That's something I've learned. But back to these treasures of yours, I think you're far too trusting, Joe. You really need an approved museum expert to come and assess them, not just somebody who's the friend of a carer.'

'Well, it's a bit late now, I expect they're on the way.'

'But it could be mid-evening when they get here, you said? After tea?'

'Aye, it might be.'

'I expect they'll be here for quite some time, Joe, if they do a full assessment.'

'You could be right. That carer woman said that they'd pack all my stuff and take it away somewhere to be valued. It could take a fair time to pack, there's a lot o' stuff.'

'So who's coming to visit you tonight? A carer woman, is it? Do you know her name?' Wayne asked again, hoping Joe's memory might have been jogged.

'As I said, I'm not very good with names, Wayne. I remember yours because Mrs Pluke pointed you out and I used to be a big fan of John Wayne, that's how I remember. The carers send different women to see me . . . it all gets a bit confusing. As I said, Mrs Pluke pops in sometimes when she's passing, just to see if I want anything but I know her well enough, Wayne, I'd always trust her.'

'I thought the carers allocated just one of their members to you on a regular basis, the same one every time so you'd get to know him or her.'

'Oh, aye, I've got a young lass called Fiona who comes most of the time, mornings and afternoons, but she's not the one who said she'd be sending that valuer. She's a bit older than Fiona but don't ask me her name, I haven't a clue. I get lots in here and forget who they all are, but this one does sometimes drop in later in the day, after tea as a rule. Checking on the young 'uns, I expect, making sure they treat us right. I think Mrs Pluke does a spot of checking on 'em too, making sure t'carers do their jobs. It's appreciated, Wayne, all the work they do for not a penny in payment and I must say Crickledale Carers look after me very well.'

'Well, Joe, the local police aren't complaining about them. We just want to make our contacts more efficient than they are. Anyway I think I should remain with you until your visitors arrive.'

'You mean you don't trust 'em? Is that why you're here undercover?'

'Joe, you're a man of the world and I'm sure you've had occasions when folks have let you down.'

'I have, Wayne. Folks you'd least expect to do so, an' all.'

'Right. Without alarming you by telling you why, I must

say I'm worried about you and your belongings. I'll stay here tonight to look after you. I can feed myself and Tesco is handy if we're stuck. . . .'

'There's enough stuff in my fridge to feed an army, Wayne, it's packed to the ginnels with ready-made meals. This is all very puzzling, I don't know what's going on but it'll be nice to have your company for a while. I get lonely on my own. So you've not come to value my things? You really are my carer for tonight as well as a detective?'

'I am, but your regular carer might turn up as well.'

'Are you expecting trouble, Wayne? Is that why you're here?'

'Let's just say we're prepared for anything, Joe.'

'Fair enough, you know what you're doing but it could be fun for an old man, seeing the police in action.'

'We're drafting in others from the uniform branch, just for back-up,' Wayne explained. 'There'll be a lot of police about, mainly outside. But some of us will have to conceal ourselves inside. . . .'

'Conceal yourselves? Is this a raid?'

'Not a raid, Joe. It's a form of protection for you. I know it sounds serious but we'll be in charge and you'll come to no harm,'

'Well if you want somewhere to hide, I can tell you now my carers never go into that front room,' said Joe. 'I don't use it either. It's cosier in here.'

'Great, that'll suit us. We can hide in there with the lights off. I'll hear anyone arriving and if they do move around the house, it'll be into the kitchen to make a cup of coffee or something, or perhaps upstairs to look at your collection, as well as this room where you live and sleep. If we do get visitors, they'll be in a rush, they won't hang about.'

'My antiques are all upstairs, Wayne, they know that, I told 'em so. Mebbe that was daft. So what do you want me to do? I'm not much of an actor and as an old man I don't hear or see very well. I'm not a man of action now either, I'm old and weak, very weak. I'm 89 you know, not long for this world. My old heart's causing problems, the carers do get the doctor to call around every so often but there's nowt anyone can do. Old age has 'em all beaten but I'm not frightened of going off into t'next world. Mind you, I want to enjoy what's left of my time in this one. I still say my prayers before I go to sleep, like I used to do when I was a lad.'

'Well, I don't want you behaving like Superman, Joe. Just go about your normal household routine and let me deal with whatever happens. If you feel tired, go to bed or put the telly on and do whatever you'd be doing this evening. If you don't know what to do, pretend to be asleep.'

'I can do that with no trouble. So who do you think is coming to see me? Will it be Mrs Pluke again? I thought it was the chap off the telly and a woman carer so what do I say to them?'

'Just behave normally, Joe, pretend to be asleep and leave it all to me. I'll be somewhere in the house within listening distance. Are you expecting another carer before tonight? This afternoon, I mean.'

'Yes, Fiona comes to get me a biscuit and a cup of tea in the afternoons, then another comes later to make sure I clean my teeth and go to the loo before I get into bed. That one stays about half an hour and when she's gone to her next client I get ready for bed – pyjamas on – and I usually get to bed quite early – nine o'clock or thereabouts. I watch the news from my bed, if I can stay awake.'

'And the carer locks up when she leaves?'

'Yes, she drops the latch so I'm safely locked in for the night. She has a key, the carers look after it. I don't know her name.'

'So if anyone else tries to get in, they'll need a key?'

'Aye, but if the chap coming to see my treasures is a carer, he'll have a key, won't he? He'd never get in otherwise, unless he breaks in, and besides, if I'm asleep or watching the telly, I'd never hear him. I lie in bed and listen to the telly but it allus sends me to sleep before the news comes on. I'm out like a light till next morning.'

'Right. So when Fiona comes to make a cup of tea and do whatever she does, I'll be in your front room, listening. With the doors ajar, I should be able to hear what's being said, but if possible I don't want her to know I'm in the house. If I think she's likely to come into the front room, then I'll come out and tell her I'm a friend of yours. OK? Call me Wayne.'

'Right, I've got that! So the others will be coming later, after Fiona? They're not likely to hurt me, are they? You've got me bothered now, all this talk of folks coming to take my stuff. You hear some funny tales about folks being let into other folks' homes at night, especially when it's dark, like it will be tonight, still being winter time.'

'What sort of funny tales, Joe?'

'Well, my pals used to come and see me once in a while, before they died that was, and they told about old folks being found lying on cold floors, all done up as if ready for the coffin. . . .'

'Who's been telling you that?'

'Can't remember, but it was somebody who lives in the town and knows what goes on. . . .'

'Well, it's not going to happen to you, Joe, not with me here, is it?'

'I hope not, Wayne. I'm ready to go, but not like that. . . .'

'So it's a good job I decided to come and see you, isn't it? With all your treasures being valued tonight. Now I must keep in touch with Detective Inspector Pluke but from now I'll use my mobile. I want to keep your line clear, I'll answer it if it rings so don't try to do so. Once he explains his plans, I'll let you know.'

'Is this what the police call a stakeout? I think I must have heard that on some of the cop shows.'

'I suppose some would call it that. We might refer to it as covert observations which sounds much, much better! So, if Detective Inspector Pluke joins me, I think it would be wise for him to come in via the back door under cover of darkness. We don't want the whole street watching and wondering what he's doing here.'

'By gum, Wayne, this is getting very exciting. I don't want to miss any of the action, do I?'

'You won't, I promise,' smiled Wayne. 'And now I'll wash the pots before things start happening. You settle down with your telly.'

Meanwhile in the Pluke household, Millicent said she would prepare something and pack a sandwich with a flask of coffee for Montague.

He had not told her what his secret mission was to be, but she knew better than ask. Millicent then told him that she also was working tonight, standing in for a carer who'd been called away on a family matter. At this stage she didn't know which house she would be attending. With Millicent busy in the kitchen, Pluke rang Wayne from his bedroom, using his mobile phone.

'Wayne?'

'Speaking.'

Pluke whispered, 'I'll come to Mr Knowles' house when his afternoon carer has left. I understand you've not seen John Furnival this afternoon?'

'Not a whisper. According to his secretary, he always gets right away from Crickledale during his time off. He visits antique shops in Leeds and Harrogate, he's keen on the small stuff like trinkets and portable items.'

'That's significant, Wayne. Getting away from call-outs, I mean. Well, it looks as though you might have pre-empted a bold attempt to steal from Mr Knowles, and who knows what might have happened to him. He's not wanting to die, is he?'

'He wants to live as long as he can, there's no sign of him wanting a mercy killing. In fact he's told me that he wants to live and enjoy this world for as long as possible. Nonetheless, he's very frail but alert and chatty. He knows his heart is weak and a sudden shock could finish him off.'

'Hmm. I'm sure his carers know that. So if they took him from his bed and laid him on a cold floor, the shock might end his life?'

'I'm not a doctor, I've no idea of the effect of that. But if these old folks have any guts, they won't just lie on those cold floors

until they die, surely? I can't see Joe Knowles letting them do
that to him, frail though he is. He's a fighter.'

'That's why I think at least two people must have been
involved in those earlier deaths, Wayne. It would require
two to carry a person from his or her bed and then to hold
them down on the floor. We're not thinking of a lone rogue
carer. You need two to carry a person even when alive. If a
frail old lady was hoisted out of her bed by someone using
the fireman's lift, it would still require two fairly fit people to
lay her on the floor without causing any injuries . . . and they
must have remained with the victim until it was certain he
or she was dead. It's murder, Wayne, there's no doubt about
it. Murder in the course of theft or burglary, always targeting
valuables. And tonight, it will be attempted murder. We shall
prevent it.'

'It won't be easy.'

'It won't, but the element of surprise will be on our side. I'm
hoping we will be the reliable witnesses to this.'

'It doesn't make the carers appear in a very good light, does
it?'

'Far from it, Wayne, which is why we need to find John
Furnival as soon as possible. We need a long talk with him!
Before this call though, I alerted Inspector Horsley and
Sergeant Cockfield-pronounced-Cofield to our plans. They will
brief the town patrols who will report Furnival's movements if
he turns up anywhere in town. I'll not reveal my whereabouts
to anyone tonight, not even my wife. This is a very secret operation, Wayne.'

'You don't still suspect Mrs Pluke, do you?'

'She's involved with the carers tonight so she remains in the
frame, as they say. That's all I can say at this juncture. I know I
shouldn't be thinking of my wife in this way but this evening's
vigil will help to prove the innocence of many and perhaps the
guilt of a few. I hope it shows there is no general CVC conspir-
acy, it's all down to a few roguish members. That's how I see
things.'

'It's all making sense now.'

'Then you'll understand why I dare not inform Mrs Pluke of my whereabouts in case she inadvertently lets it known to others, particularly the suspects. As we say in the world of criminal investigation, she might blow the gaff. Unwittingly.'

'I'll remain here, waiting and watching with Joe Knowles. He's looking forward to the police activity, but I reckon he'll sleep through it all.'

'I hope he does, Wayne. That would be one worry less! Now this is what I am planning. Once the afternoon carer has left, I shall come to the rear door. Meanwhile, back-up from the town's uniform branch will arrive under cover of darkness and conceal themselves. There is ample cover near the house. Make sure you are able to let me in.'

'I will.'

'Good. I shall then instruct a uniformed constable to position himself in the vicinity of that rear door to observe events in secret and when possible to report by radio to Sergeant Cockfield-pronounced-Cofield in the Control Room. He'll ensure he is not seen by those coming into the house – fortunately, it's January so it'll be dark early. Before I join you, I'll prepare my surveillance microphones, cameras and recording machines and when I arrive, I will secrete them in Mr Knowles' room and also upstairs where his treasures are kept. I'll not let him know where I've hidden the equipment in case he lets the cat out of the bag or glances towards their hiding places. It will take a while to install the equipment and I'll be pleased if you could divert Mr Knowles' attention whilst I'm doing that.'

'No problem, I can get him talking about his athletic successes!'

'Good. Meanwhile, Wayne, before I arrive, can you discreetly chat to Mr Knowles to identify a few good places where I can conceal the equipment.'

'Yes, there'll be no large pieces, will there?'

'No, they're all small instruments, easily concealed behind furniture or even in bookcases. I'll carry them into the house in the large pockets of my greatcoat. As our man on the ground, do these plans seem feasible, Wayne?'

'I'd say very suitable, just what we need. And very necessary.'

'It means we shall be well prepared, Wayne, but I do not expect the targets to arrive before eight o'clock. We can bring our own food from Tesco. You and I will be in touch with Control via our mobile telephones; the house phone will be left available for emergencies. When I arrive you must introduce me to Mr Knowles and give me a quick tour of the house to familiarize myself with its layout and, of course, the location of the valuables. We have no time to waste, Wayne. When crooks are about, the best laid plans of mice and policemen can often go astray.'

'At the moment, I see no difficulties. The only problem would be if the villains turn up before we're ready for them.'

'I'm sure they will not arrive until at least eight o'clock which gives us time to prepare a welcoming party.'

'Why are you so confident about that?'

'I'll explain when I arrive. Now, I'm thinking, Wayne, that if these people are seeking to remove objects in secret from Mr Knowles' house, they will not do so via the front door. Approaches to front doors can be observed by too many people; consequently we shall make good use of the back door and the cover of darkness. I'll bring some battery-operated miniature night-sight cameras to cover all exits. You will gather, Wayne, that I'm approaching this project with the utmost seriousness.'

'I'm impressed. I'll be ready and waiting. I should warn you, however, that Joe Knowles is very frail and admits to being confused.'

'Thanks for the warning but we'll cope. When I arrive, you must fully update me – and well done, Wayne, for recognizing the need for this raid.'

'Thank you, sir – but our thanks are really due to Mrs Plumpton.'

Before leaving Crickledale police station, Pluke reiterated his plans to Inspector Horsley and after approving the inspector's plans for his part in the covert operation, Pluke asked that one of Horsley's officers drive him close to Joe's house but not to the actual site. Pluke wanted to arrive there quietly in a plain car under cover of darkness. Instead of wearing his usual overcoat and hat, he wore the black coat he'd used for Mrs Langneb's funeral, along with a black hat and black leather gloves. Like all Montague's coats and jackets, this one had very large pockets.

When he arrived at 6.15 p.m., the afternoon carer had left and so he entered through the back door, then closed it and locked it with the mortise key that remained in the lock. Wayne led him through to Joe's ground-floor bedroom and introduced him to Joe. He was in his armchair reading a book and looked very frail indeed.

'Mr Knowles, it's good to see you,' and Pluke shook his hand. 'It's kind of you to accommodate us like this.'

'No problem, Mr Pluke. It's better than television, having a stakeout in my own house. So what do you want me to do? Am I supposed to fight burglars and rescue damsels in distress? I was a bit of a fighter in my day, you know.'

'Nothing quite so exciting, Mr Knowles. We just want you to do exactly what you'd do normally. Don't let your visitors know we're in the house and above all, don't mention this to anyone. That's vital.'

'Mebbe it would be better if I was asleep when they come?'

'Or pretending to be asleep!' smiled Wayne.

'Aye, I can do that. Nod off in my chair or bed or wherever I am, but when she comes, she'll wake me for my tea and a trip to the toilet before I get into my pyjamas and climb into bed.'

'One important point, Mr Knowles,' said Pluke with as much seriousness as he could muster. 'I want you to tell me whether they – or indeed anyone – have permission to remove any of your valuables from the house.'

'Well, she said they would need to be valued, not that I'm thinking of getting rid of 'em just yet, I don't want 'em going away for ever but mebbe one day I'll send 'em to a museum.

I've no family you see, Mr Pluke, so I do need to make sure they go to t'right spot.'

'A nice gesture, I'm sure.'

'It was me who said they should get a chap to come *here* to look at 'em . . . I'd be happier with that arrangement.'

'And you told her that?'

'Aye, but she insisted they went away somewhere. That's what's going to happen tonight, they're taking my stuff away to be valued, so they say.'

'And you don't want that to happen? Is that right?'

'Aye, it is right, Mr Pluke. I don't mind my stuff being valued at home but not taken away. Mebbe you can stop 'em? I tried but they don't listen.'

'That's why we're here, Mr Knowles.'

'By gum, that's a relief. Now if you'll excuse me, I must go to the bathroom, things happen suddenly when you get old, and when you've got to go, you've got to go as fast as you can. And happily, t'toilet isn't upstairs.'

And as the old man struggled to rise from his armchair, Wayne stepped forward to give him a helping hand. Pluke smiled. 'I'll wait here till you get back,' he told Mr Knowles.

As Wayne helped the frail Joe Knowles to stagger along the passage to the toilet near the kitchen, he knew Pluke would already be installing his secret devices.

It meant Mr Knowles could never reveal them or their locations. He would have no idea they were concealed or where they were hidden. When Mr Knowles' deed was done, he was helped back to his chair by Wayne as Pluke stood and waited in the passage.

'Can I go upstairs to look at your treasures?' he asked.

'Help yourself, Mr Pluke. Wayne will be along when he gets me back into my chair,' and so Pluke went upstairs to plant more of his sophisticated surveillance equipment.

After ensuring that Mr Knowles had returned safely and was securely seated in his favourite armchair to await the arrival of his carer, Pluke and Wayne concealed themselves in the darkness of the front room. Pluke had a receiver on his jacket lapel and soon they heard Mr Knowles gently snoring in his room with the sound of the television in the background.

And so began the siege of No. 17 Hauxwell Street, Crickledale.

Chapter 19

THEY SAT IN the darkness of the front room with Mr Knowles gently snoring into Pluke's listening device and with the curtains closed against the intrusion of the street lights. The two detectives consumed ready-meals that Wayne had warmed in the kitchen. Pluke had already been in radio contact with the officers concealed outside the house to announce that everyone was prepared.

'She won't be here until eight,' Pluke told Wayne. 'So we can make ourselves at home for a while.'

'I still don't know how you can be sure of that,' commented Wayne.

'I've got a copy of the CVC duty rota from the secretary,' Pluke pulled a large sheet from his pocket and opened it on a side table. Then he produced a pencil-torch from one of his many jacket pockets and shone it on the paper. 'Here we are. Mr Joseph Knowles, 17 Hauxwell Street – he's been allocated a carer from 8 p.m. until 8.45 p.m. today, Wednesday. She's one of the professionals – Juliet Jarvis – a good timekeeper by all accounts. It means we can expect her on time, Wayne.'

'I'll recognize her from our meeting.'

'You will. In age, she is the senior of the two professionals and according to Mrs Allanby, she was thought to have more suitable experience than her colleague, Mrs Frankland. Mrs Jarvis, you will be surprised to know, has nursing experience whilst Mrs Frankland's was in commerce. Both have many admin duties to fulfil, in addition to the practical care they provide, and both do a good job, Wayne.'

'I thought Juliet Jarvis was asked to leave her previous employment, a department store? Stuff and cash kept disappearing if my memory is correct.'

'She left under a cloud and got a job as a trainee nurse – I'm not saying she stole from patients because the carers were prepared to give her another chance. There was no proof she was responsible for any of the allegations thrown at her, although both the store and the hospital dispensed with her services.'

'It's quite possible Jarvis was guilty all along. The trouble with light-fingered people is that they never stop – even when it's widely known they're pilfering. They just keep on stealing. . . .'

'It's that knowledge of human frailty that helps us detect crimes, Wayne.'

'So if Mrs Jarvis has a past, she's clearly never learned her lesson if she's going to try and steal Mr Knowles' valuables.'

'Well, Wayne, she might be cleverer than we think. There's no guarantee she will get involved even if she is the prime mover. She might get someone else to do her dirty work.'

'You've reason to suspect her?'

'I remembered she was on duty most Wednesdays and she also takes part regularly in the "Thursday Special" as it's called.'

'You mean Furnival will be left holding the baby, as it were?'

'No, not Furnival. He won't be here, Wayne.'

'But I thought he was the villain behind all this . . . you said that no-one knows his past, his job application was full of errors, his references were all fakes, he's vanished from the scene today, no-one knows where he is. On top of that, he collects small antiques. He's a fireman too, so he says, able to lift people with the famous fireman's lift . . . he must be the favourite as a suspect. . . .'

'He'll have to answer to the authorities, Wayne, his CV is riddled with false information so it is a matter for his employers.'

'Surely he'll be sacked?'

'Once more, Wayne, that's a matter for his employers. I have learned from a colleague in Norfolk he was in fact a fireman but with a large commercial warehouse in that area, not working for a local authority. He dressed up his application just a little . . . but that doesn't make him a thief and a killer. It does show how easy it is to jump to conclusions. . . .'

'But Mr Knowles said his carer is bringing a man, another carer, to collect his antiques, ostensibly for valuation.'

'That's right, but she hasn't named him. It's not Furnival.'

'Well, there aren't many men working for CVC, that narrows it down somewhat. But what sort of errors did Furnival's job application contain? I can't understand how such things get past those who make the appointments. You'd think the recruitment officials would check references and factual statements. . . .'

'It seems that the higher up the professional ladder one climbs, Wayne, the fewer checks are made. Those responsible for selecting senior members of staff tend to accept the word of top professionals, even though some are outright crooks and confidence tricksters.'

'So can I ask what errors were contained in his job application for Crickledale Volunteer Carers?'

'Well, for a start, his references were all false. Earlier today, I checked them with the organizations which are purported to have written them, and all are false. Email is a wonderful invention, Wayne; I scanned his copies which meant I could check them individually. He said he had been a senior fire officer, but there is no record of him serving in any British branch of the Fire Service, and he said he had taken compulsory retirement at reaching fifty years of age. The general retirement age for senior fire officers is either 55 or 60 but that is not compulsory. He said he was a Senior Divisional Officer in Leeds City Fire Service but at the time, there was no such fire service – Leeds was part of the West Yorkshire County Fire Service. In fact, I doubt if John C. Furnival is his real name. He might have a very unsavoury past if we dug that far into it, and if we sought to prove the falsity of his application, he could be charged with the criminal offences of dishonestly obtaining a pecuniary advantage. The snag is, he has done a wonderful job with Crickledale Volunteer Carers, moulding them into an effective and trusted unit, even if some of their members have a history of dishonesty or untrustworthiness. So is he a man with a troubled past who is honestly trying to reform himself into a good citizen? Or is he a downright rogue?'

'He sounds to be a thorough rogue, sir.'

'To be honest, Wayne, I'm not sure. He might be trying desperately to reform himself. It has been known for that to happen in rare cases. Like most other people I've spoken to, Millicent speaks highly of him and his work. It is very clear that, whatever his past, he is doing a very good job here in Crickledale. But if Mrs Jarvis' accessory is a male person on the staff of Crickledale Volunteers Carers, it narrows it down a lot if Furnival can be eliminated.'

'Parkinson or Dorsey then?'

'Didn't Joe tell you she was bringing the man off the telly tonight?'

'Parky! Parkinson ... good grief ... Parky, a name made famous on television. . . .'

'Right. Now one reason I thought Furnival was our man was because of his strength and professional skills as a fireman. Those earlier old folks had been manhandled out of their beds and placed on the floor, perhaps by using the fireman's lift – and kept there despite their undoubted struggles. That would need two people, I reckon, strong people. Parkinson is strong, he's a stonemason, accustomed to lifting heavy items. And Mrs Jarvis is a former nurse so she will be accustomed to moving patients around.'

'So what led you to him, sir?'

'He lives with Mrs Jarvis.'

'So how did you discover that?'

'They share the same telephone number for call-outs. They're shown on that list of volunteers and staff. And on top of that, after my research in the library and some of my own knowledge, I think they've been using the infamous Black Pillow as an extra means of killing people, it's more reliable that a cold stone floor!'

'I've never heard of that? What is it?'

'It was used until the beginning of the last century in parts of rural England, Wayne, to help dying people to pass away more quickly and without pain. It was a small pillow, half the size of a conventional one, and full of very soft feathers. When a person was dying in clear pain and having a tough time in those final moments, the black pillow was placed over their face and held there gently until breathing had ceased. Doctors of the time knew about such tricks but their medical knowledge couldn't identify the fact that such a pillow had been used. If it was used gently even today, I don't think a GP would notice the deceased had been smothered and I question whether a pathologist would recognize any symptoms in the deceased's lungs. It is possible to identify a powerful smothering or strangulation, but a soft pillow held over the face gently in those final moments is a different matter. I doubt if suffocation by that method would be detected by an ordinary GP – but it would prevent the victims getting back to their feet and walking off the cold floor!'

'Have you any proof of all this, sir?'

'Not yet, but tonight I hope to obtain sufficient evidence to justify a charge of attempted murder at the very least. And I also believe the open doors and windows, and the covered mirrors were a decoy tactic – to throw us off the scent. To make it look like an ancient mercy killing when in fact it was cold-blooded murder committed for greed. Tonight we shall see whether I was right.'

'So you're sure this pair of villains is coming to kill Mr Knowles tonight and steal his property?'

'The indications are all there, Wayne. They will steal the valuables by telling a feasible tale to a gullible old man, and then ease him into death, which can't be far off anyway, so that he cannot inform the police or anyone else that his valuables have gone. Could it be simpler, especially when the professionals state the death was from natural causes? The perfect murder, Wayne?'

'No murder is perfect, sir.'

'In the past and well into modern times, people have helped their loved ones to die and this raises the question I asked when we began this cold-case review. Are these deaths the result of malice or kindness?'

'In this case, it's malice, sir, beyond all doubt. They're doing it to cover up their crimes.'

'I believe so too. Tonight, therefore, God willing, we shall arrest them for attempted murder. That can happen only if we can catch them in the act. We can't arrest them for attempted murder just for thinking about it. *Intent* is not *attempt*.'

'So if we are to secure a conviction in court, we must let them get very close to killing poor old Joe. In other words, they must make their attempt – and we must stop them before it's too late. It's a fine line.'

'With such an old man involved, that could be a tall order. There are considerable risks, Wayne.'

And at that point, from their hiding places they heard a vehicle ease to a halt outside the front door. Its lights lit up the room momentarily and then they were dowsed. A car door slammed and they could hear footsteps approaching the house. One set of footsteps. There was no sound of the car door being locked. Then the front door opened and was closed, followed by more footsteps across the hall into the dining room that Joe was using as his bedroom. It was precisely eight o'clock.

'Hello Joe,' the female voice was caught clearly on Pluke's recording system. 'Asleep again, eh? Come along, time for a cup of tea and a wash before you go to bed. Get your 'jamas on, I'll heat your supper. It's fish pie, you like fish pie, don't you. . . ?'

The voice faded as the woman left Joe's room and made for the kitchen where they heard the light being switched on and noises of cutlery and kitchen utensils being utilized and a kettle being filled from the tap. Then they heard the distinctive sound of the back door being unlocked. It was followed by Joe's television set being switched on – which pleased Pluke. Its noise would cover any sounds made by the police team.

Then Pluke activated his concealed radio. 'Pluke to all units, Pluke to all units. Suspect One is in the house, preparing a meal for Joe. Her vehicle is parked outside the front door. I need one constable to attend the vehicle at the front . . . and disable it, then stand guard in the shadows. She has unlocked the rear door which is near the kitchen to prepare for the arrival of the second suspect, he will surely come whilst she is in attendance, it will be his cover. He will not be regarded as a suspect by the neighbours if a carer is attending . . . allow him entry without seeing you. Joe's TV is switched on, it's a talk show so don't be misled by voices. I'll alert you when I need you all to come into the house but it is essential to prevent any escapes. Acknowledge. Over.'

One by one, his men on the outside acknowledged receipt of his instructions. The scene was set. The woman was still in the kitchen preparing the meal with a full teapot, mug and milk on a tray. They heard her footsteps leaving the kitchen as she bore the tray through to Joe's bedroom, and then her voice saying, 'Here we are, Joe. A nice supper for you. Hop into bed and I'll put the tray on your bed-table . . . and while you're eating, I'll check upstairs to see if all your windows are locked . . . then I'll come to wash up your pots. No need to rush, you can watch your telly.'

'Aye right,' said Joe.

'Car parked at front disabled,' said a soft voice on Pluke's radio, well out of earshot of the woman and even Joe. 'Plug leads and rotor arm disconnected.'

'Received,' acknowledged Pluke. 'Remain to guard car and apprehend anyone attempting to move the car or flee the scene.'

'Roger,' said the anonymous voice.

'She's gone upstairs,' said Wayne. 'I can hear her climbing the steps.'

'She's preparing to help her accomplice,' muttered Pluke.

And then the police radio burbled into action again as a whispered voice said, 'For Detective Inspector's Pluke's information, Mrs Pluke is now arriving by the front door . . .'

Chapter 20

'DETAIN MRS PLUKE,' ordered Montague. 'Keep her silent and out of sight until further notice. Tell her those are my orders.'

'Will co,' replied the anonymous voice.

Another soft voice reached their ears. 'Observer Three. Large white van, no markings, approaching rear of house. One occupant, male . . . he's going into the backyard of No. 17 . . . parked, lights off, engine cut. . . . He has not locked the van doors. No other vehicles or people in the vicinity. A man has disembarked and has taken two large suitcases from the rear. I believe there are more cases there, it looks full of them . . . he has now approached the rear kitchen door, lights are showing in the kitchen, the cases appear empty, they are swinging about a lot. He's entered the house but not closed the rear door. He's out again, retracing his steps to the van. He's taken two more large suitcases from the rear and is taking them into the house two by two. . . . I think he's coming back for more . . . yes, here he comes. . . .'

Pluke and Wayne listened to the running commentary and, from where they were hiding, they could visualize the scene. Eventually, the man had emptied the rear compartment of the van to pile a dozen or more empty suitcases in the kitchen. Then he entered the house and closed the door to pick up two cases and head for the stairs.

Pluke spoke quietly, 'He's taking the cases upstairs, no doubt to pack them with stolen goods. Observer Three – disable the van . . .'

'Roger,' said Observer Three. There was a long pause, after which the same constable said, 'Van disabled. Rotor arm and plug leads disconnected. Over and out.'

'Received thank you,' said Pluke. 'Once all the suitcases are upstairs, they will start filling them with small antique items, this may take a while. I am still concealed but the television is producing some useful covering sounds and Mr Knowles is apparently asleep, I can hear him breathing heavily as if in sleep . . . this is the critical moment. All units to rear of house – prepare to enter the house when I give the order "enter" . . . last man to enter please lock the door and remove the key. Units at front of house, prepare to enter when I give that order, lock the door and secure it internally. Now maintain radio silence as we await the next move. With Detective Sergeant Wain, I am in the front living room to the right of the front door as one enters, in darkness but with radio links. We are now awaiting two things – the probable attempt on the life of Mr Knowles, and the suspects' departure with several suitcases full of portable and varied antiques. Complete radio silence please. Over and out.'

In the ensuing silence, it was possible to hear a pin drop, apart from gentle and rather weak slumbering noises from Joe Knowles and the burbling of the television set. Upstairs in the solidly built Victorian house, there was not a sound either; they were packing the objects in cases filled with polystyrene foam particles. They were not rushing into carelessness, but not wasting a second in unnecessary chatter; each knew his and her job and each was an expert at packing in this manner. Before long, ten large cases had been quietly filled and were standing inside the bedroom.

'I'll help you down with some of those,' said the female voice which carried loud and clear through the receivers in Pluke's room. 'We can stack them in the kitchen before we load them . . . it'll give us space.'

'What about him? Is it time we dealt with him?' asked a male voice.

'I'll go and have a look. I've got the pillow in case we need it.'

'I'll come with you. I'll open the bedroom windows now and cover the mirrors.'

Pluke and Wain, with radio silence outside, heard the footsteps of the two plotters descending the stairs.

The man said, 'We can put him in the hallway, it's got a cold tiled floor, just lay him there. You can use your black pillow if he gets boisterous, that always calms them down.'

The listeners heard footsteps crossing the hall and entering the room in which Joe Knowles lay fast asleep with his shallow breathing.

'He's out like a light,' said the man.

'Good, let's do it,' responded the woman. 'I'll take his feet if you can cope with his shoulders. Put him on the floor in the hall . . . that should finish him off. Poor old chap, he was a really nice old man but is certainly on his way out. Well, he is now.'

In Pluke's room, Wayne mouthed, 'Now?'

'No. Wait. We need evidence of an actual attempted murder, not the mere plans.'

And from another of his commodious pockets, he produced a digital camera, checked that it was switched on and waited. They could hear the couple puffing and scuffling along beneath the heavy weight of Joe Knowles, as they hoisted him out of the warm bed and laid him on the bedside mat. Using that as a kind of sleigh, they dragged him through the door and out into the chilly hall with its stone floor, and there they withdrew the mat until he was lying on the stone. He had not woken up; he was still snoring but ever so lightly.

'Pillow? I'll do it if you're nervous,' said a man's voice.

'Would you?'

'It's not the first time. If you do it properly it doesn't leave any evidence.'

'It's still in the bedroom, I'll get it.'

There was a long silent pause and they heard the footsteps of the man on the bare tiles as he approached the dormant figure of Joe Knowles. On the sensitive microphone hidden in Joe's underwear, Pluke and Wayne could hear his breathing and then footsteps growing louder and louder as they grew closer and closer. Then there was silence as the black pillow was gently placed over his face.

'Go, go, go!' shouted Pluke into his microphones.

For a few seconds there appeared to be pandemonium but as Pluke's camera caught the action with Parkinson holding the black pillow over Joe's face and Juliet trying to run to freedom but finding all exits barred by uniformed policeman led by Inspector Horsley, they capitulated.

Joe slept through it all and so a couple of burly police officers lifted him back onto the bedroom carpet and once again used it as a sleigh to haul him back to his bedside where they placed him beneath the blankets, still snoring but alive and warm again. Someone switched off the TV set.

'Well, well, well,' said Pluke. 'This is most interesting. Detective Sergeant Wain, will you arrest Roland Parkinson and Juliet Jarvis on a charge of attempted murder, with secondary charges of attempted theft and burglary, the details of which have yet to be ascertained. And Inspector Horsley, perhaps you could arrange to escort these prisoners to the police station for formal processing and detention. There will be no bail.'

Neither of the accused said a word, neither did they struggle. It was pointless.

Pluke spoke again, 'For the information of Mr Parkinson and Juliet Jarvis, I shall be re-opening previous cases of death and theft that have occurred in Crickledale in recent years.'

Inspector Horsley then asked, 'Montague, I have Mrs Pluke in my car, you asked me to bring her here. . . .'

'Ah yes, thank you for that. Bring her in please.'

Somewhat mystified by what was happening, Horsley went outside and escorted Millicent into the house where Joe Knowles was still fast asleep.

'Millicent,' announced Pluke. 'As one of the Crickledale Carers, perhaps you could call a doctor and ask him to examine Mr Joe Knowles in that room. He has had something of a bewildering experience but I feel he is well and is in dream-land. The doctor might feel he should be in hospital, then we must close all doors and windows. When I have finished the paperwork concerned with tonight's outcome of my cold-case review, I shall come home. Tomorrow, however, I need to speak urgently to Mr Furnival about all this and some other related matters – but that can wait until tomorrow.'

'I shall be waiting to hear all about it,' smiled Millicent, absorbing the scene around her. 'I might even make you a cele-bratory cup of cocoa.'

John Furnival disappeared that night. His car and most of his belongings vanished from the house he had rented and he was never seen again. A description of him was circulated both in police publications and on the internet, saying the police wished to speak to him about matters relating to Crickledale Volunteer Carers but no-one responded.

Within a month, advertisements appeared in local and regional newspapers seeking professional members of staff to fill current vacancies at Crickledale Volunteer Carers. Millicent Pluke declared she would not apply, although she might con-tinue as a volunteer.